MARJORIE

MARJORIE

KATE TALBOT

DEDICATION

To my husband, John, and my children,
Jasmine, Claire, and Peter

Acknowledgements

I WOULD LIKE TO offer thanks to Pauline Bentley, who was the first to guide and encourage me; Linda Acaster, who edited the first draft; Richard Parsons, Guy Phoenix and my book club members for their valuable criticism; also Pam Edwards, for her valuable comments and proofreading.

1

JULY 1963

S HE'D GONE TO Manchester in May with Alison to see the Beatles with Roy Orbison at the Odeon, where she helped to drown out the music, screaming and singing alongside Alison and hundreds of other teenagers, the words known by heart. She would have preferred to dance to their songs at the school dance, but the teachers thought otherwise. Lessons in ballroom dancing at the local grammar school were thought to be a more wholesome preparation for an end-of-term dance. It was a long way from the excitement of the concert, but Marjorie had to admit she rather enjoyed the romance of the music.

She swirled to a stop at the end of the waltz and drew away from the sixth former whose idea of dancing was to steer her around in any direction at a frantic pace. She felt her face flush as she stood apart from him, an invitation for a new partner. The music began; there was a flurry of exchanges, and Marjorie found herself in the arms of George, not quite full grown, but already solid and dependable.

'Nice dress.' George looked with obvious approval at the scarlet shift dress, which plunged steeply, revealing her cleavage.

'Thanks. I made it myself. It's from a Vogue pattern. They're very sophisticated, you know.' She was proud of her latest creation, which she had run up on her mother's Singer sewing machine, not caring that the seams were unfinished, the pinning and tacking ignored. It was the instant overall effect that she liked, to the despair of her needlework teacher.

'You always look beautiful,' George said softly.

Marjorie looked up at her brother's friend, so familiar with his shock of straight brown hair tumbling over his eyes. 'Thanks, George.' She felt comfortable. He was a good dancer, holding her firmly, guiding her between the other couples with ease.

'No Nicholas, then?'

'No,' she answered. 'You know he's not interested in school dances. All he wants to do is draw and paint. Dad gets really mad at him.'

'Nicholas is certainly different from the other lads, but I like him.' He drew her closer. 'His sister, she's all right too.'

'You're just a friend, remember.' She liked George a lot and was used to his adoration, but he was her brother's friend, and she had known him for years—not very romantic in her view.

'Yeah, I remember,' he said, resignation in his voice.

He walked her home, his arm resting lightly on her shoulder. She felt safe with him. They came to the centre of Middleston with its town hall and cluster of shops around the green. Her house was only five minutes' walk away, but she didn't feel tired. 'Do you fancy going to the canal?'

'Yeah. Why not? I'll have to hold on to you, though. You'll topple over in those high heels.'

She laughed as she took his hand. It felt warm and firm. They turned into the pitch-black narrow lane leading to the wharf and came to the warren of streets that had been her playground as a child. They passed the end of Albermarle Street, where the corner shop sat quietly in the dark.

'I used to dream about working here. That was the height of my ambition when I was younger.'

'And now? What do you want to do when you leave school?'

'I want to be an architect, but I need to get really good marks at A level. Dad thinks I should be a secretary and forget about going into the sixth form, but I'm good at maths and science. He just grunts when I show him my house designs even though they're much better than the boxes he builds. But what about you? Why aren't you worrying about your results? You're brainy. You could go to university next year.'

'I'm not interested in going to university. I like messing around with boats. That's my dad's business, and he wants me to help him to develop it. He has two narrow boats now, and he wants more. It's a simple decision.'

'It's simple for you because you get on with your dad.' Bitterness crept into her voice as the images appeared of her father kicking out at Nicholas; she thought also of the snide remarks and the contempt in his voice aimed at her gentle, artistic brother.

As if reading her thoughts, George said, 'Nicholas and your dad loathe each other, but Nicholas doesn't want to leave Middleston either. He says it inspires him, especially these old wharf buildings.'

They had reached the five-storey wharf buildings, built of local stone, now mellowed with age to a soft, dusty-grey colour, rising from the canal as if guarding its history. At their side the cotton mill had stood proud, demolished in a day in a cloud of dust. The disused railway line abruptly stopped in front of the crumbled foundations.

'This whole area should be preserved, not torn down. It's what this town was built on,' George stated. 'The mill was a magnet for people offering employment and the security of a wage packet. I did a project on the history of the mill and these buildings at school. The council wouldn't let me in, saying they were unsafe, but I think they just didn't want people to see their potential.'

Marjorie looked up at the old buildings, such a familiar sight—like old friends. 'They're all alone now, wondering if they will meet the same fate as the mill. It was the last straw for Nicholas. He said Dad's a philistine and that these will be next to make way for new houses, but,' she pointed to the basin itself, 'who would want to live near that?'

'That, Marjorie, is the whole point. Cleaned out, this basin is a gold mine. Dad would love to have it for his boats, but that's never going to happen while the council uses it as a tip until it's developed. They keep it that way so nobody will mind what happens to it. Dad says we have to be thankful that they allow us to moor our boats in the turning bay upstream.'

'I remember the mill coming down. We were told to stay indoors because of the dust. Nicholas and I came out later to see what they'd done. I've never seen him so upset. That's when he really started to hate Dad.'

George took her hand again, and they walked towards her home in companionable silence for several minutes. 'Dad says there's so much infighting on the council that it will be years before anything happens.'

'I hope that's true, George. I can't imagine how Nicholas would react if those plans went ahead, and his wharf buildings were torn down as well. He loves them.'

'He's not alone. Lots of folk here don't want them to come down. It's the town's heritage, and they should be preserved.'

They stood in the pool of light cast by the streetlight outside the two wrought-iron gates that led into the driveway of the large Edwardian house that had been home to the Baines family for the last six years.

'Can I kiss you, Marjorie?' George tentatively asked, as if expecting the answer to be no, as usual.

'No. I keep telling you, George, I don't want to. You're our friend, and besides…' She trailed off. Max was arriving in the morning, and her heart gave a leap.

'Besides, what?' He sounded puzzled.

'Nothing.' Although she really liked George, he didn't have a part to play in her romantic dreams. 'Thanks for walking me home. I hope you're right about the wharf,' she said as she turned into the drive and waved back at him, knowing that he would wait at the gate until she was safely inside the house.

She let herself in, trying to be quiet. Her mother would be sleeping lightly, waiting for her step. As she closed the door behind her, reaching up to draw the bolts, she could hear her father's snoring in the front bedroom. Her mother had finally decided on separate bedrooms, using the excuse that his rumbles and coughs in the night were getting louder as he grew older.

The second and third stair gave their usual creak, and she sighed, knowing it would have disturbed her mother. On the first landing, she stopped to listen.

'Marjorie, is that you?'

She opened the door to see her mother leaning on one elbow, waiting for her to come in. Three greying curls were pinned above the furrowed forehead; her face, devoid of make-up, looked tired and pale. A book lay open on the candlewick counterpane.

'Who else would it be, Mum? Would you rather I were a handsome hunk, come to drag you from your bed and take you to distant lands?'

'Well, yes, frankly,' her mother answered. 'Just down the road would do to get away from this noise.' She indicated with her head the direction from which the rumbles emanated.

'OK. I'll see what I can arrange the next time I go to a school dance,' she said, enjoying her mother's company, but knowing there was no escape from the figure who lay like a sleeping ogre across the landing.

'How was it?'

'Good fun. Everyone was there, except Alison, and Nicholas of course. It's strange to see everyone out of school uniform. Everyone liked my dress, by the way, especially George.'

'I still think it's unsuitable for a school dance. However, you know best.'

Her mother's tone reminded Marjorie of the disagreement over the dress earlier that evening. Not wanting to reopen the subject, she answered simply, 'Yes mum. Good night. See you in the morning.'

'Good night. Sleep well if you can.' Marjorie began to close the door when her mother drew her back. 'By the way, Alison rang again.'

'Did she?' Alison had obviously tried again to stop her from going to the dance. 'I'll see her tomorrow.' Why Alison's parents didn't allow her to go to the school dance was beyond her comprehension. She knew Alison resented her freedom, but Marjorie loved dancing and wanted to wear her new dress.

'Good night, love. Close the door firmly, Marjorie; the noise is shaking the house.'

Her bedroom was on the next floor. A rickety staircase with a worn carpet led the way up and round to her door, her private domain since her mother's move into her old bedroom. She didn't mind that it had once been servants' quarters, but when she had asked her Dad if she could paint over the flimsy floral wallpaper, she was met with a guffaw of derision; he told her he wasn't going to waste good money when the only person to see it was her.

She closed the door behind her and looked with dismay at the bed strewn with discarded clothes, the result of several hours' preparation for the dance. She stepped out of her dress and added it to the pile, then kicked off her shoes. In her bathroom she looked with disgust at the forgotten water lying in the bath; a pink sponge was lying like an island in a sea of pale-grey scum. She bent to pull the plug out and then stopped; the water travelling through the old pipes would wake the whole household.

She washed her face, making sure all the makeup was removed, and then gave her teeth a cursory brush. Returning to her bedroom, she scooped all the clothes off the bed and trailed them to the armchair, where she wearily dropped them. Tomorrow she would get everything back into apple-pie order. Tomorrow she would call Alison. Tomorrow Max would arrive. She climbed into bed, her haven, snuggled down, and to the faint rumbling of her father's snores, fell asleep immediately.

The scratching on her door registered, but she did not stir. Without looking at her clock, she knew it was eight in the morning because Barney was ready for his walk. Nicholas would have to take him. She drifted off to sleep again as she heard her mother's voice coaxing the dog away from her door.

Her thoughts drifted. Why is a bed the most comfortable when it's time to get up, she mused? Then her eyes flew open, and excitement brought a tightness to her chest. Max was coming today. Her so called cousin at twenty-eight was growing more attractive every time she saw him since he'd landed on their doorstep two years ago.

'Tell me how we're related to Max,' she had asked her mother after his first whirlwind visit.

Her mother took up another sock and pulled it over the darning mushroom. 'Auntie Winnie was a widow when she married your uncle Walter. Max was six at the time and he took on the Baines name. As you know, Walter was killed in the war. Winnie and Max went to live with her sister down in Devon soon after. We haven't seen her for years. We've exchanged Christmas cards but that's all. It was quite a surprise when Max contacted your Dad.'

'So, he's not related to us at all, really.'

'Only by marriage.'

'Dad really likes him.'

'He's charmed your Dad, that's for sure. And don't you get ideas, he's far too old for you.'

Since then, Max had been centre stage of her romantic dreams. She must ring Alison to tell her to come early so that they could have fun watching his arrival from her bedroom window.

She dressed and took her time cleaning up the debris of the previous night before running downstairs to the kitchen. Her mother was bending over the oven, tugging at the shelves with one hand whilst holding a raw bacon and egg flan with the other.

'Marjorie. Hold this, will you, while I move the shelf?' She looked and sounded overwrought.

'Why don't you just put it down?' Marjorie's cool logic and her mother's ability to be easily flustered did not mix well.

'Just hold it, please,' her mother snapped, 'before I decide to walk out and never come back.'

'OK. What's Dad said this time?' Marjorie asked, resignation in her voice, as she took the flan from her mother.

'It's not what he said, it's the way he said it.' Her mother punctuated her words in time to her tugs at the stubborn shelf. 'If he thinks he can talk to me as though I were a servant, putting in his orders, he...'

Marjorie rolled her eyes to the ceiling at the cold war between her parents. 'Mum, he's been doing that for years, and you have been saying that for as long as I can remember, but you're still here. Anyway, you can't walk out today; Max is coming. Who would do the entertaining?'

'Entertaining!' Her mother finally wrenched the shelf free and slid it between the grooves above. 'Max is part of the family; he doesn't need to be entertained.'

'Hardly seems worth the effort,' Marjorie said, looking at the flan before handing it over to her mother to place on the shelf.

'It's not,' her mother answered testily, banging the oven door closed, 'for all the appreciation it will get. But never mind. What time is it now?' She glanced at the clock in its wooden casing sitting solidly on the mantelpiece. 'They'll be here in half an hour. Set the table will you?'

Marjorie loved the family kitchen, with its huge oak table dominating the room. Her Dad had insisted on having it when he'd bought out a small builder with 'big ideas,' as he put it. The table had been in the conference room where clients were supposed to discuss plans for building projects. 'Silly bastard thought they'd be impressed, but they never came near his fancy table, and now it's mine. Good as new,' he'd boasted as it was heaved into the back room. 'The lads will turn this into the kitchen,' he announced without discussion. Marjorie remembered her mother pressed against the wall as chairs were unceremoniously pushed aside by two of her father's workmen, and the huge table slammed in the middle of the 'telly room,' as they called it. She watched her mother's face changing from indignation to anger, but even as she opened her mouth to speak, Ernest Baines had already stuffed his cigar into his mouth and walked out of the house, slamming the door.

'It'll be like a farmhouse kitchen,' she ventured as her mother slumped into a chair, tea towel in hand, her lips firmly pursed. 'You've always wanted a bigger kitchen,' Marjorie continued, trying to get her mother to see the bright side and to take her out of her black mood.

She hated it when their mother became 'depressed,' as it was called. It made her depressed too (if that was the word), as she skirted round her mother, saying as little as possible so as not to upset her more. Be gentle with her, Dr Kerr had said the last time her mother was whisked off to hospital with yet another attack of angina. She and Nicholas had no problem being gentle, but how were they to control their father's behaviour?

Why her parents couldn't speak to one another like other people she couldn't fathom. George's parents joked with one another and even hugged in front of visitors. Nicholas had taken her with him after her father had lashed out and given her mother a black eye. She couldn't remember the reason her father hit her mother that time, but she did remember feeling acutely embarrassed at George's house. The two domestic scenes couldn't have been more different, and she had felt ashamed and enlightened at the same time. This was what home life could be like. It was a revelation.

The cooker and fridge were moved; kitchen cupboards were built and lined up against the walls; Formica tops were fitted; the old kitchen became a place to do the washing, and the telly room was transformed into a kitchen. It became the favourite place for everyone except their father, who sat like a cigar-smoking Buddha in the front room with the relocated television at full blast.

The big table served many functions: homework at one end with the sewing machine and meals eaten at the other end. Piles of books, mending, sewing basket, Barney's lead…all shared space, sometimes being transferred to the sideboard in a clear up only to find their way back to the table in a matter of hours.

Her mother came to love the big kitchen for the refuge it offered. She kept her latest library book behind the cushion of her armchair, taking it out when she knew it was safe. Marjorie loved sitting at the table in the evenings while she and Nicholas did their homework. Her mother would look up from her book and say, 'Did you know…?' They would stop what they were doing to listen. Dry facts would be transformed into a story full of colour. She brought characters to life, animating history, geography, or current affairs and handing down the gift of storytelling she had inherited from her father. He had been a gentle man, she had told them, whom she had loved dearly and missed sorely when he died suddenly soon after she married. Reading between the lines, Marjorie gleaned that her grandfather never liked her dad.

Marjorie laid the table, taking special care because of Max coming. She hadn't realised that he was already in Middleston and that he would be joining them for lunch. Alison would be disappointed that she wouldn't be sharing the excitement of his arrival. Still, there was plenty of time to talk and plan when she saw her later in the day. She brought out their best plates from the sideboard, along with napkins that they only used for very special occasions.

'Good Lord, Marjorie, it's only Max coming, not royalty.' Her mother chided her gently but allowed her daughter to clear the big table of clutter to make it look presentable.

'I know, Mum, but I want it to look nice.'

'Your dad won't notice, that's for sure.' Her mother staggered as she spoke, and her face crumpled with pain. 'Oh dear God—not now,' she moaned, her hand clutching the front of her dress.

'Mum!' Marjorie darted forward but was too late. Horrified, she watched her mother slump to the floor. 'Are you all right, Mum?' Even as she said it, she knew it was a daft question, but she desperately wanted her mother to say yes, let's finish laying the table, anything to bring her back to normal.

'No, I'm not,' she said grimly, her face contorting with agony.

A cold chill passed through Marjorie's body. 'I'll go and get Dr Kerr.'

Marjorie lifted her mother's head and put a cushion underneath, then dashed to the cloakroom to fetch a thick gardening cardigan, placing it around her shoulders before leaving the house.

She flew past the newly installed telephone in the hall, skidded to a halt, then continued out of the house and ran down the drive, through the large gates, and into the quiet leafy road, passing two other large detached houses before coming to the gates of Dr Kerr's practice. She raced into the drive past the highly polished plaque on the gatepost, noting that the bottle-green Jaguar was parked in front of the garage doors. Thank God Dr Kerr was in. Relieved, she rang the bell. It sounded through the spacious hall, and almost immediately David Kerr was there with his long grey coat on, as if ready to leave.

'Hello, Marjorie. What can I do for you on this lovely day?'

'My mother,' she gasped. 'She needs help. She's collapsed.'

Dr Kerr called into the house. 'Nancy, Mrs Baines is ill. Better alert the hospital and get an ambulance round.'

It was shortly after moving house that her mother had experienced her first attack of angina. Dr Kerr and his wife had supported Marjorie and Nicholas through the event, and would have liked to have talked to their father too, but had been met with truculence and hostility. His anger at his wife's illness, taking her away from her duties, as he saw it, was plain.

'There's no room for weakness in my family,' he growled at the Kerr's. 'Everybody has to pull their weight.' The attacks had continued in spite of the medication, with increasing severity.

On entering the kitchen, they found her mother slumped on the floor. Marjorie had a sense of foreboding as she saw how the pain had taken its toll on her mother's features. The half-closed eyes showed no life above the grey cheeks. Her mouth was open and relaxed. She looked old. Marjorie covered her mouth as if to prevent the cry of anguish she felt welling up inside her from escaping.

Dr Kerr knelt down beside her mother. 'I'll take care of you now, Lydia.' He spoke slowly as he placed a tablet under her tongue before adjusting her position. 'An ambulance is on its way. You're in good hands now.'

Straightening, he took Marjorie's elbow, guiding her to a kitchen chair. Sitting next to her at the massive table, he took her trembling hands in his own. 'Would you like me to call your father and tell him?'

'He'll be home soon anyway for lunch with Max. He won't want to be interrupted.' She felt very young and vulnerable. She didn't want to incur her father's wrath. Without her mother there as a buffer, it would all fall on Nicholas and herself.

Dr Kerr seemed to pick up the fear in her voice. 'I'll call him, even if it's just to tell him that he won't be having lunch here.'

'I can—'

'No, you can't. You've done enough for one day,' he said firmly. 'Perhaps it's time your father learnt that life just can't go on as normal when your mother is ill.'

He looked across at the shallowly breathing figure, and as if sensing that he may not have another opportunity, he said, 'Marjorie, your mother is very ill and not very strong now after all these attacks. She may not have too long to live.'

The possibility of her mother dying had not occurred to her. 'She can't die yet. She's not old enough.' She knew she was talking nonsense. She tried to digest the implications of his words, but her heart refused to let them settle where reason might make sense of them. He was talking about the future. It wasn't relevant now. Her mother would get well again. She didn't have to think about it now.

'She's very ill, Marjorie,' he repeated gently. 'People can die at any age when they're too ill.'

As he finished speaking, they heard the ambulance pull up outside the front door and two doors slam. Dr Kerr left her side to supervise her mother's journey to hospital.

Sometime later she was still sitting at the table when Barney came rushing into the kitchen, tail wagging, tongue hanging lopsidedly, pushing his wet face into her lap, demanding his ears to be scratched. Not having any success, he went round the table and sniffed the floor looking for forgotten crumbs before going on to the scullery to find his water.

Nicholas sauntered in. At eighteen he appeared awkward and lanky, accentuated by his tall but slight build. He wore his usual weekend clothes, a three-year-old Guernsey fishing sweater which he still didn't fill, and navy cord trousers. They were smeared with paint and oil. 'Hello, Sis.' He looked round. 'Where's Mum?' Loud splashing and scraping could be heard as Barney trailed his bowl over the quarry-tiled floor. 'We had a great walk, right down by the canal and along the railway line and over the bridge,' he went on, oblivious to her haggard expression. 'You get a fantastic view of the old wharf buildings from there. They might turn some into artists' studios...'

Still shocked by her mother's collapse, Marjorie stared blankly at him.

'Well don't look so interested.' He frowned at the burnt flan on the table. 'What's that? Did you make it? Where's Mum?' he asked again.

She hugged her arms together, holding her own anguish together. 'Mum's gone into hospital again.'

She hated telling him. He always withdrew into his own world whenever their mother was in hospital. Since moving into the big house, she had been taken away from them for long periods until her heart was strong enough for the world again. Strong enough for the scorn meted out by their father and the bullying.

It had been easier when they had lived next door to Auntie Ollie, in the shabby street where their old friend still lived. That was before her father made his money. Her mother used to love life then. She remembered her singing and yearned to go back to that time.

Auntie Ollie wasn't their real aunt; she was a widow. And having no children of her own, she had delighted in knowing Lydia and the children. They had shared in each other's lives with trust and love. Their father, however, had never approved of the close tie.

'Does Auntie Ollie know?' Nicholas asked, a tremor in his voice.

Marjorie shook her head. 'Not yet.'

'Does Dad know?'

'Yes. Dr Kerr will have told him by now.'

Nicholas sat next to her. With a sigh he placed his elbows on the table, cupping his chin in his hands. She saw he was having a difficult time holding back the tears. Poor Nicholas. Her own emotions were also too near the surface to speak. They'd never talked together about feelings, and they were not going to now. She didn't have the words in her head to say what she was thinking, but she felt a raw gash inside her chest at the thought of her mother struggling for life and her father not caring.

There was a crunching of wheels over the gravel as a car swept up to the front door. Doors slammed and the animated voices of their father and cousin drove brother and sister into action. They sped, shoulder to shoulder, up the stairs, leaping two at a time until they reached her room at the top of the house. Hearts leaping wildly, they helped each other to lock the door. They didn't have to speak to know that neither of them wanted to hear their father's indifference to their mother's state of health.

Minutes went by. Their breathing calmed, and so did they. Marjorie knew that they could not stay hidden forever, that they would have to face their father and be polite to their cousin. Her earlier excitement about seeing Max again had vanished after the trauma of the morning. Marjorie was the first to speak. 'We'd better go down.'

'Yeah, suppose so.'

She squeezed Nicholas's arm, encouraging him. 'It'll be all right. Mum will be better tomorrow, I expect. We'll go and see her then.'

'If Dad lets us.'

Even though she was younger, Marjorie felt she was the stronger of the two and more adept at avoiding their father's wrath. She unlocked the door. 'He will,' she reassured him. 'Besides, Max is here now. Dad won't want to appear cruel in front of Max.'

'Max doesn't care.' Nicholas spoke with unexpected bitterness. 'He just thinks it's funny and says he hopes it isn't catching.'

'When did he say that? He can't have said that!'

'He did, when he was here last time.'

'No.'

'He said it to me when we were on our own.'

She searched her brother's eyes, so like her own, not wanting to believe him, but knowing that Nicholas would never lie. 'He can't have meant it, then.'

'Marjorie,' her father bellowed impatiently. 'Marjorie, where are you, girl?'

They heard their father beginning to climb slowly upwards, pausing to catch his breath as he reached the landing.

'Marjorie, Nicholas, come down at once, d'you hear?'

She opened the door, revealing her father. Nicholas stayed behind, using her as a flimsy protection against his father's power.

A cigar held by a small fat hand was put back into its customary place between stained teeth. Her father spluttered when the smoke met the back of his throat. He was already struggling to catch his breath from the climb up the stairs. His waist-coated chest heaved; his large, florid face was taut with exertion and irritation.

Marjorie and Nicholas did not dare move. Max was behind, being solicitous. Max, the subject of Marjorie's dreams.

Due to his casual, insolent air, an assuredness in the world that belied his twenty-eight years, Marjorie was attracted to Max like a moth to a flame. He had never said or done anything to earn such a level of adoration. All he had to do was to be there, out of her reach. In that way, her imagination could do the rest, filling in the details of conversation, of being alone together on a romantic walk, holding hands, kissing. She had replayed that kiss so many times—what he said, what she said, and how he gently held her in his arms and told her he loved her. She looked covetously now at the well-built figure with his Gregory Peck film-star looks putting his arm round her father's shoulders.

'Uncle Ernest, are you all right? Here, let me help you. Let me get you a drink or something.'

Marjorie saw his eyes travelling up her long, slim, bare legs, past the flared skirt to the blouse, open at the neck, and to her face. Holding his gaze, her heart fluttered as she saw the admiration in his stare.

'Sorry to hear about Auntie Lydia,' Max said lightly.

'Don't you feel sorry for her, lad. What about me?' Ernest sprang back to life, antagonistic as usual. 'Where's that drink? You two, get yourselves downstairs when we have a guest. Where're your manners?' He glared at Marjorie, stabbing the air with his cigar. 'We need some lunch, girl.'

Marjorie followed her father and Max into the living room. 'There isn't any lunch ready. Mum was taken ill in the middle of preparing it. Didn't Dr Kerr tell you?'

'Yes, my lass, he did. But I expect you to get on with what needs to be done, instead of mooning about feeling sorry for your mother. Bloody woman.' He clapped his hands and rubbed them together. 'As it's somewhat of an occasion, let's go out, Max. Marjorie, book a table at the George for us. We'll have a slap up lunch and celebrate, eh lad?'

He reached up and placed a possessive hand on Max's back. 'Where's that pansy son of mine? Ah, there you are.' He swung round, catching sight of Nicholas in the doorway. 'Trying to sneak away as usual.' Nicholas stepped forward from the hall. 'You've missed out, lad, with your fairy ways.' He was spitting as he spoke. 'Max is coming in with me now, and he'll work his way up through the company like you should have been doing. What d'you say to that?'

Nicholas looked from Earnest's jeering scowl to the self-satisfied smirk of his cousin. 'Congratulations, Max,' he said, not bothering to conceal his dislike. 'You've done me a great favour.' He turned to go.

Ernest Baines glared after him, his face belligerent. 'You'll regret this, my lad. I'll cut you out.'

The bell rang. Max pushed past Nicholas and opened the front door with proprietary confidence. Marjorie snatched up the phone to reserve a table at the George Hotel. She heard Alison's voice, unusually merry and bright, and the velvet tones Max reserved for flattery, before he swept his arm in a grand gesture, making way for her friend to enter. Alison strutted past him into the hall, her eyes sparkling, her head held high.

'They've got a table right now,' Marjorie said to her father as she replaced the receiver. He had been pacing in and out of the living room as if trying to shake off his anger at Nicholas, who had sauntered past him and out of the door without a word to anyone.

'Let's be off then, lad. I'm famished,' he said, brushing past Alison and Marjorie, leaving a trail of cigar smoke in his wake.

'Bye, girls. See you later.' Max winked at them before turning on his heel to follow his lunch companion, slamming the door behind him.

'Isn't he gorgeous?' Marjorie turned to Alison, whose gaze was transfixed on the closed door.

'Yes, he is,' she answered simply.

'Mum's in hospital again,' Marjorie said as she started to climb the stairs to her bedroom. 'She was taken ill this morning. Dr Kerr frightened me. He said she might not have long to live.'

'She can't die yet, she's not that old,' Alison said in a matter-of-fact voice.

'That's what I think.' Marjorie drew comfort from her friend's confident declaration. Feeling happier, she continued to lead the way upstairs.

—◊—

Alison tucked a final pin in Marjorie's hair to secure her creation.

'There,' she announced proudly. 'Now you can look.'

Marjorie turned towards the dressing table and peered into the mirror, surveying the transformation. Her hair was piled high in a teetering bouffant; each curl had been sprayed generously before being pinned in place, a layered sculpture worthy of any hairdresser in the town.

'It's great. Do you think Max will notice?' She pouted her red lips and half closed her eyes, imitating Marilyn Monroe.

Alison laughed merrily. 'Now it's my turn.' She swapped places with Marjorie to have her hair put up. Alison's fine features were framed by thick blond hair cut expertly at chin length. She had perfected the gesture of running her hand through her hair and letting it fall casually, as if knowing that it would still look perfect. Eyebrow pencil and liner had been skilfully applied to the almond-shaped eyes; a light dusting of powder and a modest pink lipstick completed the picture of understated refinement.

Marjorie looked in the mirror at her friend and for the first time felt threatened by her presence. 'I better not make you look more beautiful than me. What if he looks at you all the time?'

'He won't even notice me, silly. You look gorgeous, and anyway, he hardly ever sees me.' Alison smoothed an eyebrow with her finger.

'He certainly noticed you at the door; I could tell.' Marjorie tried to sound casual.

'Only because he was so surprised how much I'd grown up since last year,' Alison parried, sidestepping the implied question and not satisfying Marjorie's curiosity.

Marjorie continued to brush Alison's hair, and the two girls were quiet, lost in their own thoughts. The brilliant plan hatched the day before, of suggesting to Max that they go to the cinema as an opportunity to get him on his own away from her father no longer seemed so attractive to Marjorie. She had imagined Max sitting between them, holding her hand and ignoring Alison on his other side, but what if…? From the record player Roy Orbison's voice reached new heights in an agony of emotion.

'He said you looked a smasher.' The hurt crept into her voice.

'Did you find out what's on at the pictures?' Alison asked, ignoring Marjorie's last remark. Getting no answer, she looked up from her perfectly shaped pink nails into the glum face in the mirror, 'Hey, dreamboat, I asked you a question.'

'No I didn't. I don't think I want to go now.' Marjorie's confidence in her own attractiveness was being sapped by the coolness of the girl in the mirror. The gold hair that really didn't need anything done to it to look stunning folded into a smooth spiral, and Marjorie expertly pinned it. 'D'you want spray?' she asked testily, unable to conceal her jealousy.

'No, nothing. I like it to look natural.'

Marjorie looked at her watch again. She couldn't understand where Max and her father were. 'Will you help me make tea before you go?'

Alison checked her hair in the mirror and looked pleased with the overall result, including her new dress. She shook her head. 'I'm sorry, I better go now. Mum and Dad will be wondering where I am.' She looked round the room, at the dressing table where makeup lay strewn, caps off bottles, tubes and lipsticks. She had tried a couple of dresses on which now lay on the floor. She tiptoed her way through the mess to the door. 'I'll see you tomorrow morning, then.' She left, delicately picking her way downstairs in her new stiletto heels.

Marjorie heard the front door slam and looked at the room. It would have to wait. Why couldn't Alison have at least helped her with this lot before she went? But then, Alison never cleared up or got her hands dirty, so it was pointless to even ask her. She had arrived late in their married life, so her well-off parents employed cleaning staff to help with the running of their house.

She looked into the mirror again and felt a little ridiculous in her piled-up hair. About to take the first of many pins out, her heart sank as she heard the car below her window. Not wanting to be found upstairs again, she quickly ran down to the kitchen and pulled out the loaf of bread and some cheese to start the cheese on toast. She found a tin of baked beans and some fresh tomatoes to go with it.

'Hello, Marjorie. All alone?'

She looked up at Max standing in the doorway. She blushed as he closed the door and came over to stand beside her.

'I saw your friend walking down the road. Is she coming again tomorrow?'

'Yes. We're going for a walk with Barney before I visit Mum.' She unwrapped the cheese and started to slice it, wanting bright conversation to come to her, but it didn't, as usual.

Max took a slice of cheese and ate it, looking at her, evidently enjoying her awkwardness. 'Does she live near?'

'Just down the road in the big house on the corner.'

'She must be rich then.'

'I suppose so. Her Dad was in business, but he's retired now. They don't let her go out much.' But why were they talking about Alison? 'How long are you staying this time, Max?' she said, changing the subject. 'Are you really going to be in Dad's business?' He was ignoring her. 'Will you live here?' Her questions hung in the air. Was he never going to speak? She blushed, remembering her hair. 'Alison did my hair. D'you like it?' she ventured.

He turned towards her at the mention of Alison's name. 'It looks bloody awful. It's like a bat's nest, but,' he said as he got up to leave, 'you smell nice.'

She blushed again, hating her hair. Why couldn't she have hair like Alison's?

'When will tea be ready?'

She looked at the clock. 'About half past five.'

'Right then, I've time for a bath. See you a later little, cousin.' He departed, leaving her to get the tea ready for the three very different men in her life.

Nicholas came in just as they were sitting down, and took his place at the end of the table without a word. Marjorie wanted to ask him if he'd told Auntie Ollie about what had happened to their mother, but their father didn't like the contact with their old neighbour, saying they were above that sort now, so it would have to wait.

Ernest thrust his face towards Nicholas from the opposite end of the table. 'I'm surprised you still expect to be fed in my house,' he snarled. Like two spears, his knife and fork were held in fisted hands on either side of his plate, as the warrior in him came out to fight.

'Why shouldn't I? It's my home too,' Nicholas answered mildly as he settled down and began to scoop up some baked beans with his fork. He continued to eat, his eyes averted from his father's bellicose posture.

Marjorie stopped eating, fear for Nicholas immediately driving away her appetite. Max wiped his mouth and poured himself a cup of tea before going on with his meal.

'You'll look at me when I'm speaking to you, my lad.' Their father glowered down the table. 'And eat with your bloody knife.'

Nicholas picked up his knife. 'Sorry, Dad, I always forget that bad manners upset you.' He looked steadily at his father as if challenging him. She held her breath, wondering what would happen. A climb-down was not in her father's nature. Nicholas was being reckless. It was as though he didn't care about the consequences.

Ernest's glower took in Marjorie, pressed into the back of her seat with tension, and Max, who had taken some bread and butter and was calmly spreading jam. 'You think you're clever with your schooling and your arty-farty ways,' he snarled, 'but you're nothing but a useless weakling. Don't think you're getting anything from me, because you're not. It's your cousin here,' he indicated Max with his fork, 'that's doing what you should have been doing. From now on, as far as I'm concerned, you don't exist.'

Marjorie saw Nicholas relax. There was nothing new in the speech, but Nicholas himself broke new ground by saying, 'Can that be a two-way arrangement, Father?'

'You little bastard,' Earnest hissed as he leapt to his feet, shaking with barely contained rage. 'Get out of here, now,' he yelled, the full force of his anger suddenly released. 'You're no son of mine unless I get an apology!'

'In that case, I'll go until Mum gets back,' Nicholas answered, scraping his chair back. 'Thanks for tea,' he said to

Marjorie, who was sitting motionless like a startled deer caught in the crossfire.

Please don't go, she pleaded silently. Was she going to be left alone to deal with her father?

'Get out, get out!' Earnest screamed at the departing figure of his son. The front door slammed.

Max held the teapot over the cup. 'Tea, Uncle Ernest?' he asked the still-standing figure as though nothing had occurred. He looked across at her and grinned. She relaxed as she watched her father subside into his chair like a deflated balloon, all the hot air having escaped. 'Tea?' Max asked, and she held out her cup gratefully to him.

Later as she washed the dishes, Max came to stand beside her. Her father had gone into the living room to watch the news on the television.

'Dad and Nicholas have never really got on,' she said to him, trying to excuse her father's temper.

'That's to my advantage,' he muttered almost to himself. She looked sideways at him, at his strong profile, the shadow of his beard darkened at the end of the day. She thought he was quite the most handsome man she had ever met in her life, or would ever meet. Here he was, choosing to stand next to her, to talk with her. The thought swelled her heart, and she blushed. Their eyes met, and he smiled.

'I'll see that Nicholas is taken care of,' he told her, as he put an arm round her shoulder. She felt the weight of his hand and thought she might die with happiness. Then she remembered her mother in hospital.

'I hope Mum will be better soon.'

He squeezed her shoulder. 'I'm sure she will. Poor Auntie Lydia,' he said soothingly. The picture of the wolf from 'Little Red Riding Hood' flashed through her head, but she pushed it aside.

'Come here,' he said, lifting her chin up and bending to kiss her lips. Before she knew it, he was holding her with one hand on her back, the other travelling up her skirt to her panties.

She struggled free. 'No, Max.' She laughed at his boldness and ran round the other side of the table.

'You're not that sort of girl, Marjorie?' he asked teasingly, following her.

'No, I'm not. I've never done anything like that,' she said, keeping the table between them.

'Didn't you like it then?'

His smooth tones unsettled her, and she stopped to think. 'No, I didn't,' she answered firmly, surprising herself at how strongly she felt. This scenario was not part of the romantic picture she had drawn.

'I can tell you're lying,' he chortled. 'I'll see you later,' he said enigmatically. He grinned at her and walked out of the kitchen.

As she finished the dishes, Marjorie's head whirled. Now what? She didn't like the thought of being alone. Her mother in hospital, Nicholas gone, her father and Max in cahoots—what was she to do? She wiped her hands on the tea towel and looked around the kitchen, wanting an answer to come to her. Her instincts were to join Nicholas at Auntie Ollie's, but she knew her father would never allow it. The sort of interest that Max had shown in her was the last thing she wanted. 'What am I to do?' she cried out loud as she wiped the table. It seemed that she had no choice but to carry on as normal and not give Max any opportunity to do that again.

Not wanting to be alone in the kitchen, she joined the two men in the front room. They were talking business. She picked up her book on modern architecture and sat down. Max and Ernest's future partnership was being discussed. Max handled her father well. Their age difference did not seem to bring inequality. On the contrary, it was as though Max was in charge. It was he who led the conversation, and it was her father who looked surprised before he readily agreed to Max's suggestions. It had never been clear to her before why Ernest wanted Max in his business, but it became apparent that evening as she half listened in. Her father had settled into his chair, a cloud of cigar smoke hanging over his head.

'Eventually, lad, we'll have the whole town in our pockets. I'll be sitting on the council and feeding Baines and Baines the contracts, legit like. We'll be seen to take in tenders, but we'll just have better proposals than everyone else.' He chuckled. 'This town will be sewn up in under five years, I reckon. Mind you, with this general election coming up, we have to make sure we're lining the right pockets. Labour will win, you mark my words, and they have their high ideals, which could get in the way.'

'We'll have to look into shares, Uncle. To be convincing, I'll need to have full partnership.'

'No lad, not yet.' Ernest shook his head. 'Not until you can buy yourself in, and that won't be for a long time.'

'If I could raise the money, would you put a time frame on that offer?'

'You could come in tomorrow if you had the capital,' he said expansively, 'but I think you're underestimating the worth of the business. It'll take you years to buy in.'

'I'm aware of that, but if I could raise the money, say in two to three years, would your offer stand? And don't forget my worth to the company as a director.'

'You don't have any worth as a director,' Ernest countered.

'I can promise I will have, Uncle. I'm going to be very valuable to you.'

Ernest regarded Max, who had taken a seat on the other side of the fireplace. His eyes narrowed momentarily, as if considering the wisdom of another rash promise.

'It'll be years before you can raise enough. You can have my word on that offer.'

'In writing.'

Ernest took the cigar from his mouth and contemplated it thoughtfully. 'Aye lad, you can have it in writing,' he said quietly, as if he knew he would regret it one day.

The evening wore on, the two men drinking, exchanging ideas, and making plans. Not once did they address Marjorie or even acknowledge her presence. She felt tired after the day's events. Her father had drunk too much and was becoming louder, burping and boasting. She knew it wouldn't be long before he passed out.

She got up. 'Goodnight, Dad.'

'Night lass,' he slurred. 'And make sure you're up early to make our breakfast. We've got a long day ahead of us.' He turned to Max. 'How's about a nightcap?'

'Thanks, don't mind if I do. What'll yours be, Uncle? The same again?'

Ignoring Marjorie, he walked past her to the drinks table behind her father's chair. He pulled the glass stopper from the decanter and poured a generous amount of whisky for Ernest into the tumbler before looking across at her. 'Night, Madge,' he said with mocking self-assuredness before continuing to prepare his own drink.

She closed the door behind her and ran upstairs to her room. She lay awake, too tense for sleep to come. Her top sheet and blanket travelled around the bed with her as she struggled with her painful feelings of sorrow for her mother and the memory of Max's unexpected advance. It was a warm night, and she kicked the bedclothes to the bottom of the bed and lay there on her rumpled sheet, willing sleep to put an end to her troubled mind.

A noise startled her. She thought it was Barney at first. Then the unmistakable sound of the door handle being turned and a faint creak as the door opened made her heart jolt. Was it Nicholas back, wanting to talk? She sat up. Her eyes widened in astonishment. Oh God, it wasn't Nicholas, it was Max.

Unmistakably Max, with his tie pulled loose at his neck, revealing a gold chain nestling between the black hairs growing upwards from his chest. He checked that the door was firmly closed before walking on tiptoe to her bed. His tall figure loomed over her. His teeth glistened from the smile which played over his face, as if enjoying Marjorie's discomfort. She began to pull the sheet up to cover herself, but he calmly removed it from her hands, throwing it onto the floor.

'Max, what do you want?' she demanded, alarmed. He had brought with him the smell of tobacco and whisky.

'You,' he said and began to undo his tie, then his shirt buttons, fixing her with his cold eyes.

'I don't like this, Max.' She sprang out of bed, crossing her arms over her breasts as she backed away. A violent trembling gripped her as she stared at Max in speechless horror as he continued to undress. This was madness. What did he want?

Naked, he turned to face her. His chest was covered in thick hair, his arms large and muscled. Her eyes travelled downwards and found his penis pointing at her from a bed of black hair.

He chuckled at her look of surprise. 'Come here,' he said, sure of himself.

She had nowhere to go. She had never seen a man undressed before. This was Max, the object of her romantic notions, but those dreams had not included his creeping into her room like this.

He took hold of her hands and locked them behind her and covered her mouth with his, her young breasts behind the thin nightdress pressed against his hard chest. His tongue insinuated itself between her lips, exploring her mouth.

She struggled against the powerful body that held her, imprisoning her. Nowhere in her dreams had she imagined this. In her dreams she could control events. Now she wrestled vainly against the determined strength of Max, unable to free herself. He released her mouth, and taking a deep breath, she opened her mouth to scream. A large hand smelling of whisky stifled her cry, preventing the sound from forming.

Struggling wildly, she was caught in his arms and lifted onto the bed, her head pinned down into the pillow by his mouth, hard and unrelenting on her lips. Max rolled on top of her, roughly pushing her legs apart. She moaned into his mouth, struggling for air, feeling sick with the reek of smoke and alcohol. Incensed with the way his hands were exploring her, his strong fingers reaching deep into her, she tried to wrench his arm away, but it refused to move. She began to feel frightened as the battle over her body was being lost by muscle power she could not hope to compete with. She was terrified. He groaned with pleasure as he thrust into her. She cried out, an animal cry, an animal in distress. Please let her father hear.

'Go on, shout and scream. I love it.' He laughed into her tortured face. 'Your Dad's drunk as a newt and won't hear a thing. You've been wagging this sweet juicy cunt in my face for years, wanting this like I have.' He got hold of her legs and held them far apart, and with a fixed stare into the face beneath him, roughly plunged in and out of her shamed body, ignoring her protestations and cries of pain.

2

'TELL ME WHAT happened,' Alison urged Marjorie. They were taking Barney for his walk along the towpath as planned. The warm sun had cleared the early-morning mist, revealing a cloudless blue sky. It was going to be a beautiful day. Alison clearly wanted to hear every detail of what had happened and been said in the Baineses' house the previous night. Marjorie refused to be drawn. Alison pouted. 'Tell me. If I didn't know you better, I'd think you didn't care about Max.'

Conscious of the soreness between her legs, Marjorie said, 'There's nothing to tell. I don't want to talk about him.' Her hatred of Max engulfed her, and she allowed Barney to pull her away from Alison's side, to walk in front at a distance from her old life.

It was as though she had been propelled into another world, away from light-hearted chatter and dreams into something sordid that would never see daylight. Max had told her to keep her trap shut. Then he'd left her to clean herself of blood and semen. It had not been necessary to tell her that.

She felt common and dirty, as if a horrible trick had been played on her. Of course she had known what men and women did within marriage. It had been the subject of intense discussion when she was about ten with her friends, and later in her early teens. Imagining her parents actually participating in that strange act left her nonplussed since they had never seemed close. It was difficult to believe they could have done such an act, but her existence proved it. Now she had knowledge of that act. Until last night she had always thought she would only gain that knowledge on her wedding night.

They passed the warehouses, and Marjorie recalled Nicholas saying something about turning them into artists' studios. *He would love that*, she thought, in a desperate attempt to take her mind off her feelings of shame. He had their mother's artistic nature; all he wanted to do was draw and paint, much to their father's disdain. It was clear that Nicholas would never be any help to the business. Physically, he appeared soft, and as their father so often put it, he was more like a girl. Ernest would be embarrassed to parade him as his son at the office. Nicholas was delighted to be let off the hook and did nothing to dispel his father's opinion.

Alison caught up with her and broke into her thoughts. 'Is your mother's illness dangerous?'

Ashamed that she had been only thinking of herself, Marjorie said what she hoped to be the truth, in spite of Dr Kerr's pessimism. 'No, she should be out in a few days.'

'I don't mean that. Is it dangerous to other people?'

Alison's question echoed in Marjorie's head. 'What d'you mean by that?' she demanded, turning round to confront her friend.

'Max said that sort of illness usually runs in families and also that it might be contagious to other people.'

Coldness entered her battered heart. 'When did he say that?' Her voice rose with indignation.

'This morning, when I was waiting for you downstairs.' Alison seemed unconcerned by Marjorie's stricken face.

Tears prickled behind her eyelids and she blinked them aside as her loathing of Max deepened.

'Marjorie, I feel a bit awkward.' But the half smile playing around Alison's lips didn't look awkward.

'Why?'

'He asked me out to the pictures. I didn't like to appear rude, so I said yes, as long as it's a matinee, to keep Mum and Dad happy. You weren't bothered about the pictures yesterday, so he's calling for me tomorrow. Anyway, you don't seem to be that interested in him this morning.'

She didn't know what to say. She was astonished at the cruelty of Max and now the treachery of her friend. She could never tell Alison what had happened, but should she warn her about Max? No, she couldn't trust her. She couldn't trust either of them not to twist round what had happened and make out that she was at fault.

The only person she could tell was Auntie Ollie, but she was too ashamed to tell her. And Nicholas, could she tell him? The thought was brushed aside as it formed. What could he do? She loved Nicholas but knew that he wouldn't be able to help her. He had stood up to her father, but his head was in the clouds. He wasn't practical; he was a dreamer. She would leave him out of it. How would her mother take it if she ever found out? It might be the last straw that made her mother leave Nicholas and her forever.

She shouldn't have let him do it to her. She should have screamed louder. If only her father had not thought so much of Max. Dad was sure to blame her. Max had said she had led him on. Had she? She didn't know that she was leading him on to do that to her. If so, then it was her own fault. From now on she would keep out of his way. She had no intention of allowing it to happen again.

Alison's insistent voice penetrated her thoughts, 'Are you interested in him or aren't you? If you are, I won't go, but if you aren't, then I've a right to accept his invitation.'

'I'm not bothered,' Marjorie shouted, surprised at her own vehemence. 'Just stop talking about him, will you.'

Heedless of the pain written across Marjorie's face, Alison looked relieved and gaily announced, 'All right, Miss Miserable, if that's what you want. I'm going home. You're not much company today.' She hurried off, taking the footbridge over the canal, leaving Marjorie alone with Barney.

She wiped her wet cheeks with her sleeve and wished she had a handkerchief for her nose. It would be better if she didn't think. Yes, if she ignored what had happened, perhaps it would be all right. She looked around at her childhood playground, the towpath leading up to the lock, the overflow sluices, and the bridge crossing the canal where she had thrown crusts to the ducks paddling in formation until chaos ensued as the bread hit the water. Across the canal the view of the wharf buildings had been a backdrop to endless games around the basin, now turned into a squalid dumping pit by the council with Keep Out signs plastered around barbed wire fencing. *It looks how I feel. Dirty and not to be touched*, she thought as she turned towards home.

She saw Nicholas hurrying towards her. His face was pale with anxiety.

'Auntie Ollie's just rung from the hospital,' he burst out. 'She said Mum's bad and we should go straight away.'

'Oh God, Nicholas. Let's run.' She led the way, tugging Barney along while leaping over the girders and expertly avoiding the barbed wire trailing over the tufted grass. Nicholas followed. 'Come on, we have to hurry,' she called over her shoulder.

'You sound like Mum could die,' Nicholas cried, the fear in his voice evident.

—◆—

Lydia Baines was already lying peacefully, her arms folded over her still chest, her closest friend weeping without restraint in the visitor's chair by her side. Olivia wept for herself and for her godchildren. What would happen to them now? Who would look after those little souls in that grand house, with that maniac rampaging about, scheming to fleece everyone who stood in his path? And that Max, a carbon copy of Ernest, dripping evil in his wake. 'Lydia, my dear, you were so kind and forgiving, and you would never admit, even to yourself, that you had made a bad choice of husband. You stubbornly returned to the ring for another bout until the bell went, and you landed back in hospital again and again. If only you had left him all those years ago when we lived like sisters, side by side.'

Olivia stroked Lydia's arm. '"It'll be better, you'll see," you said. Oh, Lydia, we used to have some good times in the old days, and now look at you.' She got up to look into her dead friend's face, trying to fathom the pain and understand how it had been for her since her move to the most desirable street in the town. 'God knows we saw little of each other after the move. You always put on a brave face, having plausible explanations and justifications for Ernest's behaviour. It seems as if we only really met in a hospital ward, at crisis times, when the charade was caught off guard, and the truth came out.'

She bent to brush Lydia's forehead with her lips. 'Goodbye, my dear. I hope you are in God's hands. You deserve to be.' Surrendering to her grief, she wept again, waiting for the children. She was the only barrier between them and their father now, she thought. They would be here soon.

—∭—

It was cold in the church. The flower arrangements looked forlorn, the heads spread out to make them look more generous. Beside her Nicholas was close to collapse. She offered her arm for support. The two leant against each other, feeling the benefit of their mutual love, as the service drew to the end with the last hymn.

Marjorie was aware of Max standing in the pew behind her. Her back felt hot with shame at the memory of his body joined together with hers. The smell of his sweat still lingered in her nostrils. The primeval grunts and sounds of satisfaction still echoed in her ears. She knew now that he didn't care a damn for her, or for her dead mother.

Since she had walked into the hospital with Nicholas to find her mother already lifeless, she had been in a sickened daze. Remembering the scene in the kitchen before her mother's attack, she felt responsible for her mother's early death. If only she had helped her more. If only she hadn't been so wrapped up in Max.

'It's my fault, Nicholas. Everything's my fault. I should have known. I could have stopped her from dying,' she whispered, tears streaming down her face, as the last verse of her mother's favourite hymn was sung by the handful of mourners.

'No, our Marjorie, that's not right,' Nicholas murmured. 'It's not your fault. It's not anybody's fault, except...' He glanced furtively at his father who was plugging the end of the pew with his bulk.

Marjorie followed his look, and she shook her head as if denying her father's part. 'It's not him. It's me that's rotten.'

She gazed into his gentle face, drained of colour, sorrow casting a shadow over the boy, forcing him into manhood against his will. She pleaded with her eyes for him to acknowledge the truth as she saw it, but he steadfastly refused. 'It's not your fault.' He said each word slowly and clearly, as if speaking to a child. Behind them, Max chuckled. Marjorie shuddered at the chilling sound, moving even closer to Nicholas, trying to block out the despised figure.

At the door, Nicholas thanked Dr Kerr and his wife for coming. Marjorie was also thankful that the Kerrs had come, but she did not trust herself to speak.

Nancy Kerr put her arms around Marjorie. 'If you want to talk, remember that I live just two doors away.'

Marjorie nodded, grateful for the offer, but wondering what she would say if she visited the Kerrs. She could not pretend to be the innocent girl they had once known.

At the graveside, Marjorie held on to Auntie Ollie, who stood, even though she was a head shorter, like a rock between brother and sister. Marjorie felt the protective shield as she said her final goodbye to her mother. It seemed as if they alone mourned her mother's passing. The other figures were taking furtive looks at watches as though her mother was keeping them away from more pressing business—which, Marjorie considered ruefully, she probably was. Her father had not interrupted his working week with the small matter of his wife's death. Her mother's death had also not stopped Max from taking Alison to the pictures as planned. And he continued to see her.

3

Six months after her mother's funeral, Marjorie had to confront Max. She had delayed too long, and now the matter was urgent. She was going to have a baby. The knowledge terrified her. Articles found in old copies of *Woman* magazine confirmed her suspicions. Yes, her periods had stopped, she had been sick in the mornings, and now when she carefully examined her changing body in the privacy of her room, the distinct bulge was obvious.

Max had been staying in the house on and off since her mother's death. He travelled between Manchester, eighteen miles away, and her home, which no longer felt like home. Scurrying about like a mouse avoiding a dangerous cat, she was careful not to be left alone with him, careful to lock her bedroom door as soon as she was there. She spent most of her time locked in, trying to complete homework assignments and worrying about her future. Nicholas spent most of his time at Auntie Ollie's, a fact that seemed to have gone unnoticed by her father. There was no such escape for her. She had to shop, cook the meals, and clean the house after school.

It was a quarter to eight, and she knew Max was alone downstairs because her father was out at a council meeting. She crept downstairs, her nerves acting as antennae to danger. She was charged, ready to flee if Max made a wrong move. The television was on in the living room, the door ajar. She tiptoed across the hall and listened. Kathy Kirby was singing about daffodils. Smoke drifted out of the spacious room, her mother's favourite before the kitchen was transformed, with its panelling and plate rack that still held her pretty collection of plates.

Marjorie tentatively knocked, as if she were the visitor. She didn't have long to wait. The door flew wide open, revealing Max, a glass of whisky in one hand, a cigarette held between his teeth.

'Ha ha,' he took the cigarette out of his mouth and spat a stray bit of tobacco at her feet. 'So you couldn't wait for your dad to go out,' he jeered. 'Come for some more, have we?' He held her chin up and leered into her face. 'Well, I don't like second-hand goods, see. And that's what you are now, little cousin.'

Shaking with hatred and shame, she tried to ignore his gibe. She had rehearsed her speech, and she would continue with it. 'I have to speak to you, Max. I need some help because I think I'm pregnant.'

She could see he was surprised and taken aback. He rubbed his chin, looking thoughtfully at her with ice in his eyes. 'And you're telling me I'm the father, you little bitch.' His eyes narrowed. 'How many more fellers have you tried this on? One lousy fuck doesn't count. Who else have you been laying?' he snarled, his teeth bared.

Shaken by his attack, she pleaded, 'No one, Max. You're the only one. Please believe me.'

He took a mouthful of whisky. 'I don't believe you, little cousin,' he enunciated slowly between clenched teeth, 'because you don't figure in my future plans. You'll have to get rid of it. If you say it's mine, I'll deny it.' He turned the knife. 'If you breathe a word of this to your dad, I'll tell him what sort of hussy you are. You're worthless trash, just like your mother.'

Marjorie backed away from the attack. 'How dare you say that about my mother? And it was you who came into my room and did this to me. It was you, and only you,' she cried, her anger giving her courage to go on. 'There was never anyone else, and you know it,' she shouted, surprised at the force of her anger, which shook her body.

He chuckled at her outburst, disarming her.

'You have to help me, Max,' she implored. 'You can't just ignore me after what you've done.'

He looked her up and down, his gaze coming to rest on her stomach. She felt naked, vulnerable.

He rubbed his chin again, a speculative gleam in his eyes. 'You're right, Madge, I need you out of the way, like your dear brother.' He was sneering now. 'I tell you what; I'll be kind and give you some money.'

Relief that he was going to help swept over her.

'Just don't come back.' He punctuated each word with contempt. 'It's your own fault you're up the spout. It's a good

job your mother's dead, or she might have had a heart attack.'
He smacked his thigh and laughed uproariously at his own
joke.

The bell rang through the house. 'Now if you'll excuse
me, I have a date with a very attractive friend of yours. She's
not soiled goods like you,' he said maliciously. He thrust his
empty glass into Marjorie's hand and opened the door to reveal
Alison. Max immediately whispered into Alison's ear glancing back with evident enjoyment. Alison burst into laughter,
looking past Max into the hall at her old friend, apparently
oblivious to Marjorie's distressed appearance. Max took
Alison's arm and, leaving the door open for Marjorie to watch
their progress, led his virginal companion down the drive and
through the gates.

Stunned, her knees crumpled beneath her. She lay her head
down on the cold patterned tiles in the hall, and drawing her
legs up, she hugged them. A long moan and a deep cry of despair filled the hall.

—⚭—

Marjorie stood outside Dr Kerr's house. It was the beginning
of January. In the cool sunshine, the black crows silhouetted
in the bare trees cawed loquaciously to each other, oblivious of
her terror on the doorstep below.

She was just about to turn away when she heard the *tap tap*
of heels on the hall tiles, before the door was opened by Mrs
Kerr.

'Hi, Marjorie, how good to see you. Come on in. I was just thinking how bored I was inside this big old house with no one to talk to.' In beautifully tailored slacks and a cashmere sweater, Nancy Kerr warmly welcomed Marjorie, concern for her young neighbour showing in her eyes.

Marjorie allowed herself to be led by the elbow to the back of the house, to what had become over the years her favourite room in the Kerrs' home. The conventions of a traditional kitchen had been put aside. Pictures were clustered together, vying for a place between bookcases. A comfortable sitting area with deep settees had been created to encourage conversation while she was preparing the meal, Nancy had told Marjorie long ago. A warm dusty-rose colour on the walls and soft furnishings complemented each other; bowls filled with fruit and fresh flowers taking their place in the room that had not been planned but had evolved in response to the Kerrs' lifestyle.

The delicious smell of an apple pie with cinnamon permeated the room, bringing the image of her mother bending down in front of the oven sharply to mind. Marjorie pushed the memory away before it took hold, before she was drawn towards the door that she did not wish to open. Not yet. It was too close to her heart. Now she had a more pressing problem.

'Sit down, dear,' Nancy Kerr said, indicating a settee surrounded by books in the corner, 'and tell me how you are. Would you like a fresh orange juice?'

'Yes, please.' She followed Mrs Kerr's neat figure as she walked to the fridge, to the cupboard for two glasses, and then back to where she was sitting, present in the room, but absent, detached from reality. She had no idea where to begin. Her head was aching, and she was exhausted with the enormity of what was happening inside her body. She chewed her swollen lip, making it bleed again.

'There we go. I crushed them this morning. Nice and fresh.' She put Marjorie's glass on the table beside the settee.

Marjorie could feel Mrs Kerr looking at her closely.

'Here, let me give you something for that lip, Marjorie,' Nancy Kerr said suddenly. 'It looks real sore.' Her high heels clattered over the tiles in the hall. She returned with a bowl of water, some cotton wool, and ointment and sat down next to Marjorie.

'Now what's been happening to you, Marjorie? Tell me.' Concern filled her voice, her eyes questioning, searching her blotched and swollen face for an answer.

Marjorie didn't trust herself to speak. She felt as if a dam would burst inside her.

Mrs Kerr patted her hand. 'Let's deal with this lip first, and then you can tell me.' She wet the cotton wool and gently lifted Marjorie's chin and began to dab the sore place. The tears began then, streaming down in response to the kindness. 'Oh, honey.'

Taking Marjorie into her arms, she held her, stroking the uncombed hair as she held the girl she had watched grow from a ten-year-old child, through the gangly early teenage years, and on into a young woman, all in the space of six years. 'Let it all out, honey. It's no good bottled up inside there hurting you.'

'I'm sorry, Mrs Kerr, It's just that I...' She took a deep breath. 'I'm going to have a baby, and I don't know what to do.' She pulled herself away from Mrs Kerr's arms and sat looking down into her hands. She had decided that Mrs Kerr was her only avenue of help. She had not even contemplated telling her father. The vision of his wrath, not directed at Max, but at herself, played before her. If her father was true to his past form, the blame would be heaped on her and Max exonerated as an innocent player.

Auntie Ollie would have helped, she knew, but she felt so ashamed. The opportunities to say something to her had come and gone without Marjorie being able to unburden herself. In a way she wanted to protect Auntie Ollie because her mother had asked her friend to keep an eye on the two children, and here Marjorie was, only months later, pregnant. Auntie Ollie would feel that she had failed. She felt Mrs Kerr looking at her, knowing that she had shocked this cool American lady.

'Have you seen a general practitioner, Marjorie?' Nancy Kerr asked her gently. There was no reproach in her voice, only concern.

'No.' She shook her head. It hadn't occurred to her to see Dr Kerr, or any other doctor. They could only tell her what she was already sure of.

'What makes you think you might be pregnant?' A glimmer of hope laced Nancy's question.

Marjorie looked up into the gentle eyes. 'I've missed my periods,' she stated without emotion, as though to quash any optimism.

'That can happen for a number of reasons, Marjorie,' Nancy said, relief flooding into her voice.

'I know, but this is different.' Marjorie had not thought that she would have to convince Nancy Kerr that she was pregnant. This kind woman was obviously searching for reasons why she shouldn't be pregnant, which she felt grateful for, but it wasn't getting her any nearer to the help and advice she needed.

'Do you know how babies are conceived, Marjorie?'

'Yes,' she answered firmly. She felt herself blush.

'And has that happened to you?'

Marjorie nodded, too embarrassed to speak of such things. Nancy's protective arm came round her shoulders. 'May I ask who with?'

She shook her head. 'I can't tell you that. Mrs Kerr, do you know where I can go?' She pleaded, 'I can't stay here, look!'

She stood up and smoothed down her sweater. 'I want to die, I just want to die. What am I going to do? Max doesn't care. My dad'll kill me. I have to get away soon. I can't tell anyone except you. What shall I do?'

Nancy Kerr looked at the unmistakable bump and asked, 'Who's Max?'

'Oh, I…' She sat down again. How had she let his name slip? 'No one.' Then she said quickly, 'He's someone who's given me some money to go away, to help me, and for the baby.'

'Is he the father, Marjorie?'

'No, no,' she lied. 'He's just a sort of cousin.'

'Mm...' Nancy pursed her lips, the evasion hanging between them. 'Is there a possibility of marrying the father if that's what you wanted?'

'No, he...You see, he's going out with someone else, and I wouldn't want to marry him anyway now,' she added, feeling stupid for having such dreams.

'I see.' Mrs Kerr didn't probe any further, as if she too accepted the hopelessness of pursuing that angle as a possible solution to Marjorie's problem. 'OK, let's look at all your options one by one, and we'll make a plan, but first of all, we have to get you examined.'

The practicalities of the situation were something that Marjorie now knew Nancy would cope with immediately. The emotional chaos raging inside her would have to wait another day.

'You can help me, then?' Filled with anxiety, she looked towards the older woman for reassurance.

'If you are pregnant, Marjorie, and it does look as though you are, I'll help you as much as I can, but it's you that has to make all the hard decisions.' She took Marjorie's hands into her own. 'This shouldn't have happened to you; you're too nice a girl.'

'I'm not now though, am I?' Marjorie said, Max's words still reverberating. She hung her head and began to chew her lip again.

'Marjorie, I'm not going to ask what happened, but my guess is that you were taken advantage of. That doesn't make you bad, it makes the guy bad.' Nancy Kerr looked at the kitchen clock. 'Look, David will be home about six p.m. Can you come back then?'

'Yes. Dad doesn't care if I'm there or not so long as he gets his tea.'

'That's settled then. Drink up your juice, dear. We'll get you examined; meanwhile, I'll make some calls.'

Nancy Kerr closed the door after watching Marjorie round the corner of the drive into the road. 'Damn men!' she said aloud. 'I wonder if Sister Agnes will be able to help?'

Marjorie hurried home, relieved that she was no longer on her own. She would have to make a cold tea for her father and Nicholas if he was there, and leave it on the table for them, before going back to the Kerr's house.

In the kitchen, she found Barney asleep in his basket and Nicholas making a pile of sandwiches. Since their mother's death, Nicholas had withdrawn into a private world. Marjorie too was shaken to the core by her mother's death, her guilty secret adding to her inability to express any grief.

'What are you doing them for?' she asked, indicating the sandwiches, just to say something.

'To eat,' he said, carefully matching the pieces of bread.

She watched him, his fragile bravado evident to the one who had been a buffer in the past, but who now desperately needed protection herself. Her sense of loss of what they once had filled her with sorrow. Their mother's death had separated them. Max had separated them.

'I'm going to make tea soon, but I have to go out again later, so it'll be cold,' she said to his bent head.

'That's all right, I won't be here either.' He didn't look up. It was as though he had detached himself from his old life, including her.

It was Wednesday, and Marjorie realised that she may not have another opportunity to tell Nicholas that she had to go away. They hardly saw anything of each other. He preferred to spend his time at Auntie Ollie's or on long walks with Barney with his sketchpad. She couldn't tell him the reason she had to go, and she wondered whether he would miss her at all. 'Nicholas.' Her tone of voice made him look up. 'I'm going away soon for a few weeks. Will you be all right on your own?'

'Where to?' he asked, knife held poised over the neat pile, ready to cut.

'I can't tell you. But I want you to promise me that you won't tell Auntie Ollie. Will you do that?'

Nicholas continued to hold the knife as though frozen in action. He stared hard at Marjorie, as if taking in her changed appearance for the first time. He cocked his head to one side. 'What shall I say?'

'Just say I'm revising for my exams or something like that, will you?' she said, trying to sound light, dismissing the obvious curiosity.

'If you like,' he said, continuing to stare at her, as if by looking long enough, the reason for her going away would become clear. 'Will you be coming back?'

'I don't know. I won't be back here though.' She had never kept anything from Nicholas before. There had never been any reason to. She felt uncomfortable asking him to lie for her. 'Will I find you at Auntie Ollie's?'

'Yeah. I think I might stay there all the time. Max'll be living here from Saturday, so there's no point my being here, is there?'

'Not really.' She acknowledged the truth of his assessment. 'Except you'll need some money sometimes.'

'That's all right. Max said he'd pay me off if I went, which suits me,' he said wryly. 'I don't want much money for what I want to do anyway.'

So Max had offered Nicholas money to leave, as he had said. Marjorie saw the situation clearly now. Max had successfully cleared a path for his own ambitions, without the encumbrance of his cousins. The fact that Nicholas was not inclined to make his way in their father's company, and was only too happy to step aside, did not seem to deter Max from treating his cousins as though they were the enemy, in competition with him. He seemed to be attributing his own rules of conduct to everyone around him, whether there was resistance or not.

'What does Dad think of your leaving?'

'Nothing. He doesn't know, and I don't suppose he'll care now that he's got our dear cousin.'

'I hate Max,' Marjorie pronounced savagely. His very name was loathsome on her tongue.

'So do I,' Nicholas agreed with equal vehemence. He finished the sandwiches and wrapped them in greaseproof paper. 'Sis, you will come back, won't you?' He looked at Marjorie properly now. 'Are you going to tell me why you're going?'

She knew she looked awful and saw Nicholas's concern at her appearance: her pasty-white face and her hair pulled back in an elastic band without being brushed. 'Oh, Nicholas, everything's gone so wrong,' she cried out, unable to hold on any longer, the pretence gone.

'Here, Sis, don't cry. You'll start me going soon. Come on. We've got each other and Auntie Ollie.' He came up to her and hugged her awkwardly, the lump under her sweater between them. He stroked her hair while Marjorie struggled with the tears that refused to stop flowing. He didn't ask again why she was leaving, 'I'll think of a good excuse for you, for school as well.'

The tears abated, and she gently pulled away from him, embarrassed at her outburst. She saw his face, grim and angry, an expression difficult to equate with her mild-tempered brother. 'When you get back,' he said gruffly, holding her by the shoulders, 'I'll be at Auntie Ollie's with Barney.' He pecked her on the cheek, picked up his sandwiches, and was gone.

—✺—

Making the tea for her father was a loveless task. A pork pie, the remainder of a tin of vegetable salad, and some lettuce leaves garnished with tomato and cucumber were all she could find. Thinking it didn't look much, she looked amongst the tins and found some peaches, which she put into a bowl, and placed a small jug of evaporated milk alongside.

The single place setting at the kitchen table looked lonely, but Marjorie knew that her father wouldn't notice the lack of company. He would be critical of his tea as a matter of course, but she didn't care. In the last few months, she had learned fully what her mother had endured during the years of her marriage. All the contempt and the sneering sarcasm had been transferred to Marjorie, making it easier for her to leave her home. She had decided to let her father think she was staying with Auntie Ollie. He would want to know to arrange for someone to housekeep for him.

Marjorie got back from the Kerrs' at eight o'clock, an address tucked in her skirt pocket. Opening the front door, she knew at once that Max was there in the front room with her father. Cigar smoke filled the house, and their loud voices were vying with each other for attention. They were well matched.

She had a strong desire to turn and go back to the Kerrs' house, but then Barney was there wagging his tail and licking her hands, telling her that he hadn't been let out for his nightly walk.

'Shush, Barney, shush.' She was afraid he would bark. 'Come on, let's go.' She got him out of the house as quickly as she could, careful not to let the door bang. It would give her time to think.

She would have to go back before they decided to go to bed, which would be probably about eleven, because her father would automatically lock the doors, thinking that everyone was in. But then, it would be better to go back soon while they were in the middle of talking. She could go in the back door, deposit Barney into his basket, and creep upstairs and lock her door.

Her plan made, she walked alongside Barney on his well-known route, a fine drizzle beginning to make itself known through her sweater. It was a cold night, but she didn't bother with a coat. Curtained windows shut her out of the big houses as she walked along the familiar streets. Coming to the corner where Alison lived, she paused at the big iron gates. She hadn't seen Alison since the day of her mother's death, except on Max's arm. Why did Alison's parents approve of her seeing Max but wouldn't let her go to a school dance? He was so much older and more experienced and so dangerous. Did they think he was too good a catch to miss now that he was working with her father? It made her feel sick remembering them together, arm in arm, laughing into her face as they went out the evening she had told him she was pregnant. Their friendship was gone forever, she knew.

The rain began in earnest. She left the circle of light shed by the lamp outside Alison's home and continued along the street. If she ever came back, it would be as a changed person. She would be the mother of a child she would never be able to hold in her arms, never love and never know. Never know. Never know. The chant kept time with her walking, filling her head as she made her way back to finalise this stage of her life.

A figure walked towards her in the gloom. She kept her head bowed as she made space for him to pass.

'Marjorie?' George Thomas's surprised voice startled her.

She was aware of him taking in her dishevelled appearance as she turned back to acknowledge him. He looked so healthy and normal, his concerned face kind and gentle. She hadn't seen much of him since the school dance. He had called at the house after her mother's death. He had talked to Nicholas for some time in the garden. He had placed a gentle hand on her shoulder as he passed through the kitchen and told her how sorry he was. She knew he would be concerned for her, but she could never divulge her secret to him. She felt dirty.

He tickled Barney's ears before saying, 'You don't look well. Have you been ill?'

'No,' she replied lamely, 'I'm just a bit tired, that's all.' She bit her lip, pleading with her eyes for him to believe her, and not to ask any questions.

'Can I walk you home?'

She nodded. He unbuttoned his coat and helped her in to it. She didn't argue. She didn't know whether he had noticed the bulge underneath her sweater. Feeling weak, she was thankful for the warmth and grateful for his sensitivity. He slipped his arm through hers.

They walked in silence, her strength draining at every step. He pulled her closer to him, putting his arm round her, supporting her. They reached her gate.

'If you ever want me, Marjorie, I'll be here,' he said huskily.

She looked into his eyes, which were wet—from tears or from rain, she couldn't tell. 'Thanks George,' she said tenderly, 'I better go in now.' She started to undo the top button of his coat.

'Here, let me help you.' As if she were a child, he undid the buttons, pausing when he reached her waistline. He looked up, searching her eyes.

Please don't say anything, she frantically thought.

He began to speak. 'Marjorie…' He stopped.

There was a moment when both of them could have spoken. She could have told him everything. He could have asked her if she were pregnant. Instead, as he helped her take her arms out of the coat, he said, 'Go straight to bed and get warm.' He drew her towards him and kissed her forehead. 'You look like a frozen sparrow. I'll call round in a few days to see you.'

Grateful for his care, she smiled faintly. She pulled away from him and walked into the drive.

As she let herself in through the scullery door, she wondered if she would have enough strength to climb the stairs.

'Where the bloody hell have you been, miss?' her father thundered. 'Max and I want something proper to eat, now, so get yourself into gear and start cracking.'

'I can't Dad, I'm sorry, I don't feel well.'

She saw his hand come up and she turned her head away, the blow landing on her exposed cheek. The force behind her father's rage lifted her backwards towards the stone sink.

Marjorie's only awareness was of sinking into an abyss and an overwhelming feeling of not caring. To struggle against oblivion was out of the question; it would be a welcome relief from all the pain. She allowed herself to slip into unconsciousness, unchallenged, unaware of the blows that continued to pound her body from her father's feet.

As if satisfied that he had taught his daughter a well-deserved lesson, Ernest Baines walked away from Marjorie's inert body, out of the scullery, and past Max, who had just witnessed his uncle's lethal temper. 'It'll just have to be fish and chips then. Off you go, lad, and get some,' he instructed Max before continuing to the living room and the television.

—⁓—

Max knelt down beside Marjorie and felt for her pulse. He lifted her up and carried her upstairs to her room, laying her down on the bed. The thought that she might miscarry was uppermost in his mind. He had to get her out of the house as soon as possible. If Ernest discovered she was pregnant by him, he would be forced to marry her. He didn't want to marry her. He had his eye on the friend down the road with money of her own, which could buy him into his uncle's business. What's more, he was sure Alison was a virgin. He was determined to take a virgin down the aisle when he married. A rich virgin would suit his plans very nicely indeed. He pulled the cover up before running downstairs and out of the house to go to the fish and chip shop.

—◊—

She drew her hand out from underneath the bedclothes and felt her swollen cheek before slipping once more into a feverish sleep. At intervals during the long night, woken by pain, she had explored other areas of her body in more urgent need of her attention. Her swollen, bruised cheek was the least of her problems. She didn't mind about the damage to her body. She wanted to die anyway. Dying would solve all her problems. She wouldn't have to feel anything ever again. She invited death to come in, to take her away. She could join her mother and tell her how sorry she was. She needn't know about the baby. It could remain a secret. She could go back to that morning and help her mother get ready for Max's arrival, then her mother needn't die, and Max wouldn't come to her room. There would be no baby. She could finish school and study architecture.

'You have to leave, Marjorie.' It was Max. She didn't want to open her eyes to let in her life again. 'It's beginning to show,' he was saying. 'I'll do you a favour and take you to the bus station while your dad's out. I'll give you fifty pounds. That should take care of your little problem. I'll tell your dad you're with Nicholas. He can get someone in to do the cooking; it's bound to be better than the muck you cough up.'

She gave no indication that she had heard him, willing permanent sleep to release her. She felt his presence, sensed his eyes crawling over her. She heard him cross her room to the window and felt the daylight flooding in as he roughly pulled back the curtains.

'Get up, you lazy cow.'

'I hate you, Max,' she whispered.

She knew that this would be the last time she slept in this room. Her carefree existence before her mother dying and before Max coming into her bedroom seemed to have dissolved into a distant memory. Her room had been defiled along with her. She was not sorry to leave it.

Her hand explored where her baby lay. She stroked the skin stretched over the tiny form. It would solve all her problems if she miscarried. She could have thanked her father for his foul temper. But there was no sign that the baby was in the least disturbed by the kicks meted out by its grandfather.

She had packed her suitcase in readiness for this moment. Soon she would be on a bus going to a destination of which she had no knowledge except that it would help release her from her present nightmare. How wrong she had been about Max. She didn't want a child of his and couldn't wait to get rid of the unwelcome growth.

4

HALF AN HOUR from her destination, the pains began. As the country bus weaved its way down unfamiliar roads through farming hamlets, Marjorie's anxiety increased. It was pointless to ask the driver to stop. As far as she could see, they were in the middle of nowhere. The two other remaining passengers on this final leg of the bus journey sat resolutely together three rows in front of her, their hats and stiff shoulders a barrier of respectability. She wanted to cry out for help. She wanted her mother. The baby wasn't due for another two months, but as the pains became more frequent, she was sure that it had decided to come now. Her breathing was shallow, and her fingers began to tingle as panic swept over her.

The bus slowly chugged its way to the top of a hill, its engine teetering on the edge of expiry, as the driver changed back again into first gear to pull the bus up the last few yards. On the crest of the hill, the engine seemed to sigh with relief as the single-decker dipped its nose to make the downhill run into Appleford. Through half-closed eyes, the sight of the village nestling in the valley filled Marjorie with relief. Her hands and lips were numb; her bruised body was ready to give birth. If only she could hold on until she was out of the bus. She closed her eyes against the impending enormity of what was about to happen. If only she could escape. If only she could say no, not now, I've changed my mind. I'll do anything else. I'll be good, I promise.

She sensed the bus draw to a stop. She heard excited voices and the footsteps of the driver coming towards her. She felt his strong arms lift her out of the seat and carry her down the steps and into an open car door.

'Thank you, driver,' a voice filled with love said. 'I'll take care of her now.'

'I didn't see her until the other two passengers had got off. I feel a bit badly about it,' he said, putting Marjorie's suitcase in the boot.

'She's safe now. We'll get her to hospital straight away. Thank you for your concern.' The car door was closed, and a nun climbed in beside her, turning the key to start the engine. 'My, you look a sorry sight, young lady,' she said gently as she pulled the car out for the short journey to the hospital.

Her feet felt like ice. Marjorie lay on the iron bed waiting for morning to arrive. If she concentrated on her cold feet, she could avoid the picture of the tiny infant that had finally slipped from her body. The first cries were seared into her mind; she tried not to listen to the sound as it returned to haunt her in the night. She wanted to comfort that cry but knew she could not.

Her part was done, she reasoned. She could leave in a few days and pretend it had never happened. Sister Agnes would take care of everything. Thank goodness she had been there to meet her from the bus. A cold shiver passed through her as she remembered the bus ride and how frightened she was.

The first light came through the long windows, pushing round the heavy grey curtains and into the room. She didn't notice Sister Agnes come in and was startled when she spoke. 'Do you want to see her, child?'

Marjorie kept her face turned towards the window.

'She's very small but very beautiful,' the soft Irish voice persisted. 'I think you should see her.'

She didn't trust herself to speak as she thought of the child she couldn't hope to love. 'I can't,' she whispered.

'She's such a dear little soul, Marjorie. She may not be long for this world. I think it's important that you see her, for your own sake. I know you intend to leave her with us for adoption, but that doesn't mean that you can't love her all the same.'

Marjorie turned to look into the eyes of the nun. She felt so dirty inside in comparison to the pure love emanating from Sister Agnes. As though reading her mind, the kindly nun stroked her forehead. 'You've had a rough time of it girl, I can tell. Where did all your bruises come from? We were quite shocked to see you in such a sorry state. Who was it who did this to you?'

Marjorie struggled, fighting back the tears, feeling unworthy of the kindness shown to her. She turned her face back to the window. How could she say it was her own father who had kicked her so forcefully that she had come close to death? She shook her head.

'Never mind that for now, child.' Sister Agnes again stroked her head. 'Let's just think about the baby. Does she have a name?'

'Helen.' Where had that name come from? Of course— it was her mother's middle name. Was she asking her mother to watch over her tiny grandchild? She was going to be left through no fault of her own, placed in a family who wanted her, but what if her new parents weren't any good at bringing up a child? She would never know what had become of her. What if she didn't survive? Already she could feel the pain of separation but knew she had no choice. The fact that Max was the father had not stopped her from the unexpected surge of love for the tiny life she had given birth to. She was surprised at the force of her feelings for her baby. So this was what it was like to be a mother.

'Helen. Now that's a pretty name.'

Marjorie allowed herself to be comforted, drinking in the kindness, thirsty for some love. She knew Sister Agnes was right; she needed to see her child. She needed to explain to Helen why she was leaving. She needed to tell her how sorry she was.

5

FEBRUARY 1964

I T WAS ALREADY dark when Marjorie turned into Albemarle Street. She let go of the handle of the suitcase and let it fall on its side. She would have left it long ago on some roadside if it hadn't contained the few clothes that she had left home with two weeks before. Auntie Ollie's house was at the end of the street, next door to her old home, the one before her dad had made his money. The distance from where she was standing to that welcome door seemed immeasurable. No longer able to carry it, she had dragged the case behind her from the bus station to this point, and it had taken nearly all her strength away.

Already the events of the past months had been categorised into a compartment, designated a no-go area in her mind. That way she could survive. That way she could live with Nicholas and Auntie Ollie as though nothing had happened. The thought of being with them urged her on. Once again she pulled the suitcase behind her, collecting torn crisp packets and discarded cigarette ends as it scraped along the street. She let go of the handle as she reached the door and with her last few ounces of strength, knocked.

Nicholas opened the door. She saw the shock register on his face. 'It's not you, is it, Sis?' he asked as though not wanting to believe that the ravaged figure on the doorstep was his sister.

'Who is it, Nicholas?' she heard Auntie Ollie call from the kitchen.

'It's Marjorie,' he called back into the house, not taking his eyes off her.

'Did you say Marjorie?' Auntie Ollie came bustling to the door, tea towel in her hand, and squeezed past Nicholas.

Marjorie wanted to run into their arms to feel their love around her but held back. Shame covered her like a dirty blanket.

'Marjorie!' Auntie Ollie exclaimed. 'Oh, Marjorie, look at you, my love. What's happened to you?' Her warm arms encircled her. 'Nicholas, get on the other side and help her.'

From his transfixed state, Nicholas leapt into action, supporting her weight against him as they led her along the narrow hall into the brightly lit kitchen. Between them they helped her to the chair beside the kitchen range, damp clothes steaming overhead on the drying line. Barney, who had been asleep until then, sprang to life when he realised that Marjorie was there and proceeded to lick her limp hands lovingly, wanting her to return his affection, but she couldn't summon up the strength to match Barney's enthusiasm, and he had to be content with just her presence.

'Nicholas, pour some tea and put lots of sugar in it, then bring in the suitcase before we forget it. Now then, my love,' Auntie Ollie said gently, taking hold of her hands and examining her face as if looking for answers. 'There's plenty of time to tell us what's happened to you, but first we have to get you fattened up and well again. Oh, love, you look awful,' she declared.

Marjorie didn't trust herself to speak. She followed the movements in the kitchen and let Auntie Ollie fuss over her. 'I've just had a baby and left her,' she wanted to shout, but the words didn't come out. Nicholas didn't take his eyes off her as she sipped the sweet tea while Auntie Ollie made some scrambled eggs. She was mute; she held her secret in, nursing her loss, which threatened to fill her chest and burst out if she wasn't careful. She knew she looked dreadful; she knew that her eyes were filled with tears, which she fought to keep at bay by avoiding the concerned glances of Auntie Ollie and Nicholas. She had to keep quiet, and hopefully the pain would go away one day. She knew she could never forget what had happened to her and the tiny baby she had finally held in her arms, examining the fingers no bigger than matchsticks, the dark shadow of hair beginning to grow on her perfectly formed head, the sweet nose, the thin layer of skin protecting the tiny body, the nappy with the over-sized safety pin reaching her chest. *Helen, I called her Helen*, she wanted to tell the watchful pair, but she didn't say a word.

She slept fitfully in the tiny bedroom that overlooked the street which she had played in so happily as a child. Auntie Ollie had tucked her up with a hot-water bottle and a cup of hot milk, with orders to stay in bed until she felt stronger. She had been more than happy to comply.

Shortly after the muted chimes of the hall clock had struck eight times, a thunderous banging on the front door jerked her wide awake. She heard Auntie Ollie open the front door then the unmistakable voice of her father. 'Where the bloody hell is my daughter? I want her home where she belongs,' he yelled for the entire street to hear. Marjorie crept to the end of the bed and peered down through the net curtains at the top of her father's head. 'You've no right to harbour my children. They're my property, and I want them back.'

'Both of them, or is it just Marjorie you want back?' Auntie Ollie coolly asked.

'You can keep that pansy son of mine you're so fond of, but I'll have our Marjorie back. Tell her she can stop school and start in the office Monday morning part-time so she can do housework.'

'I will give her your message, Ernest,' Auntie Ollie politely replied and closed the door.

Marjorie watched her father look stunned, and then he pulled himself up and breathed in, the insult fluffing his plumage to its maximum. The net curtains of the terraced houses fell back into place as he glared round at his old neighbours.

'I'll get you all out of here, you just wait and see,' he yelled at anyone that was listening. 'You don't believe I can do it, do you?' he called out maliciously, addressing the windows. 'I'm more powerful than you think.' He beat his chest with his fists as if to emphasise his strength, 'I'll flush you all out like rats.'

'Well at least one rat has left the street already,' a voice called. Ernest swung round, but the street remained impassive, a solid front against him.

Marjorie quickly drew away from the window as her father looked up. 'Marjorie, I want you home where you belong, d'you hear. I'm warning you, I'll cut you out.' He turned on his heel and marched down the road.

Moments later, there came a light knock on the door, and Auntie Ollie came in. 'Hello, love.' She scrutinised the pale face. 'How are you feeling this morning?'

'Much better, thanks.' Marjorie couldn't have been more grateful to Auntie Ollie, who sat on the chair beside the bed and didn't make any demands on her or press her to explain her sorry state.

Still in his pyjamas, Nicholas joined them, concern showing on his face as he peered closely at her fragile countenance. She drew her feet up under the covers to make room for him to sit on the bed.

As though a family forum had been called, Olivia began speaking. 'Well, that was your father, in fine form as usual.'

Nicholas laughed. 'I'm so pleased he's given up on me.' But he became serious as he turned to Marjorie. 'I'm free of him, but what about you, Sis?' He regarded her with undisguised affection. 'What do you want to do?'

'I never want to go back, never,' Marjorie cried vehemently as the picture of Max laughing at her flashed through her mind. She pulled the bedcovers up under her chin as though to protect herself from the vision.

'There, there, Marjorie dear. No one's going to make you do anything that you don't want to do. No one,' Olivia declared firmly.

'That's not true,' Marjorie blurted out, clutching the bedclothes tightly. 'People can force you to do things, can't they?' Her wild frightened eyes travelled from Nicholas to Olivia for confirmation. Worried glances passed between them. Sensing she had said too much, Marjorie stared fixedly at the candlewick bedspread, trying to control the hurt tears trying to escape. Silence entered the room. They could have asked her a thousand questions. Thank God they chose not to.

Auntie Ollie broke the spell. Getting up, she said, 'We'll talk again later, dear, when you're feeling stronger. Would you like some porridge with honey?' Marjorie smiled faintly, grateful for her tact. They heard her pad down the stairs. The sound of activity in the kitchen was Nicholas's cue to speak.

'Sis?' She gave no response, and he continued haltingly as if trying to find the right words. 'You can trust me, and you can trust Auntie Ollie. I know I don't show it much, but I care about you…and…' He trailed off, not used to making such speeches.

'I feel so ashamed, our Nicholas. I can't talk about it. I don't want to talk, I just want to forget. Give me time, that's all I want.' Wretched, unable to look directly at Nicholas, she lay back on the pillow and closed her eyes, shutting him out.

'I'm starting at the post office on Monday. I'm going to do the first delivery so that I can draw and paint the rest of the day,' Nicholas said, undeterred.

'You're too good for that, our Nicholas.'

'And you're too good for that bastard to ruin your life.'

'Which one?' she muttered.

The next few days, Marjorie began to feel stronger under the tender care of Auntie Ollie and Nicholas. She resisted answering the lightly veiled, probing questions about what had brought her to such a state. Sister Agnes had wanted her to stay at the convent until the bruising had subsided, but the longer she stayed with Helen, the harder it was to think of saying goodbye. She held the tiny bundle in her arms for one last time before giving her to the nun who she had to trust would do the best for her daughter.

'Marjorie, dear, not talking about things doesn't make them go away. The death of your dear mother, God rest her soul, is testament to that truth. There is nothing on this earth that you can't tell me. I'm on your side.'

Marjorie kept her eyes averted, the pictures in her mind clear but the captions locked away. There was no way that she would let Auntie Ollie know how bad she was. The guilt of having Helen and then giving her away lay like clay on her bruised heart, a dead weight that she couldn't imagine being without. Her future meant nothing to her as she nursed the pain, forever present.

She wrote to her father, telling him that she could never return to the house or school and that she would get a job in the city and live with Auntie Ollie and Nicholas. It wasn't an angry letter; she just stated the facts. She didn't hear from him again.

Nicholas was out with his sketchpad and Ollie was at the Co-op when the bell rang. Marjorie opened the door. She saw George gasp as he took in her appearance. She had lost a lot of weight and was aware she looked awful as he smiled his crooked smile with undisguised solicitude.

Not trusting herself to speak, she turned into the hall and let him follow her into the kitchen. She sensed him following her movements as she collected cups and saucers together and wondered if it had been wise to let him in. Her misgivings were confirmed when he said, 'Will you come out with me on Friday to the pictures?'

She didn't answer and clattered about, pretending she hadn't heard. Emboldened, he continued. 'We could go to the cafe afterwards for supper, if you like?'

Feeling defiled, soiled by Max, she pushed him away with her words to stop him from being contaminated. 'I don't want to go out with you, George,' she said angrily, her back still turned to him. 'I just want to be left on my own. Leave me alone. Can't you see when you're not wanted?' She hated herself for her rudeness but could see no other way to put distance between them.

'I love you, Marjorie. You can tell me to bugger off and I will, but it won't stop me loving you.'

She turned round at his words. For a moment she nearly gave in to his warmth, she nearly stepped forward into his arms to be held...but her body reminded her of her shame, and she held on to the back of a kitchen chair as if the power of his love would pull her towards him. 'You can't love me. That's daft talk. You're only eighteen,' she snapped, hoping that by trying to belittle him, she would stop him from saying these things to her.

'Happen I'll just have to wait then.' He grinned at her, and she relaxed, regarding his open, honest face with affection. His thick mop of hair fell haphazardly over his forehead, under which blue eyes devoid of treachery and malice played over her with love. What a blind fool she had been. Perhaps she loved him too, but he would never know.

Over the weeks and months that followed, George became a regular visitor. They never went out except to go for a walk or just sit and talk about the old days, 'the golden years,' as Marjorie thought of the time before her mother died and before Max moved in. She was comfortable with George and grateful that he never alluded to what had happened. She had found a job as a junior in an architect's office in Manchester and welcomed the bus trip away from Middleston, but she needed to get further away. She needed to get away from George before she accepted a night out at the pictures, which she was longing to do, but she knew that it would give him hope. Her lost baby occupied her heart, and she felt choked by the heavy weight of guilt at leaving little Helen to fend for herself. She couldn't imagine a time when she would think of her own happiness again.

6

1991

IT HAD BEEN raining on and off for several weeks. Confined to London, going between her flat and newspaper office, Helen Arbuthnot was not affected by the bad weather. She was happy and in love with a man who returned her feelings. If she could stop time to stay awhile in this place of contentment, she would. A future with Roderick Barclay was out of the question; loving him at the moment was all that was available. Tomorrow would just have to be postponed.

On Friday the sun decided to make an appearance. Throughout the day, strong rays beaming down into the city streets did their work, and by evening the miserable weather was a memory. Walking briskly from the tube station to her flat, head held high, nut-brown bobbed hair bouncing with health, Helen savoured the afternoon's long-distance phone call from Rod. She smiled at the memory of the tone of voice he used when he suggested that they stay in a country hotel for the weekend. She was not ready.

Instead they had compromised, agreeing to spend the following day at Henley. At the moment, the nights were off limits.

She had met Rod four months ago when she was interviewing the major auctioneering houses, starting preliminary research into the sale and movement of Russian masterpieces since the end of the Cold War. At first, as introductions were made, she had thought him a stiff personality, trapped in his pinstripe suit and clipped aristocratic speech, but there was something so endearing about him that she decided to reserve judgement and not write him off as another stuffed penguin. She guessed that he was about the same age as herself, twenty-eight, although with his classic looks, he could have been anywhere between twenty-five and forty. His dark hair fell engagingly over his fine forehead so that when he looked up from the records, he was obliged to jam it back into place with his hand, as if it were an errant child trying to escape a strict nanny.

'This is not really my field, you know,' he had said, interrupting his search in the minutiae to look up at her, his finger poised between the record cards, examining her with blatant admiration, as though seeing her for the first time.

'Is there someone else I should be talking to?' she had asked, her head on one side as she returned his gaze with wonder at the fine specimen before her.

Time seemed to stand still, their eyes dancing together in mutual discovery, and suddenly smiling, he had replied, 'No, I'm just the right man for you, Miss Arbuthnot.'

They had lunched together, abandoning work as though it were irrelevant, an irritation to be brushed aside when they had so much to say. Sitting on a park bench, laughing, tentatively touching, occasionally stopping to savour their meeting, they talked and talked all afternoon in the lazy sunshine as the first leaves began to fall, heralding the end of summer.

The note accompanying the single orchid, left on her doorstep by an unknown deliveryman, was brief. 'I love you, my darling.' There was no name, but she didn't doubt that the sender was Rod. Smiling with contentment, she let herself in to her Victorian attic flat, placed the fragile bloom in a slender vase on the tiny kitchen windowsill, and took off her coat, pleased that the days without Rod were coming to a close. He had been travelling for two weeks. They had been long days for her. She was finding it increasingly hard to be without him. Within days of meeting Rod Barclay, she had surrendered her tenacious, independent spirit to a softer, more vulnerable one, making the thought of a future without him increasingly difficult to contemplate.

She looked round her tiny garret flat where she and Rod had spent so many delicious hours together. Pictures crowded her mind: merriment at his first attempts at cooking; tranquil moments listening to music, her collection swelled by some of Rod's favourite pieces; and discussions on every subject, some light, others serious, but always in good humour, always loving each other even when their ideas seemed poles apart because of their very different backgrounds.

She took up the Arran sweater he had left with her and putting it to her nose and breathed deeply into the wool, comforting herself as she had done since he had been on his trip. This is crazy, she thought, as she switched on the radio in an attempt to dispel her longing. I must stop this. There's no future in it. Nevertheless, as she lay in her bath that evening, surrounded by luxuriantly perfumed bubbles, courtesy of Rod, she allowed her thoughts to travel down that road for the first time.

Rod proposed the following day, in the middle of an argument on hereditary titles. She was vehemently opposed to them, using wide, sweeping arm movements plagiarised from an English professor at Exeter to aid her argument. Sunshine had wrapped itself round their reunion; a long lunch in their favourite thatched pub was over, and they were walking by the river, their conversation animated.

'Will you marry me, Helen?'

She marched on, catching the end of her scarf and flinging it over her shoulder. 'That won't influence me. Play fair, Rod. I know that I'm right, and you're trying to undermine my argument by appealing to my emotions, which you have, and—' She swung round. 'What did you say?'

Rod stood still, tall and square shouldered, dappled light playing around him as a sudden breeze caught in the branches of an old white willow. Wearing a sports jacket, drill trousers, and his favourite brogues, he looked the epitome of a country gentleman. He was tanned from his travels, giving him a faintly exotic appearance, perhaps Mediterranean, with his almost-black hair falling as usual over his hazel-brown eyes.

Between them a lone fisherman sat on a stool, umbrella up, maggots in a tobacco tin at his side, sandwiches stuffed in a torn pocket. He studied the river before him, seeming to take no notice of the romantic drama being played out behind him.

Helen fought to prevent the surge of joy that was threatening to explode. People of his social class just didn't marry ordinary people like her. All the evidence in her arguments about social inequality came up against this truth, so why was Rod asking her to marry him?

The creases round Rod's eyes deepened as he regarded her lovingly. 'I said, will you marry me? I love you, Helen.'

Momentarily forgetting her reservations, compelled by the force of love, she ran forward into his waiting arms. 'I love you too, Rod, so much I ache.' She lifted her lips to his and met his kiss, tender but profound, filled with mutual longing and love. Then he wrapped his strong arms about her and held her tightly to him. Helen felt his warm, vibrant body against hers. She never wanted to let him go, to become separate again. She wanted to be with him forever. She couldn't imagine how it had been before he had first come into her life, but…her spirits subsided…it was impossible. They were dreaming. Pulling away from him, she searched her beloved's eyes for insincerity, but finding none, it was she who had to bring in unpleasant realism. 'We can't marry. Your family would never allow it.'

'Blow what my family thinks,' he pronounced vehemently. 'This is about us, just us. I won't let other people come between us.'

'Your family would make life so uncomfortable for you. Your brother Jeremy is politeness itself, but I'm sure he thinks you'll soon come to your senses, that I'm a temporary stopgap for the real thing.'

'Yes, perhaps you're right,' he said resignedly, looking beyond her into the grey, undulating mass of river.

'Leave the bugger,' the fisherman unexpectedly said. 'There's plenty out there that would put up a proper fight for you.'

Rod returned from his reverie to her hurt eyes. 'What's the matter, my darling?' he asked, tenderly lifting her chin and lightly brushing her lips.

Helen fought to keep her dignity. 'Let's go back and toast those muffins, shall we?' she said in as steady a voice as she could manage.

'Mm, yummy. And we can make plans for our wedding.'

'That's more bloody like it,' the fisherman muttered as he returned to his elusive pike.

Helen's heart surged with joy. He really did want to marry her, and soon; but what about her mother, what would she think? What would Rod think of her mother's humble home and lifestyle, which, as she saw it, compared so unfavourably with his family seat? Rod would expect so much, and she and her family had so little to give. All these thoughts crowded into her head, pushing aside the happiness of the moment.

She took a deep breath. 'Rod, I want to marry you, but I can't. It's too much. I would be overwhelmed by the social demands. I haven't moved in your circles. You would be ashamed of me.'

'I wouldn't be ashamed of you. What is there to be ashamed of?'

'I think it's time I took you home to meet Mother. I've told her all about you. She knows I love you, and...' She stopped mid sentence, remembering what her mother had said the last time she called home.

'And?'

She grinned as Rod willed her to finish what she had begun to say. She had told him so little about her family; she was aware that he seized upon any snippets.

'Well, I've just remembered that my mother told me not to be surprised when you asked me to marry you.' Helen suddenly laughed at the memory, thinking not for the first time how clever her mother was.

As the days of the week were ticked off one by one before their proposed visit to her mother, Helen still hadn't told Rod the truth about her mother's situation, feeling miserable at the thought of his reaction. She tried to think of the future with equanimity. If she was meant to marry Rod, then she would; if it were their fate to go their separate ways, divided by their background, then she would accept it with composure and dignity.

—m—

Drawing closer to Appleford, Rod could sense Helen becoming anxious. They had spent most of the four-hour journey in a playful, jocular mood, the miles dissolving as they sped on towards Helen's home. Now, as they gained the crest of a hill after a punishing climb, she pulled the little car to the side and switched off the engine. The vale of Appleford lay before them, in a swathe of lush green as it followed the tiny stream that meandered through the village and farms. The upland pastures rose out of the valley like the inside of a bowl painted in deep-green hues. In the late afternoon, the southern sun accentuated the rich colours on the far side, deepening the shadows and highlighting the honey stone cottages, the outcrops of rock in the sheep-mown meadows, the church spire peeking through the spreading yew trees, symbols of everlasting life.

Visibly relaxing, Helen said softly, 'This is where I grew up, Rod. All of my most cherished childhood memories are fixed in this valley. Isn't the view wonderful from here?'

Rod felt that he was visiting Shangri-La, so idyllic was the landscape spread before him. 'It's a beautiful spot. Where's your mother's house?' His imagination was running overtime. What could be so wrong about Helen's mother that made it so difficult for her to talk about? From what Helen had said, she sounded a thoroughly decent person, salt-of-the-earth type, doing good works in the community, with a great love of gardening and pottery. So what if she lived in a modest house? If it had helped to make Helen what she was, then he could accept it, he thought magnanimously.

'What's that place on the left?' With antennae-like curiosity, his attention was drawn to the large house with its stone wall running round the grounds. 'Anyone I might know?' he asked, wondering that he hadn't heard of Appleford before.

'I don't think so, but that's where we're heading,' she said mysteriously, not meeting his puzzled expression. She started up the car and let it run down the gentle bends into the village. He allowed relief to enter, where moments before apprehension had been. He knew quality when he saw it, just like the paintings he evaluated, and Helen hadn't fooled him. Her quality and refinement stood out like a beautifully constructed Pissarro, with all the spontaneity and life captured in a vivid impression. He studied her profile, as she concentrated on the tight bends, steering in a downward spiral into the valley. He loved the way she attended to the task at hand, never taking her eyes off the road; never looking at him as he regarded her sweet, fine features; her thick hair tousled from their last embrace; her chin, determined, set over a slender neck; her mouth, full and sensuous, a mouth he never tired of kissing that pulled him into a vortex of love and unfulfilled passion.

She glanced at him, and his heart swelled with love for her as he thought of her clever ruse. 'I suppose you needed to make sure I didn't love you for money,' he chuckled.

'There's no chance of that,' she said very seriously, too seriously, he thought. He saw her lips tighten as she changed into third gear as the car gained level ground.

It took quite some time to get through the village, in spite of it being a tiny place with no more than two hundred people living there. Helen's car was immediately recognised, and everyone wanted to speak to her and to be introduced to him. He felt as though he were sitting beside a celebrity, such was the welcome for Helen back to her village. That welcome was genuinely extended to him, and he marvelled at the warmth of feeling of these country people towards a stranger.

They reached the crossroads in the centre of the village and turned left into a one-track lane, muck covered from a recently gone-by tractor. The road followed the stream for about half a mile before suddenly turning upwards and letting the unwary driver know that it was a no-through road. Helen's car knew the way well and took the bend in its stride before making the two-hundred-yard dash towards the big iron gates straight ahead.

'This is it. I'll have to ring the bell,' Helen announced as she killed the engine and leaped out to pull a bell rope with more vigour than seemed necessary, before he could ask any questions.

The bell rang out clear and strong, and almost immediately the great door of the old monastery opened, and a figure dressed in black and white appeared, clapped her hands, and ran down the drive to open the gates for her daughter and her young beau.

Rod stared, transfixed. In none of his scenarios had he imagined that Helen's mother would be a nun. Now he climbed out of the cramped little car to meet what could be his mother-in-law if they went ahead with his very own carefully laid plans. Doubt made his movements slow, as he went forward, a social smile fixed to greet her. He could not look at Helen as this bubbly nun pulled open the gates before giving her daughter a longed-for hug. He stood at a respectful distance, wishing that he were anywhere except there.

'Rod, this is my mother. Mum, I'd like you to meet Roderick Barclay.'

'It's wonderful to meet you, Roderick.' Sister Agnes grasped his hand, which half rose to meet hers as though it had forgotten its manners. 'I hope I'm not too much of a surprise for you. Helen hasn't told you, I can see.' Sister Agnes's well-worn face, crumpled now with a mixture of sympathy and merriment, surrounded with a uniform of black and white draped around her, challenged him to cross over the divide. 'Come on in, and we'll have some tea all to ourselves so that we can get to know one another. I'm not as strange as I look, am I, Helen, you naughty girl?'

The iron gates closed behind him, and Rod, flanked on either side, was steered towards the stone building, reluctance making his gait wooden, devoid of enthusiasm, any shred of humour raked out of him when the great bell had been answered.

'I'm sorry I didn't tell you, Rod. Perhaps I should have done, but I thought—'

'What she wants to say is that she's embarrassed and always has been about me and about her home, and she thinks people won't come if they know where she lives and what her mother is. Nuns don't have children, do they, and yet here's Sister Agnes with a child. Whatever will people think?' They reached a side door. 'Come in. Helen and I have the use of a sitting room through here when she's home. Make yourself comfortable, and I'll go and ask for tea.' Seeing that Rod still looked as though he were about to flee, she said, 'And that's the best seat there, under the window.' She pointed to a shabbily covered chair until he reluctantly took possession of it. She bustled away, her habit flowing behind her.

'Why didn't you tell me?' He felt as if he had been deliberately misled from the beginning of their relationship.

'Because you wouldn't have come, would you?'

'I don't know,' he said honestly. 'At least I could have been prepared. This is awful, Helen.' He rose from the chair to confront her. 'I feel as if I don't know you. I don't know what to say to you or to a…your mother.'

'I find this difficult too, Rod. All my life I've found this difficult because of reactions like yours. But this is the person who has been my mother, who has cherished me and loved me. She's not my real mother, of course, but I was born here.'

'For God's sake, let me meet your real mother, then.' He flung his arms out with exasperation. 'Why put me through this charade? Where's your real mother?'

'I don't know. I could find out, of course, but I've never wanted to. Sister Agnes has been everything to me.'

'So you were illegitimate?' His voice rose in disgust.

'Yes.'

'Christ, it's getting worse.' He turned his back on her and stared out of the window.

Sister Agnes returned carrying a tray laden with egg sandwiches and freshly bakes scones. She set it on the low table between the faded loose-covered chairs. Seeing the turned back and the misery on Helen's face, she said, 'Helen, would you be an angel and get the other tray from the kitchen? Sister Marcia wants to say hello. Now Roderick, can I offer you one of Sister Marcia's homemade scones? She's a temptress with her home baking, and I think you'll find your resistance low after tasting one.' Her soft Irish tones drew him round from the window back into the room to continue the farce.

—⚯—

Helen left them together, hoping that her mother could weave her magic on Rod, as she had done with her school friends, many of whom still visited the jolly nun, now in her sixty-third year.

Sister Marcia had arrived at the convent the same year as Agnes, and they had taken their vows together. Both women had come from large Irish families with a strong Catholic faith. Both women missed their younger brothers and sisters, and both women had conspired to keep Helen, the baby for whom they could never find a suitable family. She had been born a full two months premature and needed constant, round-the-clock care to keep her alive. As the months went by, the two nuns become irretrievably attached to the skinny little bundle, feeling that she wouldn't survive without their love and care. Gradually, the other nuns were drawn into the circle until it reached the Mother Superior, who ordered a home for the child to be found at once, to stop this madness. More prospective parents visited but were told how fragile the infant was, how unlikely she would survive without serious problems. In exasperation Mother Superior visited the nursery to see what the problem was. Helen met the scrutiny with her first smile, reaching up to touch the silver cross dangling in front of her. The old nun looked into the deep wells of Helen's eyes, such trust there, so much universal knowledge, such peace, and she too surrendered.

The adoption order was made on the grounds that the child was not expected to live very long. It was agreed that Sister Agnes, having been trained as an intensive care nurse and having had the most contact with Helen, was the most suitable person to be responsible for her short life. The whole convent rejoiced with Sister Agnes, doting on the life that had been given to them to cherish.

In the kitchen, Sister Marcia was filling the china teapot with the boiling water from the large kettle that bubbled constantly on the Aga. Crippled with arthritis, her gnarled, bony fingers curled around the handle, making the task appear torturous. Her half glasses rested on the end of her nose, steamed up, forcing the pint-sized nun to peer over them as though she were studying an ancient manuscript. She gave a cry of delight when she saw Helen. 'There you are, my lovely. Just let me finish this tea before I crush you with my love; it's been so long. There.' Relieved that she had completed the job without mishap, she placed the big cauldron back onto the hot iron disk. 'Now come here, child. You look as lovely as ever.'

'Hello, Auntie Marcia.' Helen hugged the little nun close to her and was alarmed at how frail she had become. 'It's lovely to see you again.'

'I swear you've grown again.' Marcia held Helen at arm's length to examine her. 'Whatever are you eating?'

'It's you that's shrunk. Won't you eat any of your own scones? Are they so bad? And still selling them to the villagers I hear, for a profit. Shame on you.' She parodied the soft Irish lilt.

Sister Marcia laughed, delighting in her godchild's presence after six months' absence. 'Ah, lassie, it's good to see you.' She held Helen's hands in her own, looking up at her. 'We miss you.' And what's this I hear about a young man visiting? Will I get to meet him?' she asked, her eyes twinkling.

'I don't know. He might be gone already unless Mother's thought to lock the door.'

Rod's reaction had been worse than she had imagined. She knew he was finding it difficult to keep up an appearance of basic politeness despite his usually impeccable manners, in his anxiety to liberate himself from the net she had cast over him. She should have told him. It would have saved them both from the intolerable strain she had put them both under. But then, she would never have known; she would have always wondered. At least now it was clear. He would never reconcile himself to the circumstances of her birth and her upbringing.

'If he loves you, he'll get over feeling uncomfortable with time. Just be patient,' Marcia said, peering at her above her still misted glasses. 'Now, let's get this tray ready. See, we've brought out the china teapot. You tell him that, and he'll be bowled over by the sense of occasion and wonder that he thought all along nuns led an austere life.'

Helen laughed. What was she worried about? These precious people were worth any aristocrat ten times over. She kissed the old nun on the cheek. 'Thank you. You always get things in perspective.' She picked up the tray. 'Well, here goes.' With renewed confidence, she carried it into the sitting room.

Roderick was sitting on the edge of the chair holding his plate stiffly, his scone untouched.

'...and it soon became clear that not only was she going to live, she was growing into a strong, healthy girl, winning the hearts of all who came into contact with her. I suppose she was about six when she took over the running of the convent.'

This normally amused her listener, but Roderick barely smiled at her mother, who was so obviously trying to impress him with her stories. Helen sensed he was already planning his speech to her.

'I see my mother's telling you my life story,' she said brightly.

'Yes.' He bit into the warm scone, avoiding her eyes.

'Auntie Marcia is in good spirits as always. She said she would like to meet you too, Rod, but I'm afraid that if I open the door, you might escape,' she said gaily, sensing the hopelessness of their romance.

'Perhaps you could show Roderick the rest of the convent after tea, to take away the mystery of our lives here. Would you like that, Roderick?' Agnes was obviously trying every ploy to help him accept her.

'Well, actually, I think we should be getting back. It's a long drive.'

'It wasn't a long drive on the way here, was it?' she challenged him, and then immediately regretted her outburst. 'I'm sorry, Rod. I should have been fair to you and told you.'

Why had she thought that he might accept where she came from? She felt angry with herself for making such a mistake. He wasn't even trying to communicate.

'Perhaps next time, then,' Sister Agnes said, obviously trying to soften the atmosphere between the young people.

'There won't be a next time, will there, Rod?' There she was again, forcing him to make his choice.

He didn't answer. He put the plate on the table. 'Thank you for the delicious scone, Mother…er, Sister…' He put his hand out, and Sister Agnes took it and held it there between her own two rough hands, hardened with gardening.

'I hope whatever life brings to you, Roderick, you will find fulfilment and peace. God bless you. If you ever want to talk, I'm always here.'

'I'll wait at the gate, Helen,' he muttered, and left the room. Side by side, they watched Rod's departing figure as he let himself out of the side door to walk purposefully down the drive. They saw him swing the big iron gate open and let it clang shut, the sound reverberating around the enclosure, jarring the senses. The car door slammed.

'I'm afraid I've chased him off before he got a chance to know us. I'm so sorry, my dear. D'you think he might come round in time?'

'I don't know. Perhaps. At the moment I'm not feeling much, except angry with myself for having mishandled it all. I don't think it's all Rod's fault, but I do feel disappointed with him for not even trying.'

'You have four hours' journey back to London. Lots of time to talk. Be patient with him. Listen to him, and try not to lose that quick temper of yours.'

'I'll try. Can I take some sandwiches with me for the journey? I'm famished.'

'It's good to see it hasn't affected your appetite.'

'Nothing could keep me from my food, not even a broken heart,' she said.

They drove back to London in silence. They had planned to go on to Milford House to meet his father, but when the turnoff was signposted, she passed it. He didn't correct the mistake.

Long speeches kept forming in her mind, but it would be fruitless to unleash them, she thought bitterly as her indignation rose. She offered him a sandwich as a possible opening to restoring communication, but he shook his head as though she were offering him poison.

—∞—

It was late evening when they reached London. The lines of streetlights made continuous pools on the way to Belgravia where Rod shared a tall Georgian town house with his brother, Jeremy. It seemed to Rod that the world was full of couples, arm in arm and enjoying an evening walk after the weeks of rain, making the gulf between Helen and him seem wider than ever.

She stopped the car outside his London house, and he immediately reached for the door handle.

'You're not just going without saying anything, are you?' she asked, repressed anger evident in the question.

'I don't think there is anything to discuss, do you?' She was like a confidence trickster, and he was kicking himself for having been taken in by her.

'Now, wait a minute.' With suddenly blazing eyes, she halted his exit from her life. 'You thought that I came from a middle-class family, perhaps not as wealthy as we would like, but nevertheless with the same values as yourself. Being poor to you means not being able to afford staff or having to make do with a bottle of eighty-nine instead of a vintage year. You have no concept of what real life is like out there, Rod. To be honest, neither do I. I was brought up in a loving and trusting atmosphere, where the emphasis was on acceptance and thankfulness for the gifts we have. It's you who are impoverished, not I.'

'I was willing to overlook that, but you are also illegitimate and a Catholic,' he pronounced, as if righteousness were on his side.

'Yes, I am illegitimate,' she conceded, 'for the entire world to know. Would you rather it were hidden away? Would that make it better?' She lashed out at him, her eyes kindling with resentment. 'To wrap a nice little story around the reason for my existence, to stop the gossip. Would that suit you?'

'Probably,' he acknowledged.

'And what's wrong with being a Catholic?' she continued, fired up with indignation. 'Oh, I forgot, Henry the Eighth disapproves. A very sound reason for not wanting to marry me hundreds of years later.'

'You are being ridiculous, Helen. My views are based on generations of high principles.'

'I thought you were different, Rod, but it was just a temporary flight into the real world. You fell in love with me and for a moment my background wasn't important, but at the first indication that you'd have to make further allowances, you chicken out.'

He saw Helen's head bow as though in defeat, and his heart went out to her as the germ of an idea formed in his mind, but what he had to propose he needed to phrase carefully. After all, he didn't want to lose her. He loved her. Marriage was out of the question, but she would make a thumping-good mistress.

'How wrong I was to think that I would fit into your world,' she continued, slipping the sapphire ring from her finger and turning it, the exquisite, chiselled edges reflecting myriad colours as it caught the light. 'I suppose you'll find yourself a suitable girl from the debutante ranks who was born to partner the likes of yourself. Perhaps she'll also have a dowry for you so that you can expand your family's estate, without having to work for it.'

'I think you have said enough.' He took the proffered ring and slipped it into his jacket pocket. He had the wording now, and smiling to encourage her with his plan, he said, 'I don't want to lose you because I am inordinately fond of you. I would still like to be with you—physically, you know. So perhaps we can come to some arrangement?'

At first it seemed she didn't comprehend his meaning, but then as the full knowledge of what he was offering became apparent, she shrank from him as though he were an appalling stench under her nose.

For a moment he met her eyes. Shamed, and unable to relieve the lovely, stricken face cornered in the driver's seat, he blundered out of the car and ran up the porticoed stairs. Fumbling for his key, he let himself into the softly lit hallway, closing the door on his despicable performance. What a fool he had been. What a gaff. He'd bungled the whole thing. What an intolerable situation. He wanted her out of his life at once to get away from his own shabby behaviour.

—∞—

She received the formal note, embossed with the family crest, notifying her of the break of their engagement after two days' silence.

Dear Miss Arbuthnot:

It is with regret that I have to inform you that the arrangement made for the marriage between us has been cancelled.

If you had been honest with me from the beginning, the offer of marriage would not have been made. I am therefore under no obligation to apologise for this action.

I trust that you will not attempt to make contact with me in the future.

Yours sincerely,

Roderick Barclay

It hurt. She had been prepared for it, and yet it was a surprise. The cold message penetrated her heart. She felt sick with humiliation.

Three days later, her half-finished toast still sat on the kitchen table, where she had left it to gather up the post from the doormat. It was agony unravelling her dreams, and the suppression of the love she still felt for Roderick was a concentrated effort. Her answering machine clicked on and off with the voices of her concerned colleagues, but she could not bring herself to speak yet. She wanted to be composed when she faced the world again. No one was going to know how heartbroken she was over Roderick Barclay.

7

1991

MARJORIE WATCHED THE spades of earth land on the wooden casket that housed her dead husband. She wondered if other people felt as she did now, shaken to the point where feeling no longer registers. The black clods sounded embarrassingly loud on the wooden box. She had recoiled at the invitation to throw the first earth. *The winter is almost over,* she thought. Droplets of rain hung tenuously onto the fattened buds before they continued their fall to the earth. She was going to have spring all to herself, and then summer. It was like the beginning of a holiday.

She would live a different life from now on. Like an unexpected gift, Jack's death was going to give her the chance of happiness again. She would move away from where she had shared a strangulated existence for the twenty-six years of her marriage and change her image. Conversation would come easily in place of the monosyllables that had been the pattern of communication with Jack. She would buy new clothes to replace the sad collection in her wardrobe. She gazed down at the dark-grey coat and on to her shoes, sensible and boring, and felt a pang of longing for the days, nearly forgotten, when her appearance was her only worry.

A hand under her elbow brought her back to the burial, and she allowed herself to be drawn in whatever direction her son-in-law decided.

How clever her daughter was to choose a man like Tom. Pleasant, amiable Tom, a caricature of an accountant in his suitable dark suit and tie, with his short haircut and clean-shaven face. Able to talk easily, he let anything come out of his mouth, and it somehow always seemed right at the time. Behind the serious image, a carefree, uncomplicated spirit hovered ready to bubble to the surface. He made her laugh, haltingly at first, mistrustful of a hidden meaning. Jack's humour had been based on envy for his fellow man.

Her daughter Sally was staring into the pit. The neat features inherited from her father were translated into daintiness and yes, refinement, in Sally. In Jack, those same features had been worn with pugnacious undertones, ready for an argument, ready to insult. Sally had escaped her father's mean character; she was warm and spontaneously giving. Since her birth, she had been a constant source of joy and regeneration to Marjorie. The little girl had offered her a new beginning, teaching her how to love and trust again. It was as though Sally had held her hand while she struggled with the grief of losing her first baby.

In return, as she grew up, she encouraged Sally to seek friends and to have interests outside the home, wanting her daughter to be healthy and whole. She realised that Sally would have a very distorted view of the world if the only map was her parents' hollow marriage.

She had struggled with the question of whether it would be better for Sally to grow up in a broken home or as a witness to a loveless marriage. On balance she had decided to stay put, trying to live alongside Jack in an attempt to give her daughter a good start. He had been very fond of Sally, and proud of her, making the decision to maintain the marriage easier. Whether it had been the right decision, only Sally would be able to say. Perhaps he had been a good man after all, she reflected, as she remembered the laughter and fun Jack and Sally had had together. Revolting to his wife but a good father to Sally. She thought, *I wonder if that could be carved on his headstone?*

A fine drizzle had begun, coming to rest on Sally's wide-brimmed hat, finding it to be a tranquil place, an invitation to stay. The slim, erect figure gave no obvious sign of emotion as she watched her father's final journey. Instead, her expression was puzzled, as if wondering what her father's death meant to her.

Sally held out her hand. Marjorie gratefully took it, mirroring years of companionship. She squeezed her daughter's long fingers and gave the gentle face beside her a wry glance. Sally had inherited Jack's features and build, but the uncontrollable hair was hers. It had become a point of communication. 'You were right about the hat. Whatever must my hair look like?' Marjorie drew her daughter away from the open gash in the neatly trimmed graveyard. 'How about some sandwiches before your journey?'

'I think we should go for a meal somewhere, don't you, Sally?' Tom suggested, sounding relieved that the two women were not going to linger at the graveside.

Marjorie wished that Tom had not wanted to prolong the occasion but felt she would appear churlish if she said she just wanted to get home, so she said nothing. When Sally had proudly introduced Tom to her parents three years ago, Marjorie had made a supreme effort to present a happy family front and oddly, she mused, the last few years were the happiest of her marriage.

For the first time since Jack's death, she felt regret. Had it been his fault or her own for not making the effort before Tom's appearance in their lives? Early in the marriage, she had tried to talk to Jack, but his manner was dismissive, as if her opinion were of no importance. Like her mother, she learned to have a separate life of books and music when Jack was out at the pub or at a football match.

Tom linked his arm with Sally's and led the two women along the gravelled path; past the old, crumbling, moss-covered gravestones; and past the shiny new gravestones, some with rain-spattered plastic flowers, others with fresh flowers and neatly tended plots, mirror images of their old home. A modern headstone was without flowers. Like sentinels, clumps of coarse grass stood guard round the too-short, flat stone. A spider picked its way across with the assurance of not being disturbed to the far side, where it disappeared into the grass as though visiting a neighbour on the other side of the street. Mother and daughter brought Tom to a halt and read the inscription.

'In loving memory of a husband and father,' Sally read out loud. 'That sounds all right. It's not gushing, just straightforward.'

'I'll see.' Marjorie closed the conversation and started walking briskly along the path. Tom and Sally caught her up at the lychgate, where she had turned to survey the graveyard. 'I think I'll be cremated,' she announced to the rows of headstones.

'Oh, Mum, you can't, you always said you wanted to buried here, ever since I can remember.'

'I've just changed my mind.' The thought of being expected to lie next to Jack, even in death, was intolerable. Her image of serenely lying alone under a tree, becoming part of nature's cycle, had been hijacked by Jack's will, which had expressed a similar wish.

'Well, there's no hurry to make a decision, is there?' Tom said with forced cheer, closing the gate behind them.

They settled on an ivy-clad restaurant on the edge of a village a few miles out of the city. It was quiet and sedate, a suitable venue for a postfuneral meal. Older ladies in hats with the odd male survivor sat huddled in confidential groups around their favoured tables. Only the most ancient put manners aside and stared at the newcomers with undisguised interest, taking in the details of dress and concluding that this was a sombre occasion, reporting back to their table, drawing their friends into a huddle but having to shout to reach old ears. They had heard it all before, and they nodded, taking furtive glances at sorrow not belonging to them this time.

They didn't mention Jack. Marjorie carefully avoided Tom's attempts at bringing him into the conversation. Sally drew her mother on into other areas, asking questions, none of them listening to the answers.

'Let's not have the coffee. It's always awful in these kinds of places.' Marjorie felt exhausted and hoped that she wouldn't be overruled by well-meaning Tom. She was very anxious now to get to the shops before they closed but wanted to go on her own.

'Mum probably wants to be on her own now, Tom.' Sally thankfully rescued her mother.

'I'm sorry, Mrs Willis. I wasn't thinking. Let's get you home. Today has been a very sad day for you.'

'Yes.' And then feeling that she hadn't sounded sincere enough, she added, 'Yes, it's been quite a day.'

It was already dark when Tom drove up and parked underneath the tree outside Marjorie's gate. It was a long road with the semidetached houses set well back behind a wide pavement. They had bought the house when Sally was nine and Marjorie was in her fifth year of employment as a draughtswoman and had received a welcome pay raise. Jack was reluctant to move away from the council estate they had lived in since their marriage, but Marjorie finally persuaded him with the idea that they would be in the catchment area for the best grammar school in the city. Jack had been persuaded and further mollified when he discovered a kindred spirit living next door to their new home.

From the front passenger seat, Marjorie looked at her husband's car sitting in the driveway. It was a small red car that Jack had never allowed her to drive, even though she had passed her test the first time she sat it. She could have bought herself a car, but it seemed extravagant when the bus into town passed by the house.

She opened the door and had climbed out before Tom was able to help her. She peered back into the car towards her daughter. 'Bye, Sally. I hope it won't be long before I see you again.'

Sally got out of the car. 'Mum, are you sure you'll be all right? Why don't you let us stay for just for one more night?' she asked anxiously for the third time that day.

'No. I'll be fine. You get back. You'll need to get ready for work tomorrow.' They embraced, patting each other on the back, giving comfort to one another. Tom escorted her to the front door and kissed his mother-in-law on the cheek. She liked the smell of him and the roughness of his chin. 'Goodbye, Tom. See you soon.' And in answer to a concerned questioning look she said, 'I'll be all right, I promise. I'll call if I need anything.'

Then they were both waving from the car, and she waved back and watched the car disappear amongst all the others. She closed the door and leant against it, relieved that the ordeal was over, savouring her new state. Then as if by a hidden signal, she sprang into action. Flinging off her coat, she grabbed her jacket from the hook in the hall, checked that she had enough money and her key, and let herself out of the house and set off towards the corner shop, head down so that she wouldn't have to talk to anybody. She reached the mini-roundabout and waited whilst a double-decker bus negotiated the corner. She crossed over to the shop and with relief saw a copy of the local paper folded into the wire holder by the door. With the *Chronicle* safely tucked under her arm, she squeezed one of the last two remaining sliced loaves of bread and presented the two items to the friendly Indian lady behind the counter.

'It's turned out to be a lovely day, hasn't it?'

'Yes, it's a wonderful day now.' Marjorie smiled back warmly, relishing the luxury of saying exactly what she meant for the first time since Jack's death.

Marjorie settled down to study the property pages in the paper. She glanced across at Jack's empty chair, instantly conjuring up a picture of him, and felt the familiar loathing creeping over her. She was glad to be leaving him behind in his chair, in this house, watching the soap operas like an old woman, soaking up the gossip and ready to discuss with his friend, Chris Butler, next door. Marjorie chose to sit alone in the kitchen in the evenings, listening to Radio 4, or reading, in an attempt to elevate her mind above her surroundings.

She reflected now on their wasted years. What satisfaction had Jack derived from continually criticising her, pulling her down, and calling her foul names? She would never understand his ways, just as she had never understood her father's motive for the same behaviour towards her mother. What pleasure had he got from letting Chris Butler next door believe that they still shared the same bed, the lewd jokes, and the descriptions of night-time activities told in detail as if they had happened and were not all imagined in his head?

It would be wonderful to move away, she thought as she took up the paper again to dispel the picture of her late husband and to continue her search for a new home and a new life. Yes, a new life, that's what she wanted. Another chance at happiness. She could finish her training as an architect, go to the theatre, visit art galleries, and eat what and when she wanted. The thought of living on her own filled her with excitement. Decisions would be hers; her idea of pleasure would not be met with derision by Jack, who never tired of telling her she was stupid when she wanted to read book reviews and look at documentaries rather than *Coronation Street*. Then *EastEnders* had come along, filling the house with even more misery. Reading had been her way of transporting her out of the house into another life. She didn't want to have confirmation that the world was made up of dreariness and domestic drama. Perhaps it was all too close to the truth of her own life, a mirror that she didn't want to gaze into, she thought ruefully.

But where did she want to go to? The image crossed her mind of her leaving Middleston to escape everything that had happened there. Was it the same impulse that now urged her to move again? Marrying Jack had seemed such a logical decision to make at the time. She had first met him in the lift on her way to lunch and he joined her. For the next few weeks they met every day at the same café. She thought he was harmless, chatting about his friends, football matches and visits to the pub. She listened, offering little about herself other than her work. She asked lots of questions about his apprenticeship as a surveyor which she learned was coming to an end. When he said he was taking a job up in Newcastle, she allowed their relationship to flourish. When he asked her to marry him, she readily agreed.

What a fool she had been. And yet she wouldn't have had Sally, who had filled her life—both their lives—with such joy. She had brought laughter into the house and warmth. Jack had wanted more children, but the romantic overtures mixed with insults didn't make his advances welcome, and in time he had given up. She didn't miss that side of marriage one iota.

8

NICHOLAS LOOKED AT the letter in his hand, reluctant to let it go on its journey to his sister. It had been several weeks since Auntie Ollie had died peacefully in the small terraced house they had shared for twenty-eight years. He was still numbed by the event. He had thought she would be there forever, so this letter was the beginning of acknowledging that she had indeed gone for good.

He wondered if he would hear back from Marjorie. The memory of her wedding day, with her unhappy eyes and Jack Willis's satisfied grin, had stayed with him. He felt sure that Marjorie hadn't cared whether she married Willis or not. It was just an excuse to get away from the area. Marjorie had allowed the courtship to blossom when Jack had been offered a job up North. Nicholas remembered the brief conversation with Jack Willis after the ceremony.

'Look at her.' He had tossed his slicked-back tipsy head in his bride's direction. 'She's right uppity. Look at that nose in the air as if there's a bad smell under it. I can't wait to bring her down.' Seeing Nicholas's concern, he had added for reassurance, 'Don't worry, mate, it won't be long before I bring her into line.' He had made a vulgar gesture, making Nicholas a party to his thoughts.

They hadn't seen each other since that day. Jack Willis had not been one of his favourite people.

They had let their father know of the marriage, but Ernest had chosen not to acknowledge the event, so Nicholas had given his sister away to a loathsome creature who had crawled into their lives and taken Marjorie north. He had tried to capture on canvas the look in Marjorie's eyes as she set off on her honeymoon and a new life, but he had been unable to get the mixture of relief and bare dejection that had jostled for place as she waved goodbye.

George Thomas had also chosen to stay away from the wedding. Marjorie had spent two years rebuffing his advances, only to settle on a man not worthy to clean George's shoes, Nicholas reflected. When she arrived back at Auntie Ollie's, she had withdrawn from the world, never going out except to make the hour-long bus journey to the city where she was training to be a junior draughtswoman, her ambitions to go to university to study architecture put on one side. She hid in her protective shell, choosing to help Auntie Ollie in the house. George wanted to be close to her, but she shied away from his warmth and devotion. Nicholas suspected it was because of the baby, but his loyalty to his sister prevented him from telling George. He watched helplessly as his friend was punched and buffeted by Marjorie's rejection.

Nicholas felt sure that Marjorie would never allow Jack Willis into the inner recesses of her heart. Perhaps she had been afraid that George would have demanded that she unlock the iron grip and give up the secrets of her unhappiness. He had been very persistent, but Marjorie had won, if marrying Jack Willis could be termed as winning anything.

He allowed the letter to slip through his fingers into the box, giving it a life of its own, and turned away. He crossed the street to the corner shop and picked up the local paper. An old picture of his father was on the front page.

'I see your dad's at it again, Nick,' Ben Bainbridge observed from behind the counter, as he replenished the sweets. 'Happen I'll have to look for another shop sooner than I thought.'

'It's not final yet. Try and hang on, will you. Every time someone moves away adds fuel to their argument.'

'Nick, lad, I can't hang on for very long. This shop's worth nothing now as it is, and customers are a rare breed nowadays. It's the rush hour if I have two bodies to serve at the same time.'

'If the warehouses were renovated instead of being torn down, you'd see a rise in trade, I'm sure of that. It's your only hope, Ben.'

'You're right, me lad, but who's going to stop your dad and Max Baines? Not the likes of you and me, that's for sure.' He flung the empty carton on the floor and stamped vigorously, flattening it. 'D'you remember when I bought this place? Packed it were; bunged up with folk, all seeing who could stretch their arms longest to get served. It were a blooming gold mine.' He paused, looking at Nicholas, who was staring at the picture of his father. 'Then your dad started to put his boot in.'

'Yes,' Nicholas acknowledged, 'I've been so busy with my head in painting, it's like I haven't registered all this as being real.' He indicated the street with a wide sweep of his arm. 'I've caught it all on canvas, but not in my brain. You must have thought I was a right wet bugger, not doing anything to stop that maniac.' He struck his father's photograph with the back of his hand. 'But by God, I'm going to do my best before he gets his filthy hands on my warehouses.'

'Blooming heck. I've never seen you so worked up before. Listen,' he said, looking around for the presence of non-existent listening ears before he continued in confidential tones, 'there's a meeting this Sunday. There's a few of us getting together to see what we can do to put a stop to all this. The planning application's in this week.' He pointed to the paper in Nicholas's hand. 'According to the plans, the old buildings will be torn down to make way for a new low-cost housing estate. The land's been categorised by the council as industrial wasteland, worth next to nothing.'

'Sounds a familiar trick. What the plan doesn't say is that this area has been systematically undermined and the local people driven out. It's not about housing people in need. The low-cost housing is here, right here.'

'Local traders won't be able to afford the high rents once the whole scheme's been developed. I'll be out for sure, making way for the big chains to move in.'

'I see my father's marketing department's been busy in the press expounding the virtues of the proposal. My dad looks like a benevolent old man.' He read the caption immediately under his father's photograph: 'Two-hundred-year-old wharf warehouses rat-infested crumbling liabilities, unfit for modern day usage—an insult to the local community.' Nicholas spat. 'Bloody cretins.' His anger boiled over. He felt impotent as the wheels of local government turned inexorably towards demolishing his beloved buildings. Max and his father were on another expansionist programme, building up their empire and monopoly over the town, paying off officials, and handing sweeteners to the undecided, tipping the balance forever in the favour of Baines and Baines.

'Count me in, Ben. I'm on your side all the way.'

'That's grand. There's someone else I'd like to recruit, and that's the chap who calls himself Monet…been writing letters for weeks. There's another in today.'

Nicholas kept his head down as though concentrating on the lead article. Out of the corner of his eye, he saw Ben peering at him thoughtfully.

'It wouldn't be yours truly, would it?' Getting no answer, he chuckled. 'Ee, you're a quiet fish, Nicholas Baines. You've made up for a few years with your head in paints by the volume of letters you've written lately.' Getting no denial, he guffawed loudly and at length. 'Wait till the rest of them know.'

'No, Ben. Don't let anybody know,' Nicholas urged. 'I shouldn't have let you think it was me. It's not safe. I know my dad, but I also know that his partner is ten times worse and will stop at nothing. He's used my dad to get what he wants. My old man's an angel compared to Max Baines.'

The familiar smell of turpentine and linseed oil met him as he let himself into Auntie Ollie's house. He still thought of it as her house, even though she had left it to him, with a promise that if Marjorie ever needed a home without her husband, she was to be made welcome. He had had no difficulty in making this promise. He had read between the lines of Marjorie's rare letters tucked into Christmas cards, and knew that she felt ashamed of her husband. He was sure that this added to the reasons that kept her away from Middleston. He had proposed visits to her, but Marjorie had always put them off at the last minute, the excuses thin.

As the years had gone by, only a school photograph of her daughter Sally, taken when she was eleven in her new grammar school uniform, had arrived to break the pattern. It was still in its silver frame where Auntie Ollie had lovingly placed it on the mantelpiece in the front room. He looked across at it now, unable to get close to it because of the paintings stacked up, each stretched over its own rough wooden frame, leaning backwards, choreographed in rows.

He felt lonely now that Auntie Ollie was no longer there to encourage him. He had never married, never really thought of it. His painting was his passion. He had reached middle age without really registering his changing appearance. He still wore cord trousers and one of the selection of sweaters knitted for him by Auntie Ollie over the years. His mild manner and quiet ways had left his face unmarked. Only the distant memory of his mother and Marjorie cast a shadow, making him feel sad and nostalgic. His hair was beginning to go grey at the sides. It badly needed cutting, but he was in no hurry to have it done.

He looked wryly at his years of work, and with sudden clarity realised that his painting had been a substitute for living. The process of creation had provided the journeys he had not taken, the relationships he had not experienced. He had separated himself from the mainstream, almost heedless of the outside world, living in a timeless bubble. Auntie Ollie's death had savagely broken into his tranquil space.

He had always been a congenial, friendly person but had avoided deeper relationships, relying on Auntie Ollie and his painting for succour. Auntie Ollie had left a gaping hole which needed to be filled. Accepting this need was making him reach out to his fellow man and begin to take an active interest in what was happening around him. He was beginning to feel a new source of energy, driven by a feeling of belonging and a need to participate in the world again.

He left the front room and wandered into the cluttered kitchen where he filled the kettle before opening the paper.

His letter of protest was there.

Low-cost housing scheme
Sir,

With reference to your front-page article of March 18, 'Local Company to Save Wharf Area,' your readers are naively led to believe that planning decisions in this country are based upon democratic principles. However, it appears that certain large corporations have undue influence on this democratic process in the drive to line the pockets of a few 'interested' parties.

The low-cost housing scheme is a sham. The wharf overlooks the canal basin. With the rise of the leisure boat industry, it is not hard to project into the future and see these properties becoming very desirable residences attracting high prices.

The developers stand to make an enormous profit given that the land has been designated as wasteland worth next to nothing.

I should like to suggest that long-term high income can be made for the benefit of our community by restoring the wharf buildings and letting the spaces out as offices, shops, studios, and flats in a village atmosphere which would attract tourists and provide long-term employment while conserving valuable buildings and the existing neighbourhood.

I challenge our council to raise objections to this scheme.

Yours,

N. Monet

He skimmed over his letter and read the other letter under the same heading.

Dear Sir,

I am a local craftsman, and I can't begin to tell you how glad I am to see a plan for the wharf buildings to come down. They are a blight on our town. This plan will provide work

*for local people, and the end result will benefit those folk who
can't afford ordinary housing.*
Yours faithfully,
Dan Beazley

Nicholas read this and threw the paper contemptuously on the table. Dan Beazley. He was one of his father's 'fivers.' He would do anything for five pounds. His father also had 'tenners,' those people without much conscience who nevertheless needed a little more monetary persuasion. The whole town had been filed under the amounts needed to buy them off. 'Everyone has their price. One day I'll get the vicar to turn his church into flats,' his father had been fond of saying over the Sunday lunch table, chuckling at his own power.

The kettle came alive, bubbling, demanding attention. He picked out a cup from the sink full of dirty dishes and rinsed it out. As Nicholas prepared his solitary cup of tea, he wondered who else would be at the meeting on Sunday. He also wondered if he would hear from Marjorie.

9

CHRIS BUTLER HUNG over Marjorie's wall. Like Punch, only his head and arms moved, the rest of his body concealed behind the wall supported on kitchen steps.

'Getting on, then?' he called, leering at her as usual. Since Jack's death, he had been acting like a predatory tomcat, his territory expanded to include Marjorie's garden. She had seen him of course, from the outer range of her eye, which always went to the same spot to check if Jack's old friend was there, but she ignored his question, hoping that he would respond to the outright rudeness that matched his own.

'Airs and graces, is it today then? I like it when you put your nose up like that; it makes me think I'm living next door to the Queen. The wife will be proud.'

Marjorie lifted the wet clothes one at a time and with deliberate action rammed the pegs home, turning the rotary line towards her to keep her back to this unfortunate unforeseen complication of Jack's death.

'It's going to rain, you know,' he called out, with undisguised glee.

Her back rippled with hatred. She plucked up her basket and briskly headed for her sanctuary, the attention to her potted geraniums postponed yet again.

'Oh, Mr Butler, what a surprise, I never expect to see you there, hanging over my wall,' she shot at him before shutting him out. Several weeks had passed since the funeral, and she was feeling distraught that no one had bought her house yet to rescue her from the disgusting creature next door and propel her into her new life that she had so coveted after Jack's death.

She heard the pile of post land on the doormat as it had done almost every day since she had placed her name with the estate agents. The initial excitement and surge of energy had given way to a studied casual approach, willing herself not to get too interested in a particular property until her own was sold.

She took up the letters, identifying the individual franking machine stamps, and leafed through them on the way back to the kitchen. A handwritten letter tucked amongst the others made her pause by the door. She immediately recognised the handwriting and place of posting. It was from Nicholas. It had been so long since she had heard from him.

She finished reading the letter. She felt close to tears but fought them back. *I haven't seen her for years. Why do I feel like this?* she asked herself as she sat at the kitchen table, occasionally rereading the letter as if it would tell her the reason.

'I suppose I should tell Nicholas about Jack going.' Rummaging around in the sideboard drawer, she found a block of writing paper and wrote her address at the top.

Dear Nicholas,

    Thanks for your letter. I was so sorry to hear about Auntie Ollie. You must be feeling lost without her.

    Jack died in March of a heart attack. I'm hoping to move to a new house soon.

    Are you still painting? I'd love to know how you are getting on.

    Write again soon. Lots of love,
      Marjorie

As she wrote Nicholas's name and Auntie Ollie's address, the tears began. She couldn't hold back any longer. All the unexpressed grief of the last twenty-eight years seemed to engulf her. Rocking back and forth in her chair, her arms crossed tightly for comfort, she wept for her lost baby and for the love she had been unable to give to Jack.

Sometime in the afternoon the telephone rang in the hall.

'Hello, Sally,' she answered her daughter and shivered.

'You don't sound well, Mum. Are you all right?' Sally as usual seemed to sense her state of mind.

'I've had some bad news today from your Uncle Nicholas,' she answered, feeling the tears welling up again. 'Auntie Ollie died a short while ago.'

'You've never told me about her,' Sally said gently.

Marjorie drew in a breath, gathering strength. 'She was a very dear person my mother knew when we were little. Your Uncle Nicholas lived with her for a long time, and I lived with her after, after…' She couldn't go on. She did so want to un-burden herself, but held back. She had never discussed her past with Sally. 'I'm sorry Sally; I'm in a bit of a state.'

'Mum, I've never known you to be like this. Don't cry.' Sally's sweet voice coaxed her. 'Listen, Tom and I were won-dering if you'd like to come and spend some time with us, perhaps a week or so. I've got half term coming up from the twentieth and Tom has to work, so I thought it might be nice for us to go shopping together, or do anything you like really. What do you think?'

'I think it's a lovely idea. I need a holiday, even if it's just to get away from Chris Butler next door.' She began to feel bet-ter as Sally's warm and practical nature, which had been such a support through the years, once again helped her carry on. 'Sally?' she asked tentatively, 'do you think it would be too far to go to Middleston from you, just for the day? I'd like to see your Uncle Nicholas again. It's been so long.'

'We can do that easily from here. It's only forty miles or so, and I'd love to meet him. After all, he's my only relative, isn't he?'

Back in the kitchen, Marjorie tore up the letter she had written earlier to Nicholas and started another. Halfway through the third page, she paused, reflecting on her state of mind compared to only a few hours ago. It was strange, all those tears and feelings surfacing, and then the vulnerability she had shown to her daughter; she felt more alive. Her let-ter to Nicholas reflected this. Here she was chatting to him as though they were at their old kitchen table. She needed to talk about everything; her feelings had been on hold for too long. The well of sadness felt bottomless, but she knew that today she had begun a process she sensed would lead her out of the pit she had been living in.

—◊◊—

Nicholas read Marjorie's letter, not quite believing that she had written so much after all these years. He came to the last page and learned that she was going to stay with Sally for a week, and could they meet? Could he ring? Of course he could ring. He would go to the box outside the post office now. He felt so happy.

He saw the man on the corner, his collar up and head squeezed into his neck. He thought little of it until he returned from making the phone call to Marjorie and walked into the living room. Three of his latest paintings had been slashed. A piece of paper was stuffed into one of the gashes. He felt sickened at the wanton barbarity. Months of love and effort were represented in those canvases. He had grown through them, expanded and stretched to new heights of expression. Tears of frustration exploded into his eyes. 'Oh God, the bastard. The fucking bastard.'

He knew the content before he unravelled the crumpled note: *Keep off the wharf, or else.*

10

G ATHERING UP THE papers and trying to tie them with string was proving more difficult than Helen had anticipated. Exasperated, she let the pile slide into disorder again. 'I'll have to get a box for this lot,' she announced to Steve Brown, her new colleague at the *City Post*.

'Try the basement,' he said, his back hunched, continuing to stare into his computer and giving it the occasional instruction to fine-tune his article. Sleeves were rolled up at the elbow, a cigarette pinched between his yellow, stained teeth. A curl of smoke glanced off his sallow, pockmarked cheeks, floating upwards through his thinning ginger hair. Every inch of his unfit five foot eight was a newspaper hack, producing a steady output of good, routine reporting interjected with the occasional brilliant article.

Steve had given her the minimum of help when she had started at the paper on Monday morning. Gruff in manner, he wasn't exactly rude to her, but he made it plain that he wasn't welcoming her with open arms. She had been forced to ask him the silliest of questions, making her feel that she was constantly interrupting him. Ignoring his instructions from the editor to show her around and make her feel at home, he had not even indicated where she could get a cup of coffee. It was obvious he did not care for the introduction of the chic, confident reporter from a top national paper.

Helen left the features room and ran down the bare wooden stairs to where the daily paper was printed and dispatched. The noise and smell of a printing were things she had grown to love. Without looking she could recognise each stage of the process by the sequence of sounds. She had worked her way up from her first job after leaving Exeter, little more than a messenger and tea girl to all the departments, to being a reliable reporter with an instinct for the individual human angle in the broader context. Her special features had won her acclaim, and her colleagues in London had been devastated when she had decided to leave their fold.

She weaved through the whirring machines until she spotted a pile of boxes which she identified as containing tubs of ink. Ideal for her purpose, she snatched one up. 'Can I take this?' she called out to the tall, gangly man in his fifties who was standing nearby, checking the run.

'Help yourself, love,' he shouted, extracting a copy from the run before turning to see the owner of the voice. He looked Helen up and down, appraising her in detail. 'Any time,' he added, smiling and giving her a wink.

'Thanks,' she said, smiling. His face was friendly, and she felt an immediate liking for him. 'How do you do? I'm Helen

Arbuthnot.' She reached out her hand, which he took and solemnly shook.

'Laurie Phillips.' Looking into his blackened palm which she had just shaken, he said, 'Sorry about the ink.'

'That's all right, I only need the box.'

He laughed. 'What d'you do upstairs?' He indicated the ceiling with a toss of his head.

'Reporter. Just started Monday. I've got a lot to learn, hence the box to carry my homework in.'

'Where've you come from?'

'London; I needed a change,' she added hastily.

'Any problems, being a woman?' He jutted his face towards her.

'No, why should I? What difference does it make?' she asked defensively, a stirring of unease gripping her as his face closed in on hers.

He pulled back. 'It's dangerous out there. I wouldn't let my daughter out on the streets, poking her nose into places she has no need to. There're too many nutters out there for my liking.'

Relieved that he wasn't one of them, only a concerned father figure, she relaxed. 'That's very sweet of you, Laurie, but I'm a big girl, and I can take care of myself. Have you really got a daughter?'

'Yes, three of them, and a son, and I love 'em all to pieces, and that's why they won't be doing your job, ever.' He jabbed his finger towards her, emphasising his warning. 'How your parents sleep at night is beyond me.'

'My mother hasn't a clue what goes on in the world and sleeps beautifully.' The machines slowed to a halt. 'I better not keep you any longer. Thank you for the box and your concern.'

'Just remember what I said. This isn't a very pleasant city for a girl on her own. Be careful,' he called to her retreating figure.

—⚹—

At the end of her first week, the Friday edition put to bed, Helen felt exhausted. She carried the box of papers through the city streets to her flat. It was six o'clock, and the glass and steel shelters were crowded with tired faces waiting for the buses to carry them away from the hustle of the town centre.

In the immediate future, her evenings would be spent reading all the local newspapers in the district, as well as working out where she was going to fit in the organisation beside the resentful Steve Brown. She had to find a strong story to make her debut on the paper. She had forfeited London for the provinces for personal reasons, as she had said on her application. She had no intention of making it a backwards step, seeing it instead as an opportunity to explore her potential and to demonstrate her capabilities by diversifying into uncharted territories.

She stepped out of the lift, her heart sinking at the sight of the scuffed yellow flush door of her sparsely furnished fifth-floor flat. On the north side of a rectangular block verging on a seedy area of the city, it rarely felt the sun. She experienced an acute pang of longing for her cosy west-facing attic, which used to be drenched with afternoon light, and for her friends and her familiar stomping grounds. Had it been so necessary to run away from Roderick Barclay?

The phone was ringing as she turned the key in the Yale lock. Dumping the box without ceremony on the threadbare, chocolate-brown hall carpet, she picked up the receiver.

'Hello, Helen Arbuthnot,' she answered, automatically reaching for a pencil and pad.

'Hi, Helen. My name's Nancy Kerr. I'm a friend of Sister Agnes?' The American voice left a question in the air.

'Yes, I remember she has mentioned you. Do you live in Middleston?' Her good memory served her well, as usual.

'That's right. She called me a couple of weeks ago and asked me to make sure you were settled into your new home?'

'Yes. I'm fine,' Helen answered automatically, surveying the dreary flat. The door leading into the living room was open, revealing the leatherette settee with its ashtrays set into the arms. Her senses screamed as always at the sight, and she turned her gaze to the kitchen, with its orange decor. The filthy landing gaped outside her front door. Wherever she looked, her eyes were assaulted by her landlord's idea of a luxury city-centre apartment. Advertised as having the latest mod cons, including a security camera in the underground parking area, she had grabbed at it because of its location so close to the newspaper office.

'My husband, David, and I would love to meet you, and we'd be delighted if you could join us this weekend for lunch, perhaps on Sunday?'

'I'd love to, Mrs Kerr.' Escape from these surroundings would be divine.

'Call me Nancy, dear. Do you have a car, or shall we collect you?'

'I have a car, thank you,' she said, thinking of her dear little Beetle in the badly lit underground car park. 'What time shall I come?'

'About eleven thirty? Would that be convenient for you? It's about an hour from the city.'

'Yes, perfect. It's really kind of you to invite me.' She wrote down the address. Pleased with the phone call, she picked up the box and kicked the front door closed behind her.

She always found reading papers new to her a fascinating task. She was convinced it was the best way to tune in to the heartbeat of an area. The idiosyncrasies of local people could be felt through the pages. Important local issues, the division of the space available and whether an article appeared on the front or back page, whether it was assigned to part of the page that didn't draw the eye…All these factors registered as she began her marathon read, sitting at the glass-topped chrome table, a large cup of tea by her side.

She had prepared files for prominent issues and protracted and unresolved issues. Letters to the editor were carefully read and connected to the relevant articles of past papers. She had two months of back issues of weekly local papers and two months of the daily city paper, which also picked up stories from the locals. It would take a long time to sift through the information and store it in an easily retrievable system. It would have been faster to use the services of the paper that also ran such a system, but by doing it herself, she learnt quickly and had a better feel of the area.

It was well past midnight when the *Middleston News* found its way to the top of the pile. With an added incentive to get to know what was happening in Middleston with her visit to the Kerrs on Sunday, she started to read the lead article. As she read, the idea for her debut feature began to take form. Middleston seemed to be a very controversial place.

—⁂—

Helen headed out of town, the clear sunshine bringing a little cheer to the otherwise dismal city streets, strewn with litter and the occasional lone soul shuffling aimlessly along. There was a stark contrast between the magnificent solid administrative buildings of the city centre and the huddled homes leaning together for strength. As mile upon mile they guided her out of town towards the open countryside, they reminded Helen of the city's past. They were built on the back of the industrial revolution at great cost to humanity in terms of depleting the spirit of the individual, the breaking up of village communities, and the slave trade. All these stories were told in the city's diverse architecture. Large country houses were dotted about the countryside, away from the soot and squalor, keeping their noses tilted away from the source of their grandeur.

It came unexpectedly. Helen had become used to London's conglomeration and the battle fought each time she wanted to escape its long tentacles. Now the open countryside welcomed her as her car climbed up the dual carriageway, hugging the slow lane, letting the rest of the world pass her by on its pressing business.

Turning on the radio and pulling the sun visor down, she settled into her journey. She had a good half hour's drive before her exit. She had studied the map and had a visual picture of the route ahead. Being blessed with a good sense of direction had come in useful since she had first jumped over the convent wall and discovered the delights of the wooded hillside behind the convent's enclosure. Rhododendrons became palaces peopled with princes and courtiers; schoolrooms where she always chose to be the teacher; or just a small house with a mum, daddy, and their little girl called Helen. Hours would pass before she would feel the chill in the air and know that it was time to climb the wall again, at her secret place where two moss-covered boulders provided a stairway to the top. From there she carefully picked her way past the bird's nest and the dangerous bit that had crumbled away until she came to the coal pile. If it had recently been replenished, she could just step down and slither to the bottom. But if the coal man had not been for a while, the jump became a feat of damage limitation.

The last time she jumped into the coal, the pile began to slide away from her like an avalanche, the pieces of coal behind her falling, threatening to engulf her. Her screams of panic as she was pulled downwards in the undercurrent of coal permeated the prayers of the nuns. Alarms scattered the community as instinctively the nuns ran towards the terrified voice of their little charge. Sister Agnes reached the scene first. She threw herself on to the pile, clawing at the black rocks, trying to reach her child, whose frightened eyes implored her mother to save her before it was too late.

Planks of wood were brought from the storeroom to stop the slide, but to no avail. A ladder was delicately placed against the pile to try and reach Helen that way, but the angle was wrong in which to try to extricate her.

Sister Agnes suddenly appeared again, busily knotting a sheet along its length. Taking the ladder in a no-nonsense way, she climbed to the top of the wall and made her way along it until she was above the coal pile. She threw one end of the sheet to Helen. Helen caught hold and inch by inch was hauled from the coal pile by her mother, who never knew she had such strength but thanked God for giving it to her on that day when she needed it.

If Helen had harboured any doubts of where she was held in the hearts of the nuns and especially of her mother, they were shed that day.

Safely down the ladder, assisted by the excited nuns, Helen was held tightly in her mother's arms, who rocked her back and forth as she cried with relief. Helen cried too, for a long time, making up for the family life she had never known.

That day, Helen decided that Sister Agnes was the only mother she needed. A new era was born, one of acceptance and peace. She was nine years old.

Once she was off the main road, Helen drove slowly through the hamlets and villages, the road winding through the country lanes like a young stream taking the line of least resistance. Twice she crossed a canal, her wheels making a trundling sound as she drove over the wooden boards of the bridges. At the second bridge she stopped the car and got out to watch the boats pass under. Some teenagers waved as they disappeared from view below her. She waved back and then ran to the other side to watch them reappear and waved again.

The stocky man at the wheel in jeans and a polo shirt turned round. 'Lovely morning,' he shouted up at her in a deep, sonorous voice. 'Want to join us?' He had a kind, open face under a buff-coloured fisherman's hat. He looked relaxed and completely at home on the canal. His crooked smile was contagious.

She laughed at his friendliness. 'I'd love to. Some other time though, I'm on my way to friends in Middleston.'

'Anyone I know?' he shouted even louder as the boat chugged away from her. He quickly checked forward for on-coming traffic, before turning back, his eyes squinting in the bright sunshine.

'Nancy and David Kerr,' she yelled.

'Nice people. Say hello from George Thomas.'

'I will,' she shouted. 'Bye.'

Helen turned to find a middle-aged man standing at the end of the bridge looking at her. His paint-smeared clothes hung loosely about his tall, slim frame. What appeared to be a sketchpad was tucked under his arm, a small backpack was slung over his shoulder. She smiled as she passed him. Seeming to be flustered, he hesitated before returning her politeness.

He reminded her of the monks who occasionally visited the convent and their self-imposed austerity, seeking an inner peace for their souls, the material world a hostile, foreign place that they had no desire to join.

He continued to look at her, not bothering to disguise his interest, a mildly mystified expression about the eyes, as she climbed into the car to resume her journey. As she checked her rear-view mirror, he was still there, standing as if in a trance. *What was all that about*, she wondered.

Middleston, aptly named as the central market town of the area, was respectably quiet on this late Sunday morning as Helen drove through the tree-lined streets towards the centre. Church services were just finishing, and the newsagents in the market square were getting ready for the second wave of customers. She parked her car on the cobbles outside the town hall to check the directions Nancy Kerr had given her.

It was only eleven o'clock, and she wasn't expected for another half hour. According to her directions, the Kerr's house was not going to be difficult to find. She bought the *Observer* and *Sunday Times* from the nearest newsagent. She liked the atmosphere of the market square and lingered, taking in the details. It was as all town centres should be, she thought, a meeting place, a place for exchanging goods, a central resource area with its shops clustered around the perimeter selling essential goods. In the middle of the green, surrounded by a white picket fence, a bandstand sat, as though patiently waiting for the local brass ensemble to play.

As she walked back to her car, she saw the same man from the bridge, his aesthetic appearance unmistakable. He was looking towards her. He hesitated, as if he might approach, but apparently deciding not to, he turned and sauntered on, occasionally looking back until he disappeared down a narrow corner lane. She watched the retreating figure, making sure that he had gone before climbing back into her car. It was an odd reaction to a stranger, she thought. She had experienced some weird characters in her job, but he didn't seem weird, just harmlessly curious. Perhaps they were not used to visitors in Middleston.

She found the Kerrs' street quickly, but finding the right house was not so easy. The houses were large; some had been converted to flats, and others still stood in their original glory; less stately homes, their owners clinging on despite the rising maintenance costs, were in a stand against the developers.

By a process of elimination, Helen finally turned into the pea-shingled drive of the Kerrs' home. The front door was open, and Nancy Kerr came out to greet her.

'Hi, Helen, it's so good to meet you after all this time.' Nancy Kerr kissed both of Helen's cheeks. Bathed in a light but expensive perfume, Nancy wore cool mint–green slacks topped with an expensively tailored shirt. Her short hair, lightly brushed back off her face, fell in natural waves, the blond hair of her youth still to be seen amongst the abundant silver white. Her serene features had aged gracefully. She was at ease with her elegance, a practised hostess. 'Sister Agnes said you were a beautiful girl, and just look at you!' she exclaimed, holding Helen at arm's length so that she could admire her.

'Thank you, Nancy. It's very nice to meet you too. My mother continually embarrasses me,' she said, imagining the glowing terms her mother would have described her in.

'She's one honest lady though. Come on in, Helen. I thought we'd have lunch in the garden, it's such a beautiful day. I hope you like salmon?' she asked as she led the way into the house.

'I love it.'

They walked through the cool hall to the kitchen. One end of the huge room was used as a sitting area. French doors led into the garden, through which Helen could see a table laid for two, a gaily striped umbrella shielding it from the sun.

'David will be home later this afternoon. He's attending a protest meeting called at short notice, but I'm sure we'll find lots to talk about before he gets here. Take a seat, Helen.' She indicated a stool by the work island in the centre of the room.

'I have some photographs of my mother to show you,' Helen said as she perched on the high seat, suddenly remembering the small album she had put in her bag. 'Oh, and I brought you this. I hope you like it.' She pulled out a tiny, delicately wrapped parcel.

Nancy took the little package from Helen and carefully unwrapped the layers of tissue. 'It's beautiful. Did you paint this, Helen?'

'Yes. The sisters taught me.' She was pleased that Nancy showed such appreciation of her small gift.

'They may have taught you technique, but you have real talent.'

'Thank you. I haven't done any painting for a long time. I was encouraged to make gifts for people, and I enjoyed doing these miniatures.'

'I wonder where you get your talent from?' Nancy asked, almost to herself, as she leant the diminutive rectangle against her books.

'I've no idea. I don't know who my natural parents are, or where they came from or if they are still alive,' she said bluntly, not wanting to pursue the subject.

'Would you like to know?' Nancy asked beguilingly, as she took some napkins from a drawer, her warm tones luring Helen into her confidence.

'One day, perhaps.' Suddenly fearful that Nancy would open a Pandora's box, and startled by the introduction of the subject, she went on quickly. 'I've thought about it, of course. Mother told me the circumstances when I was little.' She didn't want to know. Not yet. Roderick's insult and rejection because of her illegitimacy were still working like splinters in her heart. 'I would like to feel a little more settled before I begin a search, if I ever do, that is.' She hoped the subject was closed.

'Let's take these photographs outside, and you can show me them over lunch. Knowing Agnes, I expect she has been a wonderful mother for you, and I know you have been a delightful daughter.' She smiled reassuringly, acknowledging Helen's choice and prerogative not to have her birth details on the afternoon's agenda. 'I'll bring the salmon. The salad's already out. Can I offer you a glass of cool wine?'

'I'd love one,' she said, relief surging through her that Nancy was sensitive to her feelings.

The stories Nancy told through lunch of Sister Agnes during their nursing days in London made Helen cry with laughter. She liked Nancy. She liked her easy-going manner, and the welcome Nancy had given her, almost a stranger, into her home. A whole new dimension was being added to her mother, a life before the convent when she was just another Irish girl arriving in London to train as a nurse.

'We met when I advertised for a roommate. My dad had taken the lease on an apartment near the hospital. I got lonely knocking around this big old mansion flat on my own. Agnes replied to my ad, and that was that. She moved in from her digs, and we spent our three years training together. It was a very happy time.'

'I can't imagine my mother having a life outside the convent.'

'Well she did, and in a big way. Next time you see her, just say "jelly beans," and watch her reaction.'

Helen laughed. 'I will. You've intrigued me.'

'Agnes taught me to cook genuine Irish stew, and I introduced her to popcorn.' A faraway look passed over Nancy's face as memories surfaced. 'I'll never forget Agnes thanking God for every new day. She lived life to the full and then at the end of her midwifery training, she announced that she was going to take her orders.'

'She's been very happy.'

'Yes, I know she has. Her contentment permeates her voice; her letters are treatises of love.' Nancy seemed to examine her hands before she continued softly. 'It's ironic that Agnes was the one destined to become a mother, and I who was living in the world...' She looked up, and her eyes were moist. 'Well, it wasn't to be.'

'I'm so sorry.' Helen's heart went out to her, at her evident sorrow at never having had a child.

Nancy smiled poignantly before continuing. 'I met David in my third year. He was a handsome intern, and we fell in love immediately. Agnes said we were meant for each other, and nearly forty years later, I can say she was right. All ideas of returning to the States as a state registered nurse trained in a prestigious London hospital dissipated within weeks. We married shortly after gaining my qualification. Agnes was a bridesmaid.'

'She treasures the photograph of your wedding.'

'Does she, Helen? It's sad that our lives have been separated in style and distance. She's a wonderful person...but of course you know that.' She poured the last of the wine into their glasses. 'Her marriage was a solemn affair but has lasted as long as mine. As far as I know, she has never wavered in her constancy and love of God.'

'She's bound to him and lives by his rules, and for her they seem to work beautifully.' Helen swirled the wine in her glass as the image of Agnes's dear face was brought before her. 'She's always joyful, and I know I've been very lucky to have her as my mother.'

Nancy reached across the table and touched her hand. 'I'm so glad to know you, Helen. Ah,' she said, her face lighting up with pleasure as she exclaimed, 'There's David.' A tall man in his mid-sixties was standing in the French windows, his head on one side, arms folded, simply watching them. Below a balding top, his wiry grey hair bushed out at the temples. Under his equally unruly eyebrows, his startlingly blue eyes, clear and healthy, surveyed the scene before him. 'David, come and meet Helen. Isn't she beautiful?'

The amusement playing about his mouth suddenly broke into an engaging grin as he came forward. 'She certainly is.' His deep, chocolate voice was warm. They shook hands, her slim, long fingers in his firm but gentle grasp. 'It's a pleasure to meet you, Helen, after all these years.' He surveyed her face, as if searching for something.

'You're early, darling.' Nancy broke the spell.

'Is that a reprimand or a welcome?' he said, releasing Helen's hand and giving his wife a kiss. 'You never know with these Americans, Helen. We think we speak the same language, but I have researched this for over thirty-eight years now and come to the firm conclusion that the differences are cleverly hidden to trip up any unguarded fool such as I. But not this time. By my watch, I make this teatime.'

'Goodness, it's four p.m.,' Nancy exclaimed. 'Helen and I have talked nonstop. Well, how about strawberries for tea, for starters?'

'Sounds wonderful,' Helen said, gathering the plates off the table. 'Nancy's been regaling me with some wonderful stories of her time in London with my mother.'

They walked amiably to the kitchen, carrying the lunch-time dishes. 'I had a friend who would have married Agnes if God hadn't got in there first.'

'David,' Nancy laughingly admonished him.

Helen laughed too at his irreverence. She liked David. She liked them both. Far from feeling this was a duty call, she was enjoying herself enormously. She wondered whether they would be able to help her out with her budding story. As she began to load the dishwasher, she decided to put out a feeler. 'Were you protesting about anything worthwhile?'

'Was I protesting about anything worthwhile?' His mock indignation as he sat on the tall stool made her chuckle. 'Have you spent time in America, young lady, or has that sort of question just rubbed off this afternoon?'

'I've never been to the States, so it must be the exposure today.' Already she had enough confidence in their company to join in their style of repartee.

'Hey, Helen,' Nancy exclaimed with exaggerated indignation, 'whose side are you on? Where's my defence?'

'She's on the side of reason and sanity, not like those developers,' David said, his voice suddenly serious. 'My word, it makes me angry how they get away with it.' His mood had completely changed. 'I'm sorry, Helen, I shouldn't have mentioned something that makes me furious, especially on our first meeting, and on such a glorious day.'

Remembering the newspaper articles, Helen ventured. 'Is that the property developer who wants to raze the original buildings to the ground and put up low-cost housing?'

'Yes, but how on earth do you know about it?' He sounded surprised at her knowledge.

'Remember, I'm a newspaper girl.' She tapped the side of her nose. 'It's my business to know what's going on.'

David rubbed his chin thoughtfully, looking across at Nancy, who was gathering cups and saucers together. Helen caught Nancy's almost imperceptible shake of her head.

'Well, I'm sure it will all turn out all right.' He stood up and began to load the tray. 'These things do.'

Helen was not going to give up so easily on a story. She was known for her persistence. She was reluctant to exploit her friendship with the Kerrs, but she must have a story nevertheless, and soon. The Kerr's seemed to be involved. 'I've read all the arguments, and it seems to me that all the issues are not being brought into the case against the project. I take it you're against, like that chap who signs himself Monet.'

David and Nancy looked at each other as if alarmed. Helen saw the reaction and wondered if she had been tactless in some way.

'Yes, Helen dear.' Nancy was suddenly treating her like a cheeky child. 'We are against it, but this is a very local issue, and I'm sure we'll sort it out. Now, let's have tea.' The subject was closed. She would have to find out more from other sources.

Back underneath the umbrella again, the conversation was easy and carefree. Ice tea, a novelty to Helen, was served like a long cocktail. Scones and cream and strawberries fresh from the garden. Nancy in a floppy straw hat, her laugh infectious. David happy and adoring. The long, slanting rays of sun played on the lawn after a perfect day. Helen reluctantly looked at her watch. 'Goodness, it's half past six already. I must be on my way. Thank you so much for inviting me today.'

'You must come and see us again.' David pulled her chair out for her. 'Any time. If you want to stay, we have four spare bedrooms at your disposal.'

'Now that would be fun,' Nancy added. 'Come for the weekend next time. We could show you round.'

'You're both very kind. I'd love to. My mother said you were very special people, and she was right as usual. Which reminds me,' she said, slinging her bag onto her shoulder. 'George Thomas sends his regards.'

'When did you meet George?' David pierced her with his blue eyes, giving her an indication that she had trod on sensitive territory again.

'This morning. We waved to one another from the bridge. He asked me who I was visiting, and he said to say hello.' She began to walk through the house towards the drive.

'I expected to see him at the meeting today. So that's where he was,' David said thoughtfully.

'Perhaps he doesn't feel as strongly as you do about the wharf development,' Helen tentatively suggested as they reached her car, trying to provoke David into saying more.

Nancy quashed her ruse. Looking directly at David she said, 'I expect he saw it was such a beautiful day today and clean forgot.'

'Yes, probably just slipped his memory,' David added, as if his lines had been cued. 'He loves his boat and likes to get out when he can.'

There was a lot going on here, Helen thought, but now was not the time to pursue the story. She opened the car door. 'Thank you both for a lovely day.'

'Thank you for coming, Helen dear.' Nancy kissed her warmly on both cheeks.

'Lovely to meet you, Helen. Don't bother your head about our wharf. Come and see us soon, and we'll show you what a splendid area we live in.'

Retracing her route, Helen headed towards the centre of town. Far from cooling her interest in the wharf development, the Kerrs' hesitancy in discussing it had intrigued her. She decided to visit it. She drove round the town hall and market place and took the narrow side street indicating the wharf, the same lane that her paint-smeared monk in the rear-view mirror had taken that morning.

She parked at the end. Two concrete pillars stood like sentries guarding the way to the canal. The street was forlorn, the area beyond the pillars desolate. Tufts of grass tried to make a living out of the gravel speckled with coal residue. Black sticky lumps, softened by the sun, argued for a place with the litter. At the water's edge, the foul smell of decaying matter in stagnant pools drifted upwards.

Looking to her right, Helen saw the tall buildings, obviously abandoned. Signs of an old, disused railway were there in the raised embankment threading its way across a bridge. No attempt had been made to make the area appealing. Any money thrown at the site would probably be welcomed by the townspeople, and a low-cost housing scheme would be seen as a beneficial use of what could only be described as an eyesore.

Puzzled at the opposition to the plan and wondering whether they had any case at all, Helen walked along to the high arching footbridge. 'What possible use could this foul stream have, or will they fill it in?' she muttered, looking over the iron railing. She followed it on the opposite bank until she could clearly see the wharf buildings. Then she realised what a tragedy it would be for the development to go ahead. As if rising from the earth itself, the eighteenth-century buildings stood mellow and benign, like old retired men who have a story to tell, if only someone would stop and listen. They were not ready to go yet. They still had something to offer. They were still handsome and upright, underneath the rags.

One side of the canal was a natural harbour. The wharf buildings overlooked the vast crater filled with garbage, now ringed by barbed wire and 'Danger, Keep Out' signs. The development of housing must inevitably be linked with the development of the whole site, Helen thought, as she stood in the centre of the industrial moonscape.

The Kerrs had whetted her appetite. Seeing the scale of the site, of which the wharf-buildings were central, it was obvious that a low-cost housing scheme was at best just the beginning of a major development; at worst it was a ploy to raze the buildings to the ground to make way for a building programme that would include the basin connected to the canal system. To get her story, she had to find out what was really in the developers' plans before it was too late.

11

'IS HE HERE?' Miranda asked the bouncer, the scars of his trade criss-crossing his bloated, pallid face.

'He's in the back.'

'Thanks, Johnny.' She slipped a note into the waiting hand and nodded to her car. 'Do you like the colour?'

'What is it...purple?' He squinted into the dark, trying to make out the colour. It was double-parked outside the nightclub, waiting for him to drive it to the rear of the building where it would be safe.

'It's maroon, silly. They don't make purple cars, do they?'

'You might have had it custom painted, m'lady,' he teased.

'Oh shut up, Johnny.' She gave him a friendly punch on the shiny-suited arm before pushing open the door to reveal the world she loved. Thick smoke and the smell of stale alcohol assailed her as she made her way down the stairs.

Couples clung to each other on the small dance floor. Bar stools were occupied for the evening by regulars, most of whom had been there ever since she first came to the Zanzibar Club at the age of sixteen and met Max Baines.

He had singled her out from a group of friends celebrating an eighteenth birthday, welcome to be with them because she could help pay for the expensive cocktails. Despite this she was largely ignored by the group, so she had been flattered by Max Baines's attentions. She had allowed herself to be drawn into a back room, where she had lost her virginity. It had all been very fast, but she liked his roughness, the antithesis of her genteel upbringing. She wanted more.

She turned the gold knob in the quilted door. Max looked up from the set of plans laid out on the table. 'OK, Ron, we'll leave it there. Come on in, Miranda,' he beckoned, stubbing out his cigar in the overflowing ashtray.

Although in his midfifties, Max Baines was still an attractive man to Miranda. His features had weathered well; he had taken care of them. His plentiful grey hair was swept back from his wide forehead, contrasting with his skin, tanned from a sun lamp. His frame had filled out, giving him a bulkiness that he carried well with his height.

She walked up to him and sat astride his knee, ignoring Ron Thompson while she turned her face to be kissed, Max exploring her mouth, taking his time. Out of the corner of her eye, she saw Ron watching. She took Max's hand and guided it into her pants to her crotch, lifting herself slightly so that he could gain access.

Ron looked on, as if riveted by the sight, his restlessness apparent as he took hold of his own crotch. 'Do you want me to go or stay?' he asked, pulling out his already-erect penis.

'What do you want, Miranda?' Max asked into her mouth. 'Do you want Ron to watch?'

'I like him watching,' she answered huskily, knowing her lines well and how the evening would proceed. She had grown used to sex with more than one man; she'd even had photographs and videos taken.

'Would you like Ron to fuck you?' Max asked as he pushed her to her feet. She groaned in acquiescence, holding onto his shoulders, letting him push his fingers further into her, spreading her wetness around, the liquid sounds exciting her even further. 'Lock the door, Ron,' he said as he carried her to the divan in the corner of the room, and roughly dumped her.

She took off her clothes quickly to catch Max's erection while it lasted, but instead he turned to the thin figure of Ron, his sidekick, his man from the Middleston Council Planning Office. 'Go ahead, Ron. I haven't time.' She watched him turn away to study the plans again, and her head filled with rejection.

Ron slowly licked his lips. Not taking his eyes off her gaping legs, he stripped off and scrambled on top of her. A few minutes later he was racked by spasms, his penis jerking deep within her. He clung to her as his orgasm subsided

'God, Miranda, you're a wonderful fuck.' Beads of sweat had gathered on his forehead. 'Did you come?'

'Yes,' she lied as usual. Even Max, the magnet who held her attention in its field, keeping her obedient to his wishes, had never taken time or thought to attend to her needs. Her last few visits he had almost ignored her. Why she didn't know.

Nothing had changed as far as she was concerned; she felt the chill in the air and felt like crying. She was quite fond of Ron, but he was no substitute for Max. For the last three years, Max had been the focal point of her life; everything she had or had not done was to fit in with his wishes, she admitted to herself as she dressed. With Max's back turned to her and Ron zipping up his trousers, desperation crept up on her. She felt it worm its way into her and coil itself around her heart. *Now what am I supposed to do? Father's dead, my friends are in London, as are my brothers. I'm all alone*, she thought. *I need him.*

'Max?'

'Ron, see Miranda out and lock the door. We need to get this finished.'

'Max, I want to talk,' she cried as she was unceremoniously bundled out of the door. She felt insulted and humiliated as she heard the lock being turned.

12

IT WAS EARLY evening. Roderick Barclay listlessly rifled through the files stacked on the large rosewood desk from which his father had ruled the house. 'Our stately pile will be turned into a funfair by the year's end unless we can see a way through this mess.'

Jeremy Barclay looked up from the book he had taken down from the library shelf half an hour earlier. 'Does it really matter when neither of us lives here?'

'For God's sake, don't you have any pride?' Roderick was exasperated at his elder brother's lack of fight for everything they held dear. 'Father would turn in his grave if he could hear you.'

'He may well do, but it was he who continued to run the place as if there were no problems. His legacy to us is a white elephant, empty except for a few entrails to pick over. We'll probably have to sell everything to pay off the death duties.' He continued to leaf through his book as if that was the end of the matter.

They were ensconced behind closed doors of the library of Milford House. Their ancestors had been landowners, expanding their territory to include neighbouring land, annex-ing hamlets and villages, taking in rent to finance the big house. Their father, Lord Barclay, was the last in the line able to reap a living from the property and investments alone. Parcels of land acquired in Ireland had been quietly sold off to maintain the in-frastructure, but these assets had been finite. Peppercorn rents for staff, old and new, did not cover the maintenance costs of housing, and as they became vacant, the village houses were put up for auction. To stave off further erosion of the estate, Jeremy had looked towards the City for a living.

Without any foreseeable inheritance, Roderick had en-tered one of the large London auction houses as a junior cata-loguer. He had risen effortlessly to become a junior expert in his department.

The death of their father two weeks ago had brought the siblings together to discuss their future, leaving a respectful period after the funeral. Their younger sister Miranda had been due to join them, but she was late as usual.

'There must be a way. There has to be.' Roderick paced the richly patterned carpet. 'Can't you show any interest in your inheritance, Jeremy, instead of continuing where you left off at the last chapter?'

Jeremy's long frame sprawled on the Chesterfield, feet resting on the arm. He put the book down on the low walnut marquetry table beside him and sighed. Like his brother, he was tall and square shouldered, with dark-brown hair and ha-zel eyes. They had both graduated from Oxford, first Jeremy and then three years later, Roderick. They had honed their reasoning powers and made lasting friendships. Jeremy judged himself to be a realist, unafraid to meet the world head-on; he did not have delusions of his place in the world, and that is where he differed from his brother. He considered his brother to be a dreamer, holding archaic notions of the order of society.

He pulled himself up to his full height. 'OK. I'll have another look,' he said resignedly, aware that Roderick was beginning to panic at his seeming lack of interest. 'But I'm sure there isn't anything. The accountants and trustees know all the assets in Father's portfolio. What I find illogical is that they knew the situation yet didn't alert Father to the financial danger he was in.'

'Father's fingers were in many pies, don't forget.' Desperation crept into Roderick's voice. 'There may be other interests if we look hard enough.'

'Those pies were not always plum pies; he had his fingers bitten more than once. Remember, it was Father's ignorance of investments that attracted me to the city. I wanted to bring some control over his dealings, and I thought he had begun to listen, but there was clearly a huge loss that I was unaware of.'

Jeremy joined a relieved-looking Roderick at the desk, casting an experienced eye over the files, exposed to close scrutiny for the first time this weekend. Their father had resisted them knowing how the 'firm' ran. He had encouraged them to seek their own fortunes, handing over the house in London and an allowance that was meagre enough to discourage an idle existence. He couldn't say no to his daughter Miranda, however. She was twelve when her mother had passed away and had been hardest hit by her death. She had spent most of her time since leaving school at Milford House, occasionally making the trek to London to socialise but mostly finding her amusement in Manchester.

Jeremy idly turned the pages of an old ledger, noting with pleasure the meticulously handwritten entries denoting the monthly incomes from the estate properties. In the last three years, the entries had become erratic and then petered out as if his father had lost interest in the upkeep of these ancient records. A piece of paper folded in four was tucked between the back pages. As he began to unfold it, the sound of a car sweeping up the long drive could be heard.

'Miranda, at last.' Roderick began to tidy the files.

As Jeremy started reading, the car came to an abrupt halt. The car door slammed. Moments later Miranda flounced into the library, bringing with her a rush of perfume and cool air. Casually, Jeremy tucked the letter into his trouser pocket.

'Here you are, my fair brothers.' Her shrewd eyes danced from Jeremy to Roderick, 'Looking guilty as usual. What are you up to? No, don't tell me.' She raised her hand as though to stop an admission. 'You've found Father's lost fortune, and you mean to keep it all to yourselves.' She laughed gaily as she strode across the room to give each brother a kiss.

'Hit the nail on the head as usual, Miranda.' Jeremy returned Miranda's kiss, her expensive perfume lingering with him while she twirled away to Roderick.

'How do you like my new outfit?' She caressed her body, stroking the expensive dusk-rose suit from breasts to hips. It would have been a demure outfit, had it not been adorning Miranda's pulsing body. Her dyed blond hair, sat like a cream topping above the beautiful desultory face. Its features were unable to be still, unable to be at peace with themselves..

'You look wonderful, as usual, Miranda,' Roderick said warmly, kissing her powdered cheeks, 'but shouldn't you wait until you know the state of your finances before splashing out on new clothes?'

'Oh, everything will be all right; it always is.' She waved the suggestion away. 'You sound just like Daddy. I hope you're not going to try and restrict me in the same way.' She looked from Roderick to Jeremy with accusing eyes.

'It's not our place to restrict you, darling Miranda,' Jeremy answered her challenge calmly, 'but you will have to demonstrate some self-control in the future when you are in charge of your own finances.'

'That's exactly what Daddy used to say. It's not fair.' She stamped her elegant foot and held out her arm. 'Come on, Roddy, let's get away from Lord Spoilsport. I need a drink.'

Roderick linked his arm through hers and with a helpless look at Jeremy, led Miranda out of the library.

Jeremy recovered the letter from his pocket, reread it, shoved it deeply into his pocket again, and then left the room. The front door was still open from Miranda's arrival. In the twilight, Jeremy stood at the top of the curved steps leading down to the driveway where Miranda's new Mercedes sports car was carelessly parked. In the distance, willow trees lined the river that flowed through the grounds on its way to the next county. The gardens were laid out in terraces towards the water's edge. A cluster of beech trees to the right, their branches intertwined like lovers, had provided hours of fun for the two brothers. The wooded hills beyond, with the old well and mysterious mound that they had decided must be an ancient burial site, reminded Jeremy of the pleasure the park had provided during the long school holidays.

As he studied the magnificent vista before him, he remembered that his father also loved to stand here surveying his inheritance. He pondered his father's death. What had caused his sudden heart attack?

The sound of Miranda's laughter drew him inside. He paused in the hallway, struck afresh by its beauty. This magnificent house was his responsibility until a buyer could be found. He felt weighed down by his inheritance—not just the house, but also the family tradition. That he had inherited Milford House just to administer its demise was depressing. Walking in the direction of the voices in the drawing room, he tried to dispel his sombre mood.

'I think Jeremy was suggesting that there is a bottom to the money pile,' Roderick was declaring to a startled Miranda. 'If we sell the house, we lose the income from the whole estate, so it will not be self-generating as it was.'

'I don't know what you are talking about.' Miranda turned to Jeremy, who had taken up his father's favourite place, his back to the fireplace. 'Of course there's enough,' she exclaimed with vehemence, but not without a note of panic catching at her voice. She looked wildly from one brother to another but receiving no confirmation, her voice rose. 'There's always enough. Daddy said he'd always look after me. You're mean, both of you. You want to keep it all to yourselves.'

'Shush, keep your voice down,' Jeremy urged her, aware that Roberts and Cook were on duty.

'Why did he have to die?' she wailed. 'Daddy looked after everything so well. I never know where I am with you two.' She regarded both of them from beneath her lashes.

The little-lost-girl look was designed to elicit protective assurances. Jeremy steeled himself against it. 'Miranda, darling,' he tried to soothe her, 'it's going to take us time to sort everything out. Meanwhile we must all exercise some restraint, for prudence's sake.'

'Screw prudence, whoever she is,' she spat at him. 'Oh, I forgot, you don't do that sort of thing, do you?' With blazing eyes she swung back to Roderick, slopping her gin and tonic as she seized on her favourite subject. 'And Roddy, poor Roddy,' she enunciated slowly, as if savouring the wounds she was about to inflict, 'your ex-fiancé is not that sort of girl, I hear. Too bad she left London. Did you pay her to?' She took hold of his tie and pulled it sharply, drawing Roderick's face towards her own, her lips curled in cruel derision. 'Or did she leave of her own free will?'

Roderick flushed. 'That's enough, Miranda. I don't wish to discuss Helen—ever.'

She laughed in his face as she released his tie, clearly loving the effect she could still have on him.

Jeremy was dismayed by his sister's idea of fun. He followed her progress as she strutted triumphantly out of the room, drink in hand, swinging her hips, laughing merrily. She slammed the door behind her.

'Come on, you need a top-up. Five minutes, and she's got to you already.' He replenished Roderick's glass and poured himself a cognac.

Roderick loosened the stranglehold of his tie. 'Damn that girl with her flock of spies. Have they nothing better to do?'

'Apparently not,' Jeremy stated, handing the glass to his brother, who appeared completely shaken by Miranda's attack.

'At least Helen was independent and decent,' he cried. 'Damn Miranda.'

'Do I detect a note of regret?' Jeremy asked tentatively. At the time of the break-up, Roderick had refused to answer his questions. Still curious, he said mildly, 'I never understood what happened between you and Helen.'

Roderick walked to the window and said stiffly, 'After meeting her mother and finding out more of her background, it was clear that she would be unsuitable as a wife.'

'I thought you loved her. Was it necessary for you to stop seeing her altogether? I liked Helen. Truth be known, I found her damned attractive myself.'

'You never said so.'

'It wouldn't have been tactful to confess that I felt jealous of you finding such a splendid girl.'

'Why not? You wouldn't have acted on it.'

'I take that as a compliment, as a sign of your trust in me.'

With a wave of the hand, Roderick dismissed the possibility of his brother trespassing. 'You would have been propriety itself.'

Jeremy had watched the romance blossom between Roderick and Helen from a discreet distance. He had seen his brother grow and expand under the influence of her warm vivaciousness. She had widened his world, opening his eyes to other possibilities; and then, with a blunt knife, Roderick had severed all contact as though she were diseased.

'It would have been an impossible alliance.' Roderick stared out of the window at the darkening park. Then he muttered almost to himself, 'If only she had come from a different background.'

Jeremy didn't press further. Instead he lightened the mood by saying, 'At least no one will marry us for our money now.' He chuckled at the irony.

Roderick met his gaze. All at once the situation struck them both as funny. They laughed uproariously, a welcome release of tension after the weeks of solemnity since their father's death.

A polite clearing of the throat drew their attention to Roberts, meticulously dressed as always, standing at the door.

'Dinner is served, Master Jeremy and Roderick,' Roberts announced with a mixture of deference and quiet confidence that marked the best of his kind.

'Thank you, Roberts.' Jeremy chose not to notice the error in address as he took his handkerchief to wipe his eyes. He watched the proud man retreat, sure that his step had slowed since his late master's death. 'I suppose it will take him a while to get used to the new regime,' he said, sobering the atmosphere. 'Of course it could also mean him being out of a job if we sell. He must be near retirement age, but even so, this has been his home for all his adult life.'

Roderick looked thoughtful. 'We all need a common purpose and for each one of us to stick to it. Miranda too.'

'There lies the weak link already. Miranda is hardly going to care about this house if it stifles her spending. I think it is better to sell it as quickly as possible. Neither of us has spent much time here since Ma died. Miranda is the one who has found it to her advantage to live here, to refill her purse. Father was far too soft.'

'Definitely one rule for us and one rule for her,' Roderick answered. 'I don't agree with you about the house though, Jeremy. You're the eldest and have the last say, but I would hate to see it go. We both have some fine memories of this place.' His voice cracked with emotion. 'Surely we can see a way to keep it?'

'We'll see.' Jeremy sighed, acknowledging the loss that Roderick was expressing for both of them. He felt the letter in his pocket. He was about to take it out and show Roderick but was stopped by his new sense of responsibility towards his brother and sister. Whatever his father had done to lay himself open to blackmail, he would keep to himself. If he couldn't help the house being taken away, at least he could preserve the memory of his father in the hearts of Miranda and Roderick.

They joined Miranda in the dining room. She had changed into slacks and a mauve roll-neck sweater with the slogan 'I LOVE IT' blazoned in silver satin letters across her chest. She was sitting at the head of the table in her father's place. The two brothers sat down on either side of her, silently ignoring her statement of power.

'Are you going to be Mother?' Roderick teased as the pie was placed in front of her.

'I bloody well hope not,' she said. 'I've taken plenty of precautions.' She laughed heartily at her own joke.

Roberts, his face inscrutable as always, continued to fill the table with dishes of vegetables before leaving them to their meal.

Miranda cut the pie into four, letting the delicious aroma escape. 'Now, which of you wants the biggest bit?'

'Neither of us,' they chorused.

'A smirk flickered across Miranda's calculating face. 'All the more for me!' She jabbed at the pie, and lifting a portion clumsily across to the plate in front of her, spilled its contents on the linen tablecloth. She handed Roderick the serving at an angle so that the remaining gravy slid off the edge.

'Now it's Jeremy's turn.' She returned to the disembowelled dish. With crazed vigour, she tore at the second quarter, pulling the innards across to the plate, continuing to tear at it even in death. 'There you are, brother,' she announced, handing him the insult. 'That's your share of the pie. And this is all mine,' she said as she served herself the remaining half. 'Mm, it looks good, doesn't it? Can you pass the salt?'

Later, in the privacy of his room, Jeremy unfolded the hand-written note. It was signed with the initial M.

> *It has come to my notice that the instalment on your payment is overdue by three months.*
>
> *I am sure that this is an oversight on your part, as I know that you do not wish our secret to become public.*
>
> *Please rectify this matter within seven days.*
>
> *M.*

It was dated March 2, the day before his father had died of a heart attack.

—⚡—

'What's the matter, Jeremy? You've gone all gloomy on us, hasn't he, Roddy?' Miranda looked up from flicking through the society pages of *Country Life*, searching for familiar faces.

They were sitting in the drawing room. A fire had been lit, but it made little impact on the vast room, so they had drawn towards the flames, seeking their warmth.

Roderick glanced up from his paper. 'For someone who's made up his mind, you do look pretty miserable. What could be simpler than selling up and having no worries?'

The note of bitterness wrapped up in a jocular delivery was not lost on Jeremy. After rereading the letter he had slept badly. He was angry and determined not to let the house go to a blackmailer without a fight. 'On reflection, I think I shouldn't be too hasty,' he said, as though conceding to his brother's opinion. 'I don't think we should make any decisions for a few weeks until we've had time to go through all of father's business concerns. In the meantime I want us to reduce the expenses in maintaining the house since only Miranda lives here.'

'We must keep Maisie and Cook, but as far as I'm concerned, the rest can go.' Miranda returned to her magazine, having delivered her cost-reduction plan.

'We have to keep all the full-time staff at the moment,' Jeremy responded. 'They have all been very loyal to this family, and if we are not going to sell immediately, then we must find ways to generate income in the short term to help with the cash flow.'

'Does that mean we might be able to keep it?' Roderick asked hopefully.

'That all depends on our ingenuity and enterprise skills.'

'What are they, Jeremy darling?' Miranda jeered.

'Something this family had a couple of hundred years ago and has now nearly lost,' Jeremy rejoined abruptly.

Miranda and Roderick looked askance. Jeremy's vehemence had taken them by surprise, and for a moment there was silence in the room.

'Actually, this could be interesting.' Roderick folded his paper. He opened the drawer of the card table and took out a pad and pencil. 'OK. Ideas time,' he announced, settling down, as though pleased to be doing something.

'A zoo,' Miranda offered. 'We could dress up the servants and put them in cages and charge enormous amounts to busloads of nearly blind people.'

'Thank you, Miranda,' Jeremy said drily. 'Unless you have a more sensible idea, please be quiet.'

'You're just too, too sensible, isn't he Roddy? And a spoilsport.' She folded her arms and pouted.

'Thank goodness someone's got some business sense, that's all I can say.'

Jeremy smiled warmly at Roderick. He would do his best for them. They would be lost without the house and the status it brought them. Whoever had been blackmailing his father was going to have a tough fight.

13

FIRED UP WITH enthusiasm for her project, Helen arrived at the *Post* early. The cleaners were finishing off, bowing out with their equipment as if they'd had an audience with the Queen. They left behind the scruffy figure of Steve Brown hunched over his computer, chewing his habitual cigarette.

'Is anyone interested in the big development at Middleston?' Helen addressed the rounded shoulders.

'Not as far as I know.' Ash dropped off the end of his cigarette onto the keyboard as he spoke. 'It's a straightforward planning decision. There seems to be some local opposition judging by the letters we get, but they haven't a leg to stand on.'

'So I wouldn't be treading on anyone's toes if I pursued it?'

'Nope. Pretty boring subject, really.' He continued tapping in the story of drugs in one of the city's nightclubs.

Pleased that she had a clear run, Helen sat at the shabby desk to which she had been assigned. The veneered edges were peeling, the writing surface was pitted by years of use, and rings from coffee cups overlapped one another, spills staining in shades from tan to black. She opened the file in which she had collected all the available information on the Middleston project. She needed to visit the council offices to see the plans. She needed to interview the developers and also the opposition, including the mysterious N. Monet. He had been very vocal in the paper but had not aligned himself with the main opposition group, to which she guessed David Kerr belonged. It would be interesting to know why. There was no Monet in the telephone directory, and he had not given his address to the paper, which would have been normal procedure. The paper had published his letters because they seemed reasonable, articulate, and in-offensive and exercised a democratic right of opposition, falling within the loose guidelines of the correspondence page. As the young trainee had said, they were good fillers.

Why should anyone want to remain anonymous? Helen thought as she sat at her desk by the window that overlooked one of the busy shopping streets in the city. Being methodical, she began a list.

a. *Fear*
b. *Known by developer*
c. *Known by council, some connection?*
d. *Own agenda for development*
e. *Dislike of developer*
f. *Green/Environment planning connection?*

She reread the letters and tried to fit the tone of them to one of her reasons for anonymity. He had been open about his own ideas for the future of the wharf area. He had been open about his concern for the environment. He had not attacked the developer as a person or as an organisation but had only referred to 'the developers.' The council planners had been given a similar treatment. Was he afraid of naming names? It seemed so. So he could be known to the council and to the developer, but he feels so strongly about the project that he is taking the risk. It seems he has no personal monetary interest but is afraid of a backlash.

Possible, possible, she thought, pleased with her deductions. Now, how can I find out who he is? Monet? One of my favourite painters. Why choose Monet? *Perhaps he's interested in painting*, she deliberated as she attempted to profile her mystery man.

—⁂—

The secretary in the planning department put Helen through to Mr Thompson, the chief planning officer.

'Miss Arbuthnot from the *Post*, did you say? Why is it so necessary for you to see the plans? What is your purpose? The developers will be giving a press release when they're ready.'

His reluctance to have press involvement was not lost on her. Eel-like, he was slithering around, evading her right to view the plans. She needed to create a benign reason. 'I just want to get an overall idea, for when we do a full-page spread on the scheme, lots of pictures of the houses, perhaps a family moving in, and so on.' She hoped she sounded convincing as she bumbled on. 'We'll show the benefit to the townspeople and the local businesses; the publicity will be wonderful for everyone involved.'

'In that case,' he said, sounding relieved, 'we may be able to manage it. When would you like to come?'

'Would this afternoon be too early?'

I've pulled it off, she thought as she replaced the receiver, *but I have to be careful. I'll try and speak to the Kerrs before the meeting. They may know this character, and they may be able to shed some light on Monet.*

She called the Kerrs and caught them on their way out for a round of golf and agreed to meet them at the nineteenth hole. Meanwhile she would get together a list of council members, local big shots, clubs, and societies in the Middleston district.

At eleven thirty, after telling Steve's back where she was going, she picked up some sandwiches from the deli on the corner, unearthed her car from the underground car park beneath her flat, and headed out of town.

It was raining, and there was an unexpected chill in the air, making the journey seem longer than an hour. She found the club on the south side of Middleston, accessed by a footbridge over the canal. The recently constructed wooden clubhouse crouched low between newly planted ornamental shrubs and trees on the bank of the canal, as though wanting to hide from any boats that might be passing.

The shower which had accompanied Helen out of town had raced ahead and was at that moment dampening the Kerrs' game. She spotted them in the distance, their body language unmistakable. They were queuing to begin the last hole. Rather than wait at the clubhouse, she walked briskly towards them on the deserted parallel fairway and joined them as they were poring over the scorecard, an umbrella shielding their faces.

'Can I be the caddy?' she asked as she drew near.

David's face registered surprise and delight at seeing her. 'So you couldn't keep away from us! What's the reason for this unexpected pleasure?'

Making sure they were out of earshot, Helen came straight to the point. 'It's the wharf development at Middleston,' she told them. 'After I left you yesterday, I went to look at the site. There has to be much more to the plan than a simple, low-cost housing scheme.'

'It's such a local issue,' David said casually as he watched the couple ahead tee off. 'I'm sure you could get a better story for your debut on the *Post*.'

'I'd like to pursue it because there seems to be a few undercurrents at work there. I'm sure it's not as straightforward as it seems, and at the moment the planners and developers seem to be winning. If the paper ran the story, it might raise a few questions and delay the final decision. It would give us all time to find out what is really going on.'

'Helen, my dear,' Nancy began in her conciliatory tones, 'this is a one-horse town. It is not very exciting, you know. I can't think that it would interest anyone, other than those living in Middleston. Why don't we think over some other ideas with you? What you need is three heads my dear, always better than one.'

Helen laughed. 'If you feel so strongly about the issue your-selves,' she said, smiling at them both as they stood huddled together under the umbrella, 'why don't you want all the help you can get? Here's a city newspaper willing to take up your cause, and you're refusing. Why?' She raised her eyebrows with the challenge. 'And who is N. Monet? You know, don't you?'

They didn't bother to disguise their concern, exchanging alarmed glances. Nancy nodded to David, as if giving her con-sent to a prearranged course of action in the event of Helen's implacable curiosity. 'If we can't dissuade you and you insist on going ahead,' David said, 'then you'll need some help to avoid some pretty nasty characters.'

'I knew there was more to this,' she said, happily ignoring David's stern warning.

'Agnes was right,' David sighed. 'Strong-willed and persis-tent. Weren't those her words?' he asked Nancy as he placed his ball on the tee.

'I can't disagree,' Helen said. 'That's why I'm a reporter and here again today.'

They fell silent as David smacked the ball with a clean swing. They followed its progress in the air as it arched to-wards the green, falling just short of the emerald pool of close-ly cropped grass but continuing its energetic journey across the far side to the bunker.

'Damn, I've done it again.'

'Yup,' Nancy acknowledged before giving her ball a satisfy-ing thwack. They all watched it travel unerringly towards its goal, coming to rest a few feet before the hole.

'Nice one, my dear.'

'I'm impressed,' Helen said, replacing Nancy's iron in the bag. She began to wheel the bag behind her down the fairway, flanked on either side by David and Nancy. 'You talked to my mother? How is she?'

'Your mom is well,' Nancy told her as they walked at a brisk pace. 'We gave her a hard time, accusing her of bringing you up to be too headstrong. She said you wouldn't stop until you had rooted out the information you were after and suggested that we give in gracefully. So between us we'll be as cooperative as possible—within agreed limitations. And by that I mean we need some ground rules for your own safety.'

'Well put, my dear.' David looked relieved that Nancy had not hesitated in getting straight to the point. 'A fountain of common sense, as usual.'

'Thank you, David dear.' Nancy bowed her head, acknowledging the compliment.

Helen was amused by their complicity. She was sure that they were overreacting, clucking about her like two mother hens. Perhaps it was because they hadn't had children. She was happy to let them play at parents, but she still needed information.

'OK, I agree. If I ask a direct question and you know the answer, will you tell me?'

'Of course,' David said, his expression serious. 'But you must inform us of your progress so that we can keep an eye on you.'

Nancy patted her shoulder affectionately. 'We feel responsible for you. Agnes charged us with looking out for her little girl.'

'Anyone would think that I'd arrived in New York or Chicago, not a sleepy town nestled in the English countryside.'

'Human nature is the same everywhere, Helen,' David said. 'Don't be deceived by appearances.'

Helen parked Nancy's bag in front of the green. 'So who is N. Monet?' she asked again, eager to solve the puzzle. She took a notebook out of her bag.

David glanced at his wife before answering. 'We believe it might be Nicholas Baines.'

'Do you know where he lives?'

'Albermarle Street. It's in the run-down area of the town. Lots of empty, boarded-up homes.'

'It's a real shame about that area,' Nancy broke in. 'It used to be a genuine community there. Everyone in the neighbourhood caring for each other, helping out in times of difficulty.'

David took up the story as he thwacked his ball onto the green. 'It was originally a philanthropic development by the owners of the local mill and, incidentally, the wharf buildings. Not all Victorian entrepreneurs were grinding the last ounce of life out of their employees; some saw their role as raising the standard of living, others put an emphasis on education. In Middleston, the factory owners built the Albermarle area as a self-contained community with its own school, local shops, and church. And it worked well until relatively recently.'

'Why did it stop working?' Intrigued, Helen urged David to continue.

'It stopped working when the council began buying up properties that came on the market and then letting them stand empty, saying they were unfit for human habitation. Then rumours began about the council's future plans. Landlords became nervous and asked the council to value their property.'

'Didn't a few fires mysteriously start around that time, David?' She plucked her ball out of the hole and returned the flag.

'Yes, that's right; coincidentally, they started just in those properties that had recently been valued, according to one source. Of course the fire damage devalued the properties further, and this led to a mass exodus. The landlords took what little they could get, and the residents were forced to find alternative accommodations.' He strode over to the bunker to find his ball.

'Is this all very recent?' Helen asked as she linked past events to the present.

'It began slowly, about twenty years ago, maybe more,' Nancy replied. 'Anyway, Helen, if you seek out your alias N. Monet, you'll see the area for yourself.'

'Yes, I thought I might try to see him before my appointment with the planning officer.'

'What are you hoping to find out there?' The alarm in David's voice was apparent as he finally neared the hole.

'I want to see the overall plan in the context of the surrounding area. Even I could see that the demolition of the wharf buildings to make way for new housing is just the first phase of something bigger. It's all right, David, I'll be fine.' She laughed, seeing him getting ready to raise objections. 'I've let Mr Thompson think that I'm concentrating on what he would consider the feminine aspect. The design, if the kitchens will be big enough, whether the residents will have a play area for the children, et cetera, stuff that he won't feel threatened by.'

'Ronald Thompson has agreed to see you, Helen dear?'

'Oh, yes,' she said, turning to Nancy enthusiastically. 'I could tell almost at once that he was hiding something. Initially he didn't want me to see the plans. Suspicious, don't you think?' Her eyes shone with animation and vitality. 'There could be wholesale corruption in this small, one-horse town, and I mean to expose it.'

Helen parked her car in Albermarle Street, certain that she must have a puncture. Broken glass and beer cans littered the area in amongst torn, black-plastic refuse bags displaying their innards, the entrails of modern life spilling out to be uncollected and dispersed, forgotten.

As she looked at the boarded-up windows and the metal sheets barring access through front doors, Helen wondered if anyone lived in the street at all. Getting out of her car, the smell of decay, the warm, rotting vestiges of existence, met her. She was pleased she was wearing flat shoes as she picked her way through the garbage, looking for signs of life. Towards the end of the road, a cluster of houses were unboarded as though they had their eyes open. With relief, Helen approached a primrose yellow door with a polished number six centred at eye level. Floral curtains were at the recently painted windows, the doorstep scrubbed, the pavement swept of debris.

She lifted the brass knocker and rapped on the door, letting the street know it had a visitor. The neighbour's door opened.

'Yes? Can I help you?' a lady in her sixties politely asked Helen. 'They're not in, but I'll take a message if you like.' Small and round with an apron resting on her ample girth, she stepped into the street in her fur-lined slippers. She peered quizzically at Helen.

'I'm looking for Nicholas Baines's house,' she informed the kindly upturned face surrounded by tight grey curls. 'Do you know where he lives?'

'He lives over there, number forty-one. He's in.'

Helen followed the pointed finger to a cream-painted house opposite. 'Thank you for your help.' She turned to cross the street.

'You look like his sister, she was a bonny girl too,' the rotund figure called after her. 'Coming to visit him today, she is.' She was plainly delighted to impart the latest news.

Helen smiled back at her, thinking that she must be starved of conversation to liken her to a neighbour's relative. 'Thank you for your help.' She crossed the street, mindful of the shards of glass scattered in the gutter.

The door was opened by a tall figure. He looked familiar. 'Mr Baines?' As if transfixed, he stared at her. Somewhat disconcerted at the silent figure, she asked, 'Have we met before?' Then she remembered her monk.

'I don't think we've met.' Confusion seemed to sweep over him as he averted his eyes from her. 'Come in, please.' He stood aside for her to go into the narrow hall, waving to his neighbour across the street, before closing the door. 'I'm afraid it will have to be the kitchen; everywhere else is taken.'

It was too late. Drawn by the distinctive smells and sight of an art studio, Helen had wandered into the front living room. Astounded by the sight before her, she forgot to ask permission to study the canvasses. Landscapes vied with street scenes, peopled by squat, bowed figures going about their daily business. River scenes with brightly painted narrow boats leant against a disused canal full of the detritus of life. The warehouses were there too, entwined in a grotesque dance between beauty and the forlornness of neglect, recorded at all angles, in all seasons. Small-town Middleston had been captured, lined up like a reel of film, only the medium was oil or daring acrylic, with unlikely colours, each demanding attention.

Awed, Helen turned to Nicholas Baines with undisguised admiration. 'This is incredible. Did you do all of these?' she asked reverently, although she knew the answer. She could see Monet, Cezanne, and of course Lowry.

Nicholas's arms were folded firmly across his chest as though protecting his thin body from too much praise. He avoided looking at her directly. 'Yes, I think I'm making progress now.'

'Progress!' she exclaimed, amazed at his modesty. 'I should say so. Where do you exhibit? I feel such an idiot for not recognising your name.'

'I don't exhibit. I haven't shown my work anywhere.'

'But you must,' she enthused, shocked that his talent was unseen. She moved them one at a time from one stack to another. 'I love this one.' She held up a picture, like the others, stretched across its wooden frame, the unmistakable barrel-like figure of his neighbour, apron strings squeezed into generous folds, scrubbing her doorstep, seemingly oblivious of her stealthy observer.

'If you like it, have it.' He smiled at her.

'You mustn't give precious paintings to any stranger who walks through your door, Mr Baines.' She laughed. She turned to him, beaming with her discovery. 'What a story!'

His smile broadened. 'Thank you for your compliments. Shall I make some tea? And you can tell me your name.'

'I do apologise. I'm Helen Arbuthnot from the *Post*.' She held out her hand.

'How do you do, Miss Helen Arbuthnot. Helen,' he added and looked abashed at his own audacity. He took her hand into his own thin fingers. 'I'm Nicholas. Do you like tea? I hope so, because that's all I've got.'

She followed him down the narrow hall into the kitchen. It was evident that Nicholas Baines's priorities in life didn't include such mundane matters as housework. Like Aladdin's cave, every surface was used, and then used again: letters were propped up on cups, sketchpads stacked on top of piles of plates, laundry drying overhead on wooden slats in between pans hanging from butchers' hooks, and thick wedges of newspapers piled on a kitchen chair. Propped against the rubbish bin were a couple of paintings, apparently destroyed.

'Good heavens, you are ruthless with your work, Mr Baines,' she said.

He laughed bitterly as he filled the kettle. 'I didn't do that to my paintings, Helen.'

'Then who did, and why? It's sacrilege!'

'I'm not sure, but I have a good idea who's behind it. But let's not talk about that. I want to know why you are here, today of all days? Sit down.' He pulled out a chair and dusted it off with his hand. 'And please call me Nicholas.'

Grateful to drop the formality, she began. 'Nicholas, I'm a reporter. I'm looking into the development that is being proposed on the wharf site. I believe that it may be you who has been writing so vociferously against the idea?'

Apprehension distorted his features. 'How on earth did you get my name? I didn't give it to the paper.' Raw fear was translated into his hands that gripped the back of a chair, the whites of his knuckles straining through the skin.

'It's all right,' she hastily reassured him. 'It was David and Nancy Kerr who suggested that Monet might be you.'

She saw the tension visibly seep from him. 'What made you contact the Kerrs?'

'They're friends of my mother.'

She told him about her need for a debut story and how her interest had developed at the Kerrs' obvious opposition to her involvement. 'It intrigues me. Why the secrecy? Who or what is being threatened here?'

Nicholas filled the teapot. The temporary reassurance had left him. Now he regarded her, anxiety criss-crossing his face. 'I suppose it would be fairly transparent to anyone who knows my hobby that the letters were mine.'

She couldn't let his discomfort stop her investigation. 'Why have I come on this day of all days? What's happening today?'

'I can see why you work on a newspaper.' His sombre mood lightened. 'You don't miss much, do you?' he said wryly. 'This is a special day because my sister, Marjorie, is visiting me.' For the first time, he looked at her directly, scanning her face.

She blushed. 'I'm sorry, Nicholas. I've barged in and taken up your time without asking if it was convenient.' She got up. 'I'll come another time if you like.'

'No, don't go, Helen. Please, I want you to stay. My sister isn't due for an hour or so. I'm going to take her out for a meal. As you can see, I don't have much room for visitors. My niece, Sally, is coming too. Please stay for a while.'

His sudden torrent of words caught Helen by surprise. 'If you're sure.' She settled down again, comfortable in his company, not really wanting to leave. She looked across at the paintings leaning against the bin, the attempts at restoring them clear. 'You should have an exhibition, you know. You could sell your paintings easily.'

'Thank you, but I'm not as confident as you. There are lots of good artists out there with training who still don't sell.'

'I think you underestimate your talent. Why don't you let me find someone to view them? I have contacts in London who would be glad to see them.' Roderick came to mind, but she dismissed the idea, instead thinking of the many people she had met through him; she had attended so many preview shows and galleries with Roderick and was sure that she could persuade someone to view Nicholas's work.

'I'll think about it. It would be nice to show my later stuff, which I'm quite satisfied with. Unfortunately three of the better paintings are now standing in tatters.' All at once his anger was uncontained and spilled out. 'Bloody philistines,' he spat, tears of rage gathering.

'Who do you think was responsible? Can't you go to the police?'

'I could,' he said with a note of bitterness, 'but the repercussions are not worth it.'

She caught the raw edge of his helpless indignation and wondered at his reluctance at reporting the damage. Surely the police would want to catch the culprit, but what were the repercussions if he did? More damage to his paintings probably. But who would do this, and why?

'Is this connected to the wharf development, by any chance?' she blurted out as the thought formed.

'Yes, but it's better for you not to get involved. You mustn't,' he implored.

'I appreciate your concern, but this is a good story,' she answered firmly, not wanting to be put off. 'By bringing it to a wider audience, there may be sufficient interest to investigate the real reasons for the development. At the moment it looks from the outside that they are doing the town a favour, but from the strong feelings of your group, evidently there is more at stake. I can help you.' For a moment, as anxiety again gripped him, she feared that he would refuse to cooperate. She had an urge to reach across the table to touch his hand to reassure him. 'I guarantee that I will not let your involvement be known.'

Nicholas got up and pottered about the kitchen, taking his time rinsing out two cups, drying them carefully before setting them on the table between them. He seemed to have been weighing up the advantages and disadvantages of letting her have more information. 'I'll see if I can answer your questions.' He sighed as he sat down again. 'Ready for some tea, Helen? I can see that this is going to take some time.'

She left Nicholas, promising to return. She had enjoyed her time with him. He was obviously talented and had a deep care for those left behind in the street after the mass exodus. It was apparent that he was not only fighting for the wharf buildings but also for the remnants of his community. He knew that it was only a matter of time before the Albermarle Street area would be demolished. As she surveyed the desecrated street, she thought that the bulldozers wouldn't be long in coming if she didn't get her story out quickly. The developers would have their way.

Ahead of her was a man leaning against a wall of an empty house, a cigarette cupped in his hand. He wore a black leather jacket several sizes too large for him. He was looking down, his cap pulled forward, concealing his face. As Helen started the car, thankful that her tyres were still inflated, she looked across at the slinking greasy figure. *Strange place to pass the time of day*, she thought as she pulled away from the curb to keep her appointment at the council offices.

14

For several miles, as they drove along, her mother had been quiet. Now and then she would burst out of her reverie as if a memory had surfaced. She would appear to panic, before subsiding again, sometimes closing her eyes tightly. As Sally drove steadily on, she occasionally glimpsed the tortured face. At times she saw her mother fighting to hold back tears and losing the battle. She felt such sorrow for her mother as she saw another tissue drawn covertly from the navy handbag to surreptitiously dab the itinerant drips that landed on her pale cheeks. As they drew towards Middleston, her mother began to recognise familiar names and landmarks.

Sensing her mother's apprehension, Sally spoke to lighten the mood. 'I'd like to see where you grew up and your school. If you give me the address, I can look for myself.' She had her mother's attention now. 'It would give you a chance to talk to Uncle Nicholas on your own.'

'That's an idea.' Her mother turned to her, brightly blinking away the traces of emotion. 'I think we're nearly there now,

just a mile or two up this road, and then a turn off to the left.
Oh dear,' she wailed, as she had done several times on the journey, 'what if we don't recognise each other after all this time?'

Sally tried to reassure her. 'You will, Mum. He can't have
changed all that much, just an older version.'

'Yes, you're probably right.' Her mother subsided again
until she said, 'Look at all those new houses, and that never
used to be there.' She pointed at an office block sitting squarely, incongruously alone in a meadow of poppies.

'It says Baines and Baines. Any relative? That was your
maiden name, wasn't it?'

Marjorie didn't answer. That had always been her way,
thought Sally, resenting the door being slammed in her face
again. In the last few days, she had tried to broach the subject of her mother's past, her family, her childhood, her own
mother and father. She had been met with avoidance, as usual.
'You don't want to hear about those days.' Windows had been
cleaned, cupboards cleared, even the garden had been given a
treat. Talking was unwelcome. It had been her father, usually
inarticulate in comparison to his intelligent wife, who grunted
answers to his daughter's questions but had still not shed much
light on those early years.

'I just want to see Nicholas and then leave.' Marjorie stated.

They passed a sign by the side of the road. 'Middleston,
here we are, Mum,' Sally exclaimed. 'You're home at last.'

Her mother looked ill. 'Can you stop the car a minute.'

Sally pulled up on the verge, bumping along on the uneven
grass edge until she brought the car to an ungainly stop.

Marjorie leant back against the headrest and closed her eyes. 'I'm sorry, I'll be fine in a minute. It's just been so long, and we've got here faster than I thought.'

'I think I understand, Mum,' Sally ventured tentatively. 'You've told me so little about where you grew up and your family. Why did you stay away all this time?' She chose her words with care, her voice compassionate. 'What happened that was so terrible for you?'

Her mother opened her eyes. Please let her tell me, Sally thought, as she regarded the still-attractive face that had forever worn a cloak of sadness.

'I wanted everything to be nice for you. I wanted you to have the life that I didn't have.'

'I know that, and I'm grateful, but I would have liked to have known you better, warts and all, instead of you keeping up appearances. Sometimes it's been difficult for me too. There have been so many no-go areas when we talk.'

'Have I made such a mess of things?'

'No, you haven't,' she reassured her. 'Nobody's perfect, but you think you ought to be. I'm glad I met and married Tom, because he loves me just the way I am. I thought I had to be perfect at first, but he's taught me a lot about accepting the bad bits as well as the good and trying to work things out.'

'I think, Sally Willis, you are a wise girl. How you've survived as well as you have with the example your dad and I set, I'll never know.'

'I survived because you loved me, and Dad did too. I think he loved you a lot too.'

Marjorie looked at her sharply. 'Being called a slut and a whore several times a day is a very funny way of showing love.' A lorry thundered past, interrupting the moment of intimacy. 'I suppose we should get on. Thanks for stopping. I'm feeling a bit better now.'

They passed the Albermarle Arms and turned into a cluster of streets that seemed to be in the process of demolition.

'This can't be right. What's happened? These were good, clean streets. Turn right here.' Her mother indicated as she guided her way through the desolation.

Sally negotiated the squalid streets in silence, understanding Marjorie's shock and bewilderment.

'Nicholas said on the phone that the area had gone downhill, but this is appalling. Sally, whatever must you think?'

'They must have been nice houses once. I suppose they still are underneath the boards.'

'Albermarle Street is the next turn. I hope it isn't as bad as this.'

It was almost as bad, but as they drew up outside number forty-one, happy faces met them. Nicholas had been chatting to his neighbours, and they had all come out to greet Marjorie and her daughter, delighted to share in his reunion.

15

HELEN LET THE heavy glass door of the council office swing behind her. The sun greeted her like an old and trusted friend. She breathed in the clean air, thankful to be out of the slimy presence of Ronald Thompson, head of planning.

He had taken lessons from Uriah Heap, ingratiating himself with a gruesomely insincere smile, guiding her to what he wanted her to see, and no more, with tactics as old as time. Showing an absorption in the plans was met with a ringed hand stroking her back. She squirmed away from his touch and yet was anxious not to offend him. She knew his game and tried to outwit him with guile. After all, she was the shining lady reporter just arrived from London to work on the *Post*, but the story she had invented sounded shallow even to her own ears, dressing her in an ill-fitting camouflage that Thompson was beginning to break through. She needed to get out before the game was up.

She held out her hand. 'Mr Thompson, you've been most helpful. I'm sure we can present this development as a picture of all that is good in modern architecture in terms of the well-being of the residents.' She hoped her bright smile was convincing.

He held on to her hand for an unnecessarily long time. 'It has been a pleasure to meet someone so refreshingly young and attractive from the *Post*. I hope we will see more of each other.' His damp, limp fingers squeezed her hand as he met her steady gaze with his leering, dark-ringed eyes. 'I could arrange for you to enjoy yourself in these parts if you like?' He wet his lips with his tongue, waiting for her answer.

Revolted by his physical contact, she pulled her hand away more sharply than she intended, her disgust ill disguised.

'Thank you, but I have friends in the area.' Thank God she could say that truthfully.

'Oh? And who are your friends? Might I know them?' He cocked his head on one side, his question suspended in the air.

Panic rose as she tried to think clearly. She was caught by the intricate web of this large spider who waited, observing her, his eyes bulging with anticipation of the meal he thought he was about to devour. If she had been the bona fide home-front features reporter that she had portrayed, then there would have been no reason not to give the Kerrs' name. But she wasn't, and she didn't want Thompson to know of the connection with the Kerrs. Who else did she know in the area? Nicholas Baines? No, he was on the other side too. She needed someone outside this drama. Who else did she know in the north? 'I'm a friend of the Barclays at Milford House,' she declared, surprising herself at her own ingenuity.

'Really?' He sounded unbelieving. 'Then you know my friend Miranda?'

Miranda, that was Roderick's sister. Fancy this slimy toad being a friend of the family. 'No, I only know Roderick. We know each other from London.' She turned away, closing the conversation.

He cleared his throat as she reached the door. 'We'll need to approve your article before publication.'

'Yes of course. I'll send you a draft copy. Goodbye, Mr Thompson.' She escaped with a weak smile, feeling outsmarted and angry with herself.

She needed a refuge and drove straight to the Kerrs'. 'I hope I'm not interrupting,' she called as she walked towards David and a chunky companion.

'Come and join us, Helen.' David beckoned her to the garden table. 'We were just talking about you. George, I should like to introduce you to Helen Arbuthnot. Helen, this is a good friend of mine, George Thomas.'

She recognised him as the man from the canal. Without his hat he appeared older, his greying hair mixed with a rich tawny brown, streaked with the sun. His tanned, leathered skin showed through the thinning patch where his hat had been. He had the makings of an old sea dog, his open, friendly features deeply lined. He wore an open-necked shirt; his jeans rested on his hips, a leather belt fastened across the well-nourished girth. He was an outdoors man, honed and weathered by the elements.

'Hello,' she said as he shook her hand vigorously, deciding her first impression had been pretty accurate. She liked him. 'You waved to me from your boat yesterday.'

'Of course. You declined an offer of a trip. We must put that right sometime.'

'I'd love to, George. I'm not much of a sailor, though, I have to warn you.'

'No need to be, does she?' he said, addressing Nancy, who joined them, handing Helen a welcome glass of wine.

Nancy laughed. 'Don't go if you don't like to get wet, Helen. His sudden manoeuvres will have you overboard in no time.'

'That fellow was trying to ram me, I swear it,' George soberly told them. 'In fact, as time has gone on, I'm certain it was connected to this wharf business.'

'Helen, I think it's important that you listen to what George has to say.' Nancy's tone matched the serious note introduced by George.

'Let's not waste any time.' David pulled out a chair for Helen. 'George can't stay long in case he arouses suspicion.'

'You're making me feel nervous,' she said, taking her seat.

'Good,' George said. 'You're treading on dangerous ground. This is not as straightforward as it seems. We're dealing with a ruthless character. Max Baines will stop at nothing. It's only threats at the moment, but I'm sure he won't stop at that. When you saw me yesterday, I'd been warned off. You see, I instigated and organised the opposition group to this development scheme. Without me, he must have thought the group would be weakened and perhaps cave in.'

'How did he warn you off?'

'He used the most effective way. The note said my sons would suffer if I continued the campaign. Sunday was one of our prearranged meetings, and I had to be seen to have taken heed of the warning.'

'What did you say this man's name was?' She took out her notepad.

'Max Baines.' George enunciated each word with contempt.

'Is he any relative of Nicholas Baines?' she enquired, but she already knew the answer.

'They're distant cousins,' David said. 'But I don't think they would have had much contact over the years.'

Reasons, motives, connections. What a fool she was to think she could ride into this homely market town to find a story without taking into account the history of the people 'I saw Nicholas this morning. He's the mysterious N. Monet, who's written so much in the *Post*.'

'Yes, I know Nicholas well,' George replied. 'We were school chums. Knowing his love of painting, I made the connection between Monet and Nicholas. It wasn't difficult for me or others either, apparently.'

'You think Nicholas has had contact with his lovely cousin?' Nancy asked.

Helen answered, 'Not directly. A couple of weeks ago, three of his paintings were slashed in his house while he was out. Unfortunately, no one saw who it was, because whoever did it went in through the backyard. From what you say,' she said, turning back to George, 'it sounds as though he was also being warned off.'

'Fellow must have been watching the house, waiting for his chance,' George said thoughtfully.

'Did you see Thompson?' David asked her.

'He's another slippery customer,' George declared.

'I think I might have blown it,' Helen said, blushing at the memory of her own stupidity. She didn't want to recall the meeting, but she did, telling them every detail. 'It isn't the first time I've played a bimbo to get a story.' She laughed.

'If we are to be effective,' George said, patting her hand as if understanding her youthful rashness, 'we have to coordinate our activities so that there are no surprises. You could play a very useful role in helping us, but you must be careful.'

'Why are you against the housing scheme?' She needed as many arguments as she could against the development.

'I'm against the Baineses gaining an even stronger foothold in our town. It won't stop at the wharf, it will go on until they've paid everybody off, and they'll own the town. By fighting for some old buildings which are of historical and architectural value, we can stop the final destruction of the whole community. Look what's happened to Albermarle already. These people have to be stopped. There are only a few left who aren't in their pockets. Do we want a town made up of bland flats and smart boxes that locals can't afford to buy?'

'I admire Nicholas Baines for standing up with us,' David said, his esteem clear. 'He has guts.'

'I don't think Ernest Baines ever got over Nicholas and Marjorie walking out on him to go and live in Albermarle Street again.' George chuckled.

Nancy rose abruptly and began to collect glasses together. 'I think it's time to break up the party.'

Something in what George said had a startling effect on Nancy, Helen thought as the discussion was brought to an end. What was it? Something about Nicholas's father and sister. That must be Marjorie, who was visiting today.

David got up to leave to make up a four in a game of tennis, jocularly complaining that he would be handicapped by too much wine.

—⁓—

George also took his leave, walking into the street, glancing round occasionally to see if he was being followed. Satisfied that he had shaken off the cloth-capped lean figure on his way to the Kerrs' house, he made his way back to his home via the green. He sat on the seat he often used until he saw the figure he was expecting leaning against a tree. 'You are a worm, my friend, but watch out, the birds are coming to eat you,' he muttered, shaking open his paper, determined to bore the man to death.

—⁓—

In the late afternoon, Nancy and Helen sat companionably in the garden together. Helen was staying the night, accepting the invitation gladly to hear more of life in Middleston. She was reading the *Post*. Steve Brown's first article on drugs was in this edition. It was well written and researched. *He must have some good informers*, Helen speculated, as she read through the allegations made. *I hope he's wrong, though. The Zanzibar club is near my flat.*

She turned the pages, looking for interesting pieces. Nothing else caught her eye, just advertising, so she folded the paper and put it beside her on the canopy-covered seat, closing her eyes, enjoying the late afternoon sun. The image of a bold advertisement looking up at her played in her mind. *That's advertising for you*, she mused, as she tried to dispel the image. *Why can't I let it go?*

Exasperated, she looked at the paper again and saw what had penetrated her subconscious. A large advertisement surrounded by thick black lines, announcing the opening of Milford House's conference and exhibition facilities. Beautiful surroundings. Experienced staff. Substantial discounts for this summer's bookings...She sat upright.

'Have you seen this?'

Nancy glanced up from her book, her big hat shading her eyes as she lay back in the sun chair. 'Milford House. Isn't that the Barclays' place?'

'Yes, I knew Roderick Barclay. We were...we were engaged briefly.' The memory of those love-filled months tore at her heart, but it was his astonishing insult to her that still raged inside her like a self-contained storm.

Nancy rested her book on her knee. 'Ah, that must have been tough on you, Helen. Agnes told me you were feeling a little tender and that was probably the reason you left London. I didn't know it was one of the Barclays.'

'Do you know them?' she asked, thinking how ironic it was that she was mentioning the Barclay name for the second time that day.

'Oh, yes. David was their family doctor. He went out on call one evening years ago as a locum, and they liked him. They used to save up their illnesses to make the hour's journey worthwhile. But wait a minute.' She sat up, her expression keen with interest. 'Barclay senior died recently, a few weeks ago. He had a heart attack, quite unexpected.'

'So Jeremy will be taking over the title and the house.'

'I expect so. Being British, you know the rules better than I do,' she said, reading through the advertisement.

'Sounds as though they're a bit strapped for cash, as Roderick would put it, doesn't it?' Helen considered and then rejected the notion as she watched Nancy.

'It sure does, unless it is a particular pastime of Jeremy's?'

'Not as far as I know. I didn't get to know him well, but he had something to do with the city, a stockbroker I think. He seemed to work twenty-four hours a day. I can't recall Roderick mentioning any interests, such as hosting conferences and exhibitions.'

'It does sound a bit incompatible with stockbroking. What's Roderick's line?'

'He works for one of the big auction houses. That's how we met. I was doing a feature on the recent influx of impressionist and postimpressionist paintings coming out of Russia as well as the risks involved in transporting these priceless objects from country to country, the crooks, the fake artists, and so on.'

'So this could be Roderick's interest.' Nancy smacked the advertisement with the back of her hand.

'I hardly think that he would want his ancestral home turned into a public arena. I never went there, but it just doesn't fit in with all he told me. Anyway, Roderick and Jeremy only visited to see their father and sister. I didn't think they were interested in turning the house into a business.' Ironic, she thought, moving away from London to the provinces to get away from Roderick, only to find that he might be spending more time in this area.

'Unless they need the cash.' Nancy saw Helen shake her head. 'Could be!'

'Roderick never indicated that there were any problems. I think he would have told me. After all, he didn't have to impress me. I had already fallen in love with him before he told me of his illustrious background. He could have been the son of a dustman, it wouldn't have made any difference, except that we would probably have been married by now. It was his wealth and position in society that finished us, or my lack of it,' she added.

'Men can be such bums,' Nancy said with conviction.

Helen burst into laughter. 'You're great, Nancy. You've put everything into perspective. Have you ever thought of being an agony aunt?' she asked playfully, to disguise the pain swelling in her heart.

'Now there's an idea. Does it pay well?'

David returned in his tennis gear. He looked younger than his years as he strode across the grass towards them, taking a swing at an imaginary ball.

'Hi, honey, did you have a good game?' Nancy smiled up at him.

Helen observed the couple. Nancy lifted her head to be kissed by David. The deep love between them was apparent as they acknowledged each other like a faithful pair of swans. She thought she had her feelings under control, but watching David and Nancy, her loss of what might have been hurt her anew. She blinked away the tears that threatened to erupt and hastily excused herself, going straight to her room.

This is silly, she thought as she fought to steady her emotions. She had tried not to think, to fill her life with new projects to block out the memories, but here they were again at a mere mention of his name. Would it always be like this? She heard the doorbell ring as she stepped into the shower to wash away the unbidden memories.

'Nancy,' David whispered, 'I think I've just met Helen's half sister.'

'What do you mean, honey? It's OK. Helen's upstairs,' she reassured him as he looked round anxiously. She closed the fridge door. 'That can wait.'

'There was a girl at the door in her midtwenties.' He lowered his voice further. 'She was looking for the Baineses' old house. She said her name was Sally and that her mother lived there once. When I asked her who her mother was, she said Marjorie Baines, and had I known her? I'm afraid I said that I hadn't.' He looked at his wife helplessly.

'Oh, David, why did you say that?' She touched his arm.

'Because I didn't want to get involved in a conversation with Helen as our guest. Now I feel rotten for denying I knew Marjorie.'

'She must have had another child. Don't blame yourself.' Seeing David's distress by what had happened, she reassured him. 'If Helen hadn't been here, it wouldn't have occurred to you to say you didn't know Marjorie. It's done now. Unless we can put it right. Do you think she's still around?'

'No, she asked me where the grammar school was. I gave her directions, and she drove off.'

'She could be visiting Nicholas?'

'So could Marjorie.' He rolled his eyes to the ceiling.

'Golly, you're right, and Helen was there this morning.'

'We need to tread carefully. We may have to tell Helen about Marjorie, before she stumbles over her mother unexpectedly.'

'I'm more concerned that she doesn't meet her father or grandfather. It makes me shudder to think of Helen encountering those two evil characters. Oh, Agnes, where are you?' she implored.

'We'll manage, you'll see.' David took her into his arms. 'It's a bit like having a daughter of our own, don't you think?'

'Why didn't we think of adopting her all those years ago?' She looked up, meeting his loving eyes.

'Because, my darling, we were still trying to have our own baby.' His arms encircled her, and they hugged each other tightly, woven together through their memories and love. As they drew apart, he said, 'Perhaps I should go to Albermarle Street before Helen comes down.'

'Give my love to Marjorie,' Nancy said as David left the house.

16

I T HAD BEEN a wonderful day for Marjorie. Walking back to Albermarle Street from the café, they followed the old railway track, coming to the bridge and then on across the waste ground back towards the now-forlorn group of streets which held their happiest memories. Brother and sister talked nonstop as if they had been saving up their news from all the intervening years, as indeed they had.

Nicholas's enthusiasm for meeting Marjorie's daughter for the first time had evidently been a mutual pleasure. Sally had returned his admiration and warmth, cutting through his natural shyness with undisguised pleasure at the meeting.

His delight clear, he said, 'I can't tell you what it means to me, having your Sally and Tom so near.'

Marjorie smiled wistfully. 'I'd love to be nearer to them too, now that Jack's gone.'

'Why don't you come and live in Albermarle again? Get away from that awful neighbour of yours.'

'I'd love to get away from him, but I don't know if I could come back to Middleston. There's Max and Dad and...bad memories.' It was the first time she had referred to the disintegration of their childhood.

'And some good memories too,' Nicholas insisted. 'Don't forget Mum and Auntie Ollie and all the neighbours. Look at the reception they gave you.'

'I thought you said the street was scheduled to be pulled down,' she replied, wriggling away from the discomfort talking about the past brought up.

'I don't think it will. The time has come to make a stand against those bastards, Baines and Baines,' he announced. 'I can feel the winds of change.'

Surprised at her brother's optimism, Marjorie smiled as though joining in some madcap idea.

'It might be interesting for you to be here,' he added mischievously.

They passed the wharf buildings in silence, as though paying their respects. Nicholas had told her of the plans. She remembered his youthful ideas and dreams for them. They were almost laid to dust and concreted over.

She sensed his dwelling on their shattered lives, but she didn't want to talk about it yet. She wanted this to be a happy day. They would see each other again. It could wait for the future. Her heart was too tender now with stirred-up memories, and tears would not be too far off if they talked of such matters now. She had to think of Sally. She would be back soon. Her daughter had tactfully left them after lunch. Marjorie imagined Sally now, outside the big old house trying to fill in the pencil-line picture she had been given with colour and depth.

'It's been pulled down, you know,' Nicholas said as he steered her through the mounds of rubble and refuse.

'What has?' she asked sharply. 'The house?'

'Yes, there's a block of flats there now.'

'Why didn't you say before?'

'Because I didn't want to spoil Sally's reason for being tactful.' He smiled broadly. 'She'll be able to report back and we can be surprised. Meanwhile we've had a chance to talk.'

She smiled, thinking how much more confident Nicholas had grown and how easy it was to be with him. He had changed. His voice was deeper, and he readily voiced his opinions, the gangling awkwardness of his overlong legs replaced by a mature stride. But the old sensitivity lay just under the surface of the thickened skin. His middle years seemed to suit him. He was the strong one now. 'I wonder why we didn't do this years ago? Let's not leave it long before we see each other again. This has meant a lot to me.'

'And me, Sis.' Nicholas slipped his arm through hers. They walked on companionably. Their relationship had become familiar, like putting on a favourite old sweater, wearing its shabbiness like a dear friend.

'Marjorie?'

Something in the way he said her name made her wary.

'I wish you'd tell me about the time you went away,' he said gently. 'I do know what happened.'

'Do you?' she whispered, her first baby's face still graven in her mind.

'Was it Max?' He held her closer, giving her courage to acknowledge the truth.

She supposed subconsciously she had always been aware that he had known. She nodded imperceptibly.

They walked on, her arm held firmly through his, going down the road she had avoided all those years back.

'She must have been a beautiful baby,' he said after a time.

She looked up into his face, seeing compassion and love, not judgement as she had assigned to everyone. 'Yes. How did you know? I haven't told anybody.' The tiny creature, struggling with life after being born two months prematurely, was there now with her. Alongside the image came the accompanying emotion. 'I don't even know if she lived,' she cried out, turning a distraught face to her brother, daring to expose the rawness of her loss to him at last.

'I'm sorry.' His voice trembled as he shook his head, sharing her grief. 'It can't have been her then,' he muttered.

'What are you talking about?' She searched inside her sleeve for a tissue to wipe her tears.

He looked uncomfortable and hesitated. 'It sounds a bit daft now, but I've seen this girl. In fact she was in my house early this morning. She's a reporter on the *Post* asking questions about the redevelopment around here,' he rushed on. 'What struck me was that she looked so much like you when you were younger, all except the hair, which is straight, a bit like Max's, really.'

'Are you thinking she may be my baby?' Her heart raced. The possibility of her daughter not only being alive but in Middleston was too incongruous. She dismissed the idea. 'You must be wrong. If she did live, why would she be here, of all places?'

Nicholas shrugged.

'Unless Mrs Kerr...?' She broke off.

'Was it them who helped you?' he asked, as if putting a piece of the jigsaw in place. 'I wish I could have helped you more, but I didn't know what to do.' He turned to her with earnest intensity and placed his hands on her shoulders. 'I'm sorry it happened, Marjorie. I've felt rotten all these years for not being stronger for you.' He pulled her to him and gently rocked her in his arms. 'I've wanted to say that for so long.'

'I didn't realise how much I loved my first baby until I had Sally,' she murmured against his shoulder. 'I was ashamed of what happened, especially as Max was her father. When I first held Sally, all my feelings for my first baby came out. I cried a lot then. I told Jack about it, which was a mistake.'

Nicholas stroked her back, comforting her.

'It gave him the ammunition he'd wanted to pull me down. He never let go, Nicholas. He was like a terrier, and I was down that hole. When he died, I thought it would be easy to come into the daylight. Only I found I'd been there so long, I didn't know my way out.'

'I think it'll take time,' he responded gruffly, 'but we'll get you out.'

'It's been awful, all these years, not knowing, not being able to talk about it. If only I'd been able to confide in you before! I've been a silly bugger, our Nicholas.'

'That makes two of us.' He bent and kissed her wet cheek.

When they neared Albermarle Street, he asked, 'What did you call her?'

'Helen, Mum's middle name. I thought she needed a guardian angel. I don't suppose if she did live they would have kept the name. What's the girl's name, do you know?'

Nicholas smiled broadly. 'Helen.'

She felt dizzy with expectation. 'Oh, God, wouldn't it be wonderful?'

As they turned the corner, Dr Kerr was standing in the road.

'It seems you can have your answer now,' Nicholas observed before stepping forward to shake hands.

'Dr Kerr.' Marjorie stepped up to him shyly, his kind and trustworthy face now pleasantly creased.

He grasped her hands in recognition and studied her face. 'Still as lovely as ever,' he said kindly. 'I've just seen a beautiful young lady called Sally,' he declared, smiling broadly.

'Is she all right?' Marjorie asked anxiously, images of an accident, her daughter lying broken and dead in the road immediately springing to life.

'She's fine. I think she's looking at your old school.'

'That's a relief. I thought something might have happened.'

'The reason I came, Marjorie, is because I'm afraid I wasn't very helpful to Sally this afternoon. She came to the door asking if I knew where your old house was. I'm ashamed to say I told her I didn't know the house or you. Meeting her like that took me by surprise. Nancy and I thought that I should put the record straight in case you thought we had forgotten you.'

It seemed that was all he had come for. Her hopes subsided as he offered no more information. She withdrew her hands from his as the possibility of her first child being alive began to ebb away.

Nicholas gave her another opportunity. 'I'll have a word with you later, Dr Kerr. I know Marjorie would like to talk with you.' He retreated into the house.

She was stricken with nerves, frantic that he would leave before she plucked up her courage. What if he told her that the baby had died, as Sister Agnes had prepared her for? The baby had been so little, and she had been little more than a child herself. She remembered Sally at sixteen and thought of her having that burden, thanking God that she didn't have to make awful decisions. How can anyone make a sensible decision at that age with the limited knowledge and understanding of how the world is? Giving you own child away is a most unnatural act, and yet she had had no choice. Had she? She had pondered this question many times.

'Marjorie?' Dr Kerr interrupted her thoughts. 'Come and walk with me awhile.'

She was grateful for his suggestion and for his strong arm as he linked hers. They retraced the steps she and Nicholas had taken towards the canal. He allowed her time, staying mute, patiently waiting.

'Nicholas knows what happened to me all those years ago.' Embarrassed, she paused and took a deep breath. 'He thinks my baby might be here…in Middleston. I was wondering if you or Mrs Kerr might know about her? It was Mrs Kerr who gave me the address of the convent, and—'

'Marjorie,' he said gently, 'I know that you'll treat the information that I am going to give you sensitively, bearing in mind that your first daughter hasn't any idea that her natural parents came from this area. At this stage she hasn't expressed any desire to search for you.'

'So she did live, and she is here,' Marjorie cried in wonder.

'She is. In fact she's in my house at the moment. That's why Sally arriving at my door flummoxed me.'

'What is she like? Is she all right? She was so tiny, I can't believe this is happening.' She felt her heart leaping with boundless joy. 'Is she happy? Was her adoptive family nice?'

'Steady on, my dear.' He laughed at her delight. 'Yes, yes, and yes answers all of those, I think. Helen's a lovely girl.'

'Helen! Nicholas thinks he met her this morning. Does she work for the *Post*?'

'Yes, she's a reporter and a very bright girl.'

Marjorie savoured the news, happiness surfacing in bubbles as she allowed her mind to expand to include her daughter Helen. She felt light-headed.

'Helen's healthy, happy with her life, and, I should say, clever,' Dr Kerr was saying. 'She's fun to be with—all of those things. When the time comes, I'm sure she will be pleased to know you too.'

'Do you think she might want to soon? I don't think I can wait long, now that I know where she is.' Never before had she felt such anxious expectation.

'It's asking a lot of you, but will you trust Nancy and I as to the timing of your meeting, if that is what Helen wants? It has to be her decision as well.'

'Yes of course. It will be difficult to wait, but I can see that it all has to come from her.' Her excited apprehension subsided a little, but her curiosity was not satisfied. She wanted to know as much detail as possible. 'Was she placed in a good family?'

'Yes. You couldn't get kinder,' he replied with enthusiasm. 'She never left the convent. Sister Agnes became quite spellbound by your daughter and subsequently became Helen's legal mother. She has been treasured by that dear lady, and it shows.'

She pictured Helen running in the convent grounds, safe in the care of Sister Agnes. All the years of worry and wondering were over in a few sentences. 'I'm very grateful to Sister Agnes. She mothered me too.' The memories were being uncovered layer by layer as she spoke. 'I'll never forget looking down at Helen's tiny face. She was crying, and I cried all over her, thinking that I would never see her again. She was so little. Sister Agnes talked to me a lot about what I should do. I've never forgiven myself for leaving her, so vulnerable, without a mother.'

The guilt of not loving her baby enough because of the father still sat uncomfortably, like undigested food. 'What sort of person am I?' she implored, turning her anguished face to him as she struggled with her actions.

He drew her close. 'Under the circumstances, it was the only thing you could have done, Marjorie.'

As they completed their circuit and walked into Albermarle Street, she saw Nicholas standing at the door looking towards them with such evident anxiety that Marjorie rushed towards him, flinging herself into his waiting arms. 'She's alive, and she's here, our Nicholas,' she cried before tearing herself away and dashing up the narrow staircase.

Through the thin walls, a dam of grief could be heard bursting through the years of suppression. Nicholas listened to the emotional outpouring that he could only begin to comprehend. That it was his sister, Marjorie; that it was in this house after years of absence; that a piece of information could unlock wails and moans, pushing the black sludge of accumulated hurt before them, filled him with awe. He felt humbled by the power of raw emotion. None of his previous experiences had prepared him for this. 'Should I go to her?' he asked the older man.

'I should let her be. It's doing her a power of good,' David replied. 'Come, you wanted to speak to me, and I should like to look at your work.'

Nicholas relaxed as he led the way inside. It appeared there was nothing he could do for Marjorie at this moment, and he appreciated Dr Kerr's calm and practical approach. In light of the afternoon's events, he looked at his paintings with new eyes. He still had a long way to go before he could truly reflect life, he mused, as the distance between the real picture upstairs and the flat canvasses in the room before him illustrated. What did he know? He had never been a participant, only an observer.

'This is extraordinary. Quite extraordinary,' David said, peering closely at the paintings, his admiration clear. 'I hope you're going to let the world see your collection, Nicholas old chap.'

'Perhaps, one day,' he answered noncommittally. 'I need to develop my work more,' he added.

David rubbed his chin thoughtfully. 'Nicholas, I heard about your paintings being damaged. You're placing yourself in danger, and for that reason you need to be vigilant.'

'My father and Max are hell-bent on razing old Middleston to the ground,' Nicholas stated bitterly. 'It seems to bring inordinate delight to both of them. Unfortunately wrecking other people's lives doesn't seem to bring them lasting happiness. Like needing the next fix, they go on to find new victims. I'm ashamed to be related to them.'

'Someone has to stop them, and our small group is grateful to have your support.' David glanced towards the canvasses as he spoke. 'What we need is a person of influence on our side.'

'Unfortunately the power brokers of Middleston all seem to be under the spell of Baines and Baines. Helen Arbuthnot from the *Post* called this morning and thinks an article in her paper might bring some weight to our argument.'

'Helen may be right, although I hate to think of her getting so involved. Do you realise that she is Marjorie's daughter?'

'And Max Baines's daughter. I saw the likeness straight away but thought it was impossible until you arrived. What Marjorie must have gone through...' He trailed off as the sound of his sister's grief continued to reach them.

'We have to stop those men. They are a disgrace to the community on so many levels. Your paintings sitting here like undiscovered treasure might be the key. I'm serious,' he added enthusiastically, as Nicholas showed incredulity at the suggestion. 'You never know, maybe, just maybe, you could be the weight that will tip the balance.'

'Thank you for your confidence in my work.' Nicholas laughed wryly at the conflicting thoughts and ideas bumping against each other. 'But I hardly think it will determine the outcome of the next incursion from Baines and Baines.'

Through the window they saw Sally arrive.

Nicholas went to the door. 'I better tell her Marjorie's OK.'

'Yes, and I must be leaving. If you need me, let me know. He glanced up the stairs. 'I'll be in touch anyway about those paintings if that's all right with you?'

'Yes, yes, sure,' Nicholas answered, his mind on what he would say to Sally to explain her mother's grief. It wasn't for him to tell her the real reason.

Sally came towards them as they stood at the door. 'I don't understand,' she said as she regarded David with a puzzled expression. 'I thought you said you didn't know my mother.'

'I did, and I came here to put the record straight. You took me quite by surprise. I did know your mother and her family. In fact I was their doctor for several years…but I wasn't quite sure…'

'Is that her crying?'

Both men looked at each other. 'Yes,' they both stated in unison.

'But she will be fine, just a lot of memories surfacing.' David uncharacteristically faltered. He clapped his hands together. 'Well, mission accomplished. I must be on my way. It's been a pleasure to meet you.' Sally took his outstretched hand.

'Your mother holds a precious place in my memory, and my wife's. She was very fond of Marjorie.'

'Goodbye. You're the first person from Mum's mysterious past that I've met, apart from Uncle Nicholas and his neighbours, of course. I'm glad you were there,' she added unexpectedly.

'Your mother had a difficult time. Listen to her, and try to understand.' With a brief wave to Nicholas, he walked briskly away.

Marjorie and Sally travelled back that night. Promising to return soon, they left Nicholas's waving figure on the doorstep and turned out of Albermarle Street. Marjorie, conscious of the distance lengthening and taking her away from Helen, took a deep breath, and encouraged by her daughter's sweet profile, she began to tell her story.

17

THE LONDON HOUSE had become a dormitory. Late, sometimes in the early hours of the morning, Jeremy would let himself in, careful not to disturb Roderick. Exhausted, he would fall into bed only to find the night too short before leaving for the city again.

The two brothers had decided to put all their effort into Milford House. Friday would come, and sometime in the early evening they would drive north, sometimes together, sometimes separately, for their weekend's work. Roderick, not reliant on the vagaries of the international money markets, was able to be more flexible, a sympathetic senior encouraging him with the exhibition project, no doubt looking into the future and seeing that a house of that stature could indeed be a valuable out-of-town arts venue.

Jeremy, happy to let Roderick get on with the artistic side, had taken over the finances and organisation of the infrastructure; they consulted each other, acknowledging their individual strengths, an easy partnership based on years of trust.

At Milford House, their father's library had become a nerve centre of the project. Extra desks, a fax, computer, a sophisticated telephone system, and security arrangements had all been put in place. A surprised and flattered housekeeper had been enrolled to handle the flow of communications, exposing a flair for her new role.

The initial capital outlay had been kept to a minimum. Heavy discounts had been negotiated through Roderick's contacts, resulting in a glossy brochure, depicting the house and grounds. The drawing room, dining room, and east room had been designated as gallery space; the pictures belonging to the house had been hung elsewhere or stored.

A lover of classical music, Jeremy had mooted the idea of a concert on the lawns, a notion welcomed by Roderick but scoffed at by Miranda. The suggestion of a gift shop linked with the gallery was on hold until the interest generated was measured and established, but a cafe serving tea, coffee, and scones was a basic necessity. Miranda's scheme of a bar with music had been left hanging in the air.

Enquiries were slowly trickling in, but actual bookings were all for the following year. The advertisement in the *Post* had been one of many placed in regional papers trawling the market to net some fish, however small, in their attempt to ameliorate their set-up costs, but their optimism was diminishing by the day.

Since he had discovered the blackmail letter three months earlier, Jeremy had sifted through his father's paperwork and his personal effects, rereading business letters, looking for any nuances that might have suggested that all was not right.

He had telephoned his father's friends, casually referring to the spot of bother his father had been in, hoping that someone might take him up on the hint, but none were forthcoming. His father, it seemed, had led an exemplary life—to the outside world, at least.

The accountants had opposed the disposal of the gilts and bonds, advising his father that he would be losing considerable sums of money cashing in, but it had become apparent to Jeremy in the conversations with Trude and Williams that they were as baffled as he. They had been careful to show Jeremy his father's clear instructions.

Looking back at the previous correspondence, it became evident to Jeremy that his father had needed quite large sums of money to be made at quarterly intervals. In earlier letters, excuses were made: the money was for essential roof repairs; a new drainage system; decoration, internal and external. As the years had gone by, the excuses had petered out, and a straight demand to release monies was made in what became a standard letter of instruction. Jeremy had found no invoices to substantiate the demands. The accountants had called a meeting with the trustees of the estate, including his father, when it became clear that the realisable assets were coming to an end.

His father had died before the trustees had made their report. Looking at the neatly bound folder, Jeremy read the concern about the fabric of the building, the scheduled land-drainage system that had never transpired, the renovation programme delayed indefinitely. The house, grounds, and home farm, thankfully protected from sale by the trustees, were the only assets remaining. Funds allocated for the upkeep of the estate had depleted to a dangerous level.

From a generous lifestyle, his father had of necessity become parsimonious, leading a threadbare existence; his only luxury was in continuing to spoil his daughter. The report had recommended a strict control should be placed on expenditures to safeguard the future. Criticism of the accountants for not calling matters to the trustees' attention before that date had been put on file. The accountants had returned with a statement saying that they were in no way responsible for the disposal of income generated. Their brief was to maximise those investments in hand and reduce the tax burden. They had no authority over the Earl's wishes. They could only offer advice, which they had done repeatedly, as could be seen from the file.

Jeremy asked all concerned to put a line under the matter. What was important now was to try and retrieve the situation, to try and generate an income to maintain the house for as long as they could. A two-year time limit had been voluntarily placed on the project before a full review of the situation by the trustees. The accountants would be in constant consultation, their advice welcome. If after twenty-four months the house was not paying for itself, and if all avenues had been explored to that end, then the trustees could recommend the sale of the estate.

This weekend Roderick was absent. He was overseeing an exhibition nearing its closure in Amsterdam. Drawn like a moth to a flame, Miranda was in Manchester, having left at her usual time for the hour's journey to the bright lights. Like a sleeping giant in the valley, the great house was quiet. Jeremy lay awake, feeling defeated. With nothing to indicate the reason for and the author of his father's downhill journey culminating in his death, it seemed that he had exhausted all leads.

'There has to be evidence somewhere, but where, where?'

He mentally travelled round his father's office and into the files. In his mind's eye, he went into his father's bedroom and his dressing room, pulling out each drawer again, looking for clues.

It was 2:00 a.m. when he decided to look in the cellar. Slipping into his dressing gown and slippers, he made his way down the back staircase to the kitchen, the slumbering fridge the only sound in the cavernous room. In the moonlight cascading through the tall sash windows, he saw the Aga surrounded by copper pans, the dresser laden with family china, taking him back to the times he and Roderick used to sit on the table during school holidays and chat with Cook, fascinated by her life outside the house in the real world.

As he took the key from its place in the locker, he imagined Cook's voice berating him for going into the cellar when he had no business there. The feeling of guilt remained as he unlocked the heavy wooden door, turning the key with care, knowing that the final turn would make an abrupt sound if he didn't tease it gently round. He switched on the light and started down the cold stone steps, a trickle of fear mixed with excitement creeping into his senses as it had always done, even as an adult. Now in the middle of the night, this sensation was heightened. The decaying, musty smell of vintage ports and wines lying in their shrouds was stronger at night when the damp air penetrated the stone walls.

He didn't know what he was looking for, only that he had not found it, whatever it was. Perhaps there would never be evidence of his father's indiscretion; the only clues he had were the letter M and an approximate date of the beginning of the blackmail, deduced from the regular quarterly payments reaching back for a period of three years. But M must have an address and probably lived in an exaggerated lifestyle. If he needed the money so badly, he must have been poor to begin with, so surely someone somewhere must be suspicious.

Jeremy peered into the racks, hoping for inspiration or a sign leading him to where he could discover the truth. Finding nothing, his eyes searched the walls in the flickering strip light. Generations of his family knew all the crannies in the old stones, and Jeremy automatically found them feeling for information. There was nothing. A table and chairs with wine glasses for tasting were huddled in the corner of the vaulted cellar. He drew a chair out and sat down, weariness gathering with defeat.

'Can I get something for you, Master Jeremy?'

Jeremy leapt up with fright, knocking the chair backwards. The figure at the top of the stairs waited for an instruction, the time of night making no difference in the role play of master and servant. 'No, Roberts, I don't need anything, thank you,' he called. Retrieving the chair, he sat down again, casually crossing his legs and leaning back in an attempt to look self-possessed. Aware that the man deserved an explanation, he continued. 'I couldn't sleep, so…' He trailed off as the incongruity of the situation left him without words.

'I see, sir.' Patience and understanding enveloped the reply. Roberts descended the stairs and joined Jeremy at the table, standing by his side. 'It's a cold night. Shall I see you to your room, Master Jeremy?'

Grateful for the solicitude, Jeremy tried to allay the old man's concern. 'I was looking for something which I thought might be down here, but it isn't. Silly of me, I suppose. I could have done this in the morning, but as I said, I couldn't sleep.'

'Perhaps I can help you with your search. What is it exactly?'

'That's just it, I don't know.' Seeing the puzzled brow, he decided to take a risk. 'Look, I'll be straight with you. It seems that my father may have wanted to conceal some information somewhere. I'm trying to think of all the places that he may have hidden something. Have you any ideas, Roberts? This is confidential, you understand.'

'Yes, I understand, and no, I can't think of anywhere. We're clearing out His Lordship's—I beg your pardon, sir—the late Lordship's room on Monday. If Maisie finds anything, I shall let you know immediately.'

'I've already looked. I've searched everywhere. This was the last place, my last hope.' His shoulders slumped with fatigue. Feeling desperate, he decided to take another chance. There was no reason why he shouldn't trust this man who had been loyal to his father for over forty years. 'Look, Roberts, can I ask you something in the utmost confidence?'

'Of course, sir. It's clear that something is worrying you, and I shall be only too happy to be of assistance, and please take my word that nothing will be repeated.'

'Thank you. Won't you sit down.' The older man drew out the other chair and deferentially waited.

Jeremy chose his words carefully, looking at the caring face before him. 'Do you know of anything my father has done that might have been used against him if exposed, in exchange for monetary reward?'

There was an almost imperceptible blink. 'That sounds a little like blackmail, sir.'

'Well, yes, it is…in fact, as you say, blackmail.'

A gentle shaking of the head as Roberts seemed to cast his mind back over the years, the dismissing of each possibility erased from the years of data, until it seemed within a few minutes, the life and relationships of his beloved master were checked and scanned for indiscretions. 'No sir. I can honestly say there is nothing that I am aware of that could have been used against His Lordship. He was a very kind and honourable man. He loved your mother dearly and wouldn't have done anything to hurt her, as you know, even after she died, God rest her dear soul. I did, however, think that something was worrying your father.' He looked embarrassed, as if disclosing a confidence.

'Go on, I'm interested in hearing anything that was out of character or unusual.'

'Well, Sir, I thought that perhaps it was just Miss Miranda… out very late. A young lady driving on the roads alone at night; it worried us all. They had a little rumpus a couple of months before he died which put him out of sorts for a long while. He seemed to be desperately worried about her late sorties, and then…'

He looked at Jeremy as though asking for permission to continue. Jeremy nodded his head, comprehending that telling his father's business was difficult for him.

'Cook commented on something a few weeks before His Lordship's death. It seemed that he had gone off his food. You know how he always liked a good meal with wine. Well, he announced that he would be eating in the dining room only when all the family were gathered. He would be happy with sandwiches, lunch and dinner. Miranda too would be served simpler fare.'

'I think he had got himself into a financial corner and was looking for any way out, even if it meant not eating properly. Poor Father. If only he had been able to confide in Roderick and me.'

'He did seem distracted towards the end, as though he were greatly distressed over some issue. I regret now that I never enquired whether there was something I could have done to help alleviate the problem. Since his tragic death, I have often wondered what was troubling him. It hadn't occurred to me that it was blackmail.' He shook his head. 'No, Master Jeremy, blackmail would not have occurred to me. I hope who-ever it is…rots in hell.'

Jeremy reached across and covered Roberts's hand. 'Thank you for that sentiment. I share it completely. Come on, I've kept you out of your bed for long enough. Thank you for your support. Tell the staff how much we appreciate their help to keep things going here. By the way, where exactly does Miranda go in the evenings?'

'Your father asked me to find out for him. It's an establishment known as the Zanzibar. It's a nightclub in the centre of the city run by a Mr Max Baines.'

They had reached the kitchen and closed the cellar door when they heard the front door bang.

'That'll be Miranda. Thank you for that, Roberts.' Both men made an imperceptible bow to one another before Roberts climbed the back stairs. Jeremy walked down the corridor towards the main stairs where Miranda had already reached the first landing. Staggering to her left, she half walked, half dragged herself up the remaining stairs before reaching the gallery.

'Miranda, are you OK?' he called up to her.

'What the hell are you doing up this time of night?' she slurred. 'Or is it the morning?' She sank to her knees under the portrait of her mother and peered through the balustrade. 'Shouldn't you be in bed getting your beauty sleep, big brother?'

'You're drunk.'

'And well fucked. I feel wonderful.' She pulled herself up and continued weaving her way to her room, kicking the door behind her.

Jeremy followed, a hand on her door handle, listening to her being sick. Standing there in the middle of the night, undecided whether to go in, he wondered what kind of joy Miranda got out of life. Roderick and he had been so close, in age and interests. They had barely got to know her when she arrived eight years after Roderick. Boarding school and then university had created a gulf that had never been bridged. She lost her mother when she was twelve. A heartbroken father who was nursing his grief sent Miranda off to school, thinking it was best for her. She had fallen into a no-man's land, except, as Jeremy wryly thought, she had become every man's doxy.

He left her door and made his way to his room. He had told Roberts that he had no wish to move into the master suite; his old room was comfortable territory, his boyhood memories around him, adventure books alongside his history and philosophy volumes from Oxford, model aeroplanes, the battleship kit still waiting to be finished. Tired, with little accomplished by his night wanderings, he crawled into bed and let sleep overcome him.

Sometime before his alarm sounded in the morning, Jeremy had resolved to do four tasks. The first was to call Dr Kerr to see if his father had confided in him about the beastly business. The second was to question the gardener to see if he had been asked by his father to dispose of any papers—a long shot, but it was worth pursuing. The most logical action would be to burn the blackmail notes in the fireplace in the library, and Jeremy suspected that his father had done just that. The third was to ask Miranda why their father had been so angry with her. The fourth was to see for himself where Miranda spent her leisure time.

18

J EREMY EXAMINED HIMSELF in the mirror, appalled at how little it took to change his outward persona. The gold chain, borrowed from his mother's jewellery box nestled in the dark hairs of his neck; the shirt a hideous mistake he had rediscovered in his own wardrobe. He had purchased a cheap aftershave and some Brylcreem to complete the effect; his hair was slicked back, and the smell enveloped him.

'Do you think I'll do?' he asked, adjusting the buckle on the crocodile belt.

'Yes sir, I think that completes the picture, and if I may say so, sir, I never thought I would be entertaining a person attired thus in this house.'

Jeremy laughed. 'Splendid. Now, I just need a roll of notes in my pocket and a lot of nerve. You don't think I've gone over the top, Roberts?'

'No sir, I think with the type of gentleman you are trying to portray, one can never go over the top, as you say. I rather regret that you wouldn't take my advice on the shoes. In my view they tell a lot about a man.'

'I daresay, but the socks are already a blow to my sensibilities.'

Roberts held out a buff envelope. 'Your directions are in here, and I have sought out a street map in case you lose your way. Parking is difficult, but there will, no doubt, be places behind the old market if you can't get near. I understand that the district is a little seedy at night, and there will be unsavoury characters about. My advice is to walk as if you know exactly where you are going.'

'Thank you for your help. Wish me luck, and I'll see you in the morning.'

'I will listen for your tread, sir, to ascertain all is well with you.'

'Good man.'

Both men looked at each other with warmth and understanding generated in the twenty-four hours since their clandestine meeting in the cellar.

It was odd, Jeremy thought as he drove towards the city, that one could know and even live with someone for years under the same roof and never fully appreciate his qualities until a situation out of the ordinary order of events changes the dynamics, and other characteristics appear for the first time. That was how it had been with Roberts. In him he had found a person of remarkable steadfastness and loyalty. He had adopted an avuncular tone of voice when asked his opinion or advice. It was as though he were head of the family, holding it all together, as indeed it was in his interests to do so. Roberts didn't want to leave Milford House, but it was the inherent gentility of the man that Jeremy admired. His manner was respectful, not subservient. He seemed to consider each step in his day as though he were calling upon an inner voice to tell him which way was the wisest.

Those qualities made Jeremy decide to place an enormous amount of trust in him. They both wanted truth and justice to prevail. Whatever had driven Miranda to such extremes of behaviour had to be forgiven. She had begun this style of life at such an early age that to condemn her for the consequences of that behaviour now would be of no use. She needed compassion, not accusations. She undoubtedly would need help to get back on the road that she was on before her mother's death. Whether she could ever accept that she needed help would be the uncertainty.

He had not told Roderick of his suspicions and plans. He didn't want to burden him unnecessarily when all his energies were needed in Amsterdam. The trip to the nightclub was a fact-finding mission only, and it may not reveal any answers. The amber glow in the sky drew him on into the heart of the city.

—◊—

Jeremy ordered another drink. A full hour had passed since he had steeled his nerve and negotiated the narrow stairs leading down to the dimly lit club. The place was beginning to fill up with a surprising assortment of customers, young and older—the older being men and the young being women dressed provocatively, some in groups and others already hanging on the arm of a man who could be their father—but Jeremy knew that was not the case. A mirror behind the rows of drinks afforded a good view behind him. He tried to appear casual, but he felt totally out of his depth in these surroundings. Smoke filled the atmosphere and mixed with the stench of stale alcohol and myriad perfumes and aftershaves. He was desperate to get out but was keeping an eye on the padded door in his corner of the room. He had watched a tall man with a proprietary air usher in a young girl, a hand on her buttocks. She couldn't have been more than seventeen or eighteen.

'Haven't seen you here before, mate.'

Jeremy was startled to find someone sitting beside him.

'No,' he faltered. He had not prepared for conversation. 'Just passing through.'

The man cocked his head as if expecting further explanation.

'Up from London. Business.' He forced himself to look appreciative of his surroundings. 'Nice place. Who owns it?' There was a long pause as the question hung in the air. Jeremy knew that he hadn't sounded convincing. He didn't know the language of such places.

'Chap called Max Baines,' the other man unexpectedly offered. 'Controls half the city. Fingers in lots of pies, has Max. He's usually here wheeling and dealing behind his padded door.' He jerked his head sideways.

'Sounds like you don't have a lot of time for him.' Jeremy ventured.

'Indifferent mate, indifferent. What'll be yours? Whisky is it?'

'Cognac, Courvoisier preferably.'

'Not the usual punter, are you?' The man smiled as if he had already rumbled the sham.

'Just wanted some company,' Jeremy found himself replying weakly, determined now to leave as soon as he could politely do so.

'Company! It's whores, drugs, and booze down here, mate. What are you really here for?'

Jeremy turned to look at the man full in the face. 'As I said, company,' he enunciated slowly to the pockmarked face. A bad case of acne, poor fellow, he thought. He had an impulse to move away, but his own appearance, he remembered, was just as revolting. He fingered the chain around his neck. Had he gone too far?

The other man laughed, showing yellowing teeth. 'Well, then, the night is young, we may as well keep each other company. Company.' He chortled. 'That's a new one.' He held his glass up. 'Cheers.' He touched Jeremy's glass.

'Cheers.' Jeremy smiled at the other man. *Evidently not the usual punter either*, he thought.

His senses became alert with a familiar perfume and Miranda's unmistakable presence behind him. He stared in the mirror, holding onto the bar, willing himself not to turn round. She was trying the door handle and then banged the padded door with her fist. When there was no reply, she took off her shoe and smashed it against the door.

'Max, I know you're in there.' She put her ear to the door. 'I haven't any money,' she cried, regardless of who heard her. 'I'll do anything, Max, I need you.'

The door opened. Miranda went to push past the figure who closed the door behind him, denying her access.

'You can't go in.'

'Who the hell are you to say what I can or can't do, Ron Thompson?'

'Max doesn't want to see you, Miranda. He made that plain last time. Come on.' His voice softened. 'Let's get you a drink, and we can talk.'

She allowed herself to be steered towards a table where she slumped down, arms folded, a pout already formed. Jeremy peered at the familiar figure, fighting his instinct to snatch her up and take her home to safety. He was so close to her, yet he dare not move. He knew she hadn't noticed him hunched over his drink. His senses flared with life as he fine-tuned them in her direction.

'Two scotches,' her companion barked at the bartender before settling beside Miranda. 'There's nothing for you here anymore, Mandy. This place is for clients who have money. You don't,' he stated bluntly. 'But,' he said, putting up his hand to silence her, 'I know a way you can get some.'

Miranda visibly perked up.

'Max has said he will give you the opportunity to work in one of his client service centres.'

'And what does one do at a client service centre?' she sneered.

'You'll do what you're good at and be able to buy your stuff. Ideal, especially if I can be one of your regulars.' He put his hand on her knee before letting it travel further up. She didn't attempt to stop him.

Jeremy drew in his breath and gripped the bar edge as the reality of the situation dawned on him. Rooted to the spot, he felt sudden perspiration turn cold on his back. Was this really happening? Had Miranda not noticed where this man's hand was? She actually appeared to be weighing up his suggestion.

'When would I start?' she asked flatly.

'I can take you there now, and I can be your first customer.'

She turned her face to him and met his lips with her own.

'Come on, Mandy,' he said huskily. 'I need to get you installed.' He took her arm and led her through the darkened club.

'One of Max Baines's floozies. Rich, apparently, or was before.'

'Before what?' Jeremy was wrenched back to the man sitting beside him. He had an overwhelming desire to smash this man's face and any other man who insulted his sister. He needed to get out of this pit. Surely he didn't need to know anything more, other than his sister was being used by disgusting individuals for their pleasure.

'Rumour has it he fleeced her old man of all he had. She's high as a kite most of the time. Her credit with Max ran out when her old man died.'

Jeremy felt as though he had been struck. He finished off his drink in one gulp.

'Wife? Girlfriend?'

The directness disarmed him.

'Sister,' he said, turning an anguished face to his companion.

'Ah, then, bloody hell, you must be…shit. Listen, mate, I'm sorry about what I said. Bloody hell.'

'And who are you?'

'Steve Brown. *Post*. City paper. Look, I'm on your side, mate.' Jeremy smelled Steve Brown's bad breath as he leant in close to his ear. 'I'm investigating the drug racket being run out of here and a prostitution ring.

Jeremy was relieved on one hand but appalled on the other as he thought of Miranda's involvement. He offered his hand. The other man wiped his hand on his trousers and with a surprisingly strong grip, grasped Jeremy's.

'Faces down, mate.'

Jeremy felt the man's arm go around his shoulder, half hiding both their heads. He became aware that the padded door had opened, that a man was walking past them.

'That's Max Baines.'

Jeremy sprang up but was grabbed by Steve Brown. 'Not now,' he hissed into his ear. 'You're too emotional; we need to choose our time. Let's get out of here so we can talk.'

The cold hit him when he staggered into the street after Steve Brown.

'Steady on, mate. Look, where's your car?' Jeremy nodded to the left, and the two men leant on each other as they walked unsteadily into the night, an unlikely duo.

—◊◊—

She lay on the crumpled sheets. Ron had left. She had been told that she would have a maximum of fifteen minutes between clients, a few minutes to wash and get ready for a complete stranger to be at his disposal, to give him whatever he wanted because he would have already paid Ruby, the large, red-lipsticked woman who ran the place. Six girls in a shabby house with a B&B sign swinging outside with No Vacancies permanently displayed.

She padded to the shared bathroom. As she showered, she wondered why she had agreed to do this so readily, but then the money she was promised was enough for a couple of days' supply. Did she have a choice? Her father was dead, her brothers told her to find a job—*as if*—and now Max was tired of her. She peered into the cheap plastic mirror and thought that if she had known how the evening would end, she would have brought her makeup bag and perhaps a drink or two to get her through. *If you're going to do a job, you may as well do it well.* Isn't that what her mean brothers would say?

Out on the landing, the sound of someone weeping drew her towards a half-opened door. Another voice, foreign, was trying to soothe the girl. Curious, she tentatively knocked and looked round the door. Two young girls sat side by side on the edge of a blood-smeared bed; one of them couldn't have been more than fifteen. When they saw her, they both flinched, drawing close to one another, grasping each other's hands.

'Hello, are you all right?' Stupid question, she thought.

'Help us, please, lady, help us,' the older one cried, reaching out her hand towards Miranda. 'He take our passport. We have no money. He promise job, not this.' The disgust in her voice was clear as she indicated the sordid room.

Miranda's mind was racing. She had heard of girls being brought into the country to work as prostitutes, but the reality of their plight had not registered until this moment. 'Listen, I want to help, and I will help, but I can't right now,' she said earnestly. She had no idea how she could help, but the least she could do was think about it. She heard heavy steps on the stairs below. *Could be for me*, she thought. 'Bye girls, see you soon,' she said before retreating to her room and forgetting the foreign girls in her eagerness to be ready for her next customer.

Later though, she did remember. The last customer had been brutal in his needs. Ordering her onto her knees, he had not cared where he penetrated. She felt humiliation and shame as he used her body, grasping her buttocks and grunting his way to satisfaction. She buried her head in the pillow and wished she were anywhere else but there. What on earth had she been thinking? Did she need money so badly? What would her brothers think if they could see her now? Shame swept over her like a dirty blanket. All for what? The next fix? Despair filled her heart as she felt the man's juddering orgasm spilling into her. She didn't look up when he left; she curled herself into a foetal position and rocked herself, trying to find some comfort in her situation but found none. Had Max cared about her all these years? *Of course not.* She understood that now. Ron Thompson's words came back to her. Max wasn't interested in her now that she didn't have any money. What a fool she'd been to think he cared. She had been young and full of hope and romantic dreams. Then she had met Max Baines. Those foreign girls had come into contact with him and his cronies, and they were now trapped without a passport or money to escape. At least she could walk away. Could she do anything for them? If she went to the police they would question what she was doing there. She would think about it later.

She showered for a long time, trying to wash the disgusting man's body fluids away. She dressed quickly and stepped downstairs.

'Where do you think you're going?' With surprising energy, Ruby had leapt up from her chair and grabbed her arm. 'Get back upstairs, you're not finished yet.'

'Let go of me at once.' Even to her own ears, her accent sounded incongruous in her surroundings. 'You can't keep me here.'

'That's where you're wrong. Sluts like you belong here.'

'How dare you speak to me in that manner.' She prised the red nails from her sleeve, brushing Ruby's hand away as if a cockroach had landed on her. 'Tell Ron I don't need him anymore or his bastard friend, Max.'

'We know where to find you. You'll be back.' Ruby sneered. 'Go on, get out of here.'

It was early morning, and not knowing where she was, she asked a milkman to direct her to the town centre. With hands full of milk bottles, he made a vague gesture to her right, so she began her long walk towards her uncertain future.

—∿—

'Where are we going?'

'Anywhere, to shake the bugger off.'

'Which bugger?'

'The one following us.'

Jeremy felt liberated in the anonymity of the night, walking the city streets strewn with litter and tramps until they had shaken off their shadow. Yet he was appalled by the other man's personal habits: the chain smoking, the picking at the multitude of pimples on the back of his neck with dirty fingernails, his reaching down the back of his open-necked shirt to reach a boil—recently burst, he told him. 'Keep coming up—can't get rid of the blighters. Need a woman to look after me. Any takers, d'you think?' He laughed at his own sardonic humour. A fleeting sadness crossed his face before he rallied again to 'The Cause,' as he had named their shared enterprise. 'The Cause' being the cesspit that was Max Baines.

They parted at midnight having exchanged telephone numbers with a date for a meeting to show Jeremy all the information Steve had on their quarry. Steve had also promised him he would keep Miranda's name out of the papers.

—⚬⚬⚬—

As Jeremy tossed and turned, sleep eluded him as he thought of Miranda being caught in Max Baines's web and at this moment being used in one of the 'guest houses,' as Steve Brown had put it. He had promised not to go rushing in, not to go to the police; he now understood Max paid most of them to look the other way. He had to wait to get the last pieces of evidence in place, evidence that could bring Max Baines down, but oh, this was hard. *I'm sorry Miranda, I'm so very sorry.*

19

'I'VE LOOKED INTO bringing major artwork here, Jeremy, but there's no way it will happen. The insurance costs alone would be prohibitive; the house is just not protected to any acceptable standard to satisfy the curators; and it would cost a fortune to upgrade. I'm afraid it's a no no.'

'Damn; that leaves what, two weddings, one concert for next summer, and one tentative enquiry for conference facilities. It's just not enough.'

'Don't forget Miranda's game park. Where is she, by the way?'

'Here I am.' Miranda flounced in, flung her bag on a chair, lit a cigarette, and inhaled deeply. She stood unsteadily, feet apart for balance, inviting comment.

'Miranda, you look appalling,' Roderick stated flatly. 'Have you just come in?'

'Yep,' she snapped, her chin jutting out, ready for another fight with Roderick. 'Any chance of breakfast?'

'I'll make you some eggs if you like?' Jeremy offered. He wanted to show her all the affection she was able to accept. She did look appalling; she didn't have her usual layers of make-up to disguise the real Miranda. She looked vulnerable; her eyes were softer—it could be the lack of warpaint, but when she lowered her head as though studying the carpet, he said, 'Miranda, I've decided to make you an allowance until you find some employment. It won't be much, but it will mean that you won't have to go into the city so much. Especially at night,' he added, looking at her steadily.

She pulled on her cigarette as though absorbing the information. As she blew the smoke out, she said, 'Thank you, Jeremy, how kind.' She dropped her cigarette into a coffee cup. 'I'll be down in a jiffy; I need to put my face on.' She picked up her bag and walked unsteadily out of the room.

'Like father, like son. You're far too soft, Jeremy.'

'No, I don't think so. Miranda needs our help, Roddy.' It may have been his imagination but Jeremy felt there was a change in Miranda's manner. She had not been sarcastic when he made his offer but had seemed to accept it without argument or condition. The thought of what she must have been through made his stomach turn. This was his little sister, and he hadn't been able to protect her.

He glanced at his watch. 'Look, I'm meeting David Kerr at one in Middleston; will you join me?'

Roderick shook his head and stretched his legs out where he sat on the window seat. 'No, give him my regards,' he said, making himself comfortable before closing his eyes.

Jeremy felt relieved that Roderick had declined his invitation without asking why he was meeting with David Kerr.

His brother's unexpected appearance after an early flight from Amsterdam had been an unforeseen complication. He wasn't ready to tell Roderick of all he knew; indeed, he hoped to keep the sordid details of their sister's life to himself.

—∞—

When Jeremy entered the dining room of the Hare and Hounds, David Kerr stood to greet him at their preferred table in the bay window with views over the town. It offered some degree of privacy, being well tucked into the deep bay and separated from the nearest table by a console laden with flowers and trays of condiments. The pub served good home-made food and had excellent beer. Over the years the Hare and Hounds had become an offshoot of David's surgery for the Barclay family. Jeremy enjoyed the contact and had invited the Kerrs up to Milford House on several occasions. Jeremy had called him early that morning, asking for an urgent, nonmedical meeting, and when David had agreed readily, he had booked the table.

Food and drinks ordered, pleasantries exchanged, Jeremy came straight to the point. 'David, it appears that my father was being blackmailed, and last night I had the unpleasant experience of discovering the culprit. Does the name Max Baines mean anything to you?'

The older man looked shocked at the mention of blackmail and then resigned at the name of Max Baines.

'I am all too familiar with Max Baines—he has been a blight on Middleston, and I am not surprised that he would sink to blackmail. But what on earth would he have on your father?'

'I was hoping that he might have confided in you?'

'He never mentioned blackmail or Max Baines, but I do know that he worried about Miranda. He thought that she had got in with some dubious characters in the city.'

'At the Zanzibar. It's a nightclub in the centre of town owned by Max Baines,' Jeremy explained. 'It seems that it's a den of vice in every way.' He lowered his voice, even though they were out of anyone's earshot. 'There's a chap at the *Post* who thinks he has accumulated enough evidence to have him put away for a long time.'

'I think we'd be dancing in the streets if that were the case. Chap at the *Post*, did you say? I know someone else who works at the *Post*,' he said thoughtfully. 'But what about young Miranda in the middle of all this? Is she safe?' Jeremy was about to speak, but David suddenly raised his hand to silence him. 'Wait a minute, wait a minute, I'm just remembering something your father spoke of that didn't mean anything to me at the time.' He leaned forward. 'He asked me if I knew anything about videos and photographs on computers and if I knew how to erase something. He talked of getting rid of old photos that he didn't want—it was a rambling tale, and I have to confess I probably gave some glib reply, not having embraced videos, let alone the Internet age.'

'You were not to know the significance, if any,' Jeremy replied. 'Photographs of what, I wonder?' He felt his face flush and struggled with the images in his mind. 'I strongly suspect the photos may have been of Miranda in compromising situations,' he said, finally looking at David, grim-faced. 'Father would have gone to any lengths to protect her and the family name. It grieves me that he didn't confide in me; it must have been a terrible burden to endure alone.'

David nodded in agreement. 'I feel that I let your father down. In his way, I realise now he was asking for help, and I didn't pick up on his distress.'

'My father's sense of propriety and of what was socially acceptable even in a doctor's surgery would have kept him silent. I don't blame anyone except Max Baines if he proves to be the blackmailer. Now we have to think of Miranda.'

'Poor child, I dread to think what that foul man has done to her. She will need some help. If there's anything I can do, let me know.'

'I didn't know what an awful life she has been leading. I've always assumed that she would pull her socks up and join the working world. I've been so wrapped up in London, I wanted to believe that all was well. It makes me even more determined to hang on to Milford House. We need to fight for everything my father held dear, even though he's gone.'

'I saw your advertisement. Have you had much interest?' David asked.

He was relieved at the change of subject. 'We were hoping to get some significant artwork at the house, but in spite of all we have done, it's not enough for the insurers. We have to rethink. It's a pity because the rooms are ready and looking good. Roderick has put an enormous amount of effort into this project. It's all very disappointing.'

'What about local artists? Would you consider a new artist?'

Scepticism at David's suggestion must have shown on his face.

'No, hear me out. There's this chap, Nicholas Baines, a distant cousin of your very own Max Baines, whose been knocking out paintings over the years and now has a houseful. Never been seen in public, but I have to say I was really impressed when I saw them for the first time the other day. I admit that I'm not an expert, but you may be pleasantly surprised.'

20

NICHOLAS ANSWERED THE knock to find David Kerr standing on his doorstep with two tall, well-dressed young men flanking him. He had been feeling nervous since Dr Kerr had asked him if he would let some people from Milford House, a place he had never heard of before, come to view his work. At first he had refused, fearing that his work was of no value whatsoever and not wanting to hear that judgement. Painting had been his life. What if it were taken away with the sweep of a hand, dismissing his work as amateur nonsense? Rather let his dreams survive than be snatched away in a few seconds.

Dr Kerr had been very persuasive, citing Helen Arbuthnot's enthusiasm for his paintings and of course his own, and so he had gradually come round to the idea that now may be the time to let the world see his work. Nevertheless, he felt nauseated as he opened the door.

'Nicholas, I'd like you to meet Jeremy and Roderick Barclay. Roderick is involved in the art world, and Jeremy works in London.'

Nicholas shook the proffered hands, feeling further intimidated by the expensive suits and bearing of the Barclay brothers. 'Come in. It's a bit crowded. Mind the canvas on the easel as you go in; it's still drying in places.' He stood by to let Roderick and then Jeremy squeeze into the small living room. 'I've no idea if they have any value, but my paintings have been my life. It's funny having people look at them after all these years.' He found himself babbling on.

He stopped talking when he realised he was not being listened to. He stood in the doorway with David Kerr as the two brothers murmured to each other as they bent over the canvasses piled against the walls; Roderick, the younger one, pointed out details to his older brother, an exclamation here and there. Time went by; a painting held to the light, clothes smeared with oil residue and dust ignored as they seemed to revel and delight in the discovery. There were snatched pieces of conversation. 'I need Paul to come up and confirm. Milford House. Huge interest. Catalogue and profile. The press.'

David smiled at him, and he found himself grinning back, feeling very foolish as his eyes filled with unexpected tears of relief.

'You might be Middleston's saviour if you let the world see your work. Will you?'

'I think it's time.'

21

I T WAS DUSK when Helen negotiated the ramp down to the car park under her block of flats. She was tired, having spent the day with Steve Brown in a remote cafe on the moors. He had insisted on the venue, wanting total security from eavesdroppers, he had said. In a rare moment of real communication, she had told Steve of her problem with being forced into the position of writing an insipid article on the Middleston wharf development when her real interest was in supporting the opposition to the development plans.

At the mention of Ron Thompson and Max Baines, Steve turned his computer off, took his jacket from the back of his chair, and told her they needed to get out. Ten minutes later they had collected her car and were driving out of the city.

Separated from his computer, Steve Brown was extraordinarily talkative given that Helen had only previously received grunts as an acknowledgement of her existence. She tried to ignore the continual scratching at the back of his neck as his animation mounted.

'Bloody hell, why didn't you tell me you were getting mixed up with the bloody mafia? Max Baines rules the bloody city; he's not some genteel fraudster—nobody's been able to pin anything on him because of all the bloody protection he gets. He's trampled over anybody that's stood in his way, including his own uncle.'

'The other half of Baines and Baines?'

'He's languishing in some bloody old people's home on the other side of the city, going bonkers with none of his family aware of it; it took me months to find him. He's been incarcerated until he signs his share over, but he told me he'd rather snuff it before he signs over to his dear partner. He was a bloody rogue, but he was an angel compared to bloody Max Baines. Max Baines has laundered all his ill-gotten gains through Baines and Baines, and he must be wetting his pants thinking he can't get hold of it. I hope Baines senior dies soon with his shares in Baines and Baines hidden under his stinking whisky-soaked mattress.'

'I've met his son, Nicholas Baines. Why isn't he aware of his father's situation?'

'They fell out donkey's years ago, don't know why.'

'Nicholas is an artist. I don't think they would have much in common.'

'Next turning,' Steve said, pointing to a road snaking upwards onto the moors. 'My aunt owns a cafe at the top. Perfect place to be private.'

'Surely the office is private. Is there any need for this cloak and dagger stuff?' She laughed.

'Are you kidding? We've been bugged before, and there's no reason to believe that the place isn't riddled. I don't trust anybody.'

'I wondered why you didn't speak to me.'

'Well, now I am.' He grinned. 'We have to start working together so that we don't mess each other's stories up. I had a near miss the other night at the Zanzibar. Fellow was watching out for his sister and nearly blew my cover. Bloody Lord so and so of Milford House and his drug-head tart of a sister.'

'Miranda?'

'Oh God, don't tell me you know them. You've only just arrived.'

'I knew Roderick and Jeremy in London.'

'Course you did. You people all stick together,' he said acidly.

'I'll have you know, Steve Brown, that I'm from a very humble background, and I will not be pigeonholed by some northern person.'

He threw his head back and laughed, yellow teeth exposed like a rocky ridge between crusted lips. 'There's nothing humble about you, Miss Toffee Nose.'

'If we are flinging insults at each other, there's nothing refined about you, Mr…Mr…I'll think of something.'

They smiled spontaneously at each other, barriers down.

'Good, we've established an excellent working relationship. As soon as we get to Auntie Daff's, I'll tell you all I know about Max Baines: the blackmailing, gun-running, drug-dealing, brothel-running bastard that I intend to personally bring down and get locked up.'

—◊—

With keys in one hand and briefcase in the other, she walked towards the lift, her head buzzing with all that Steve Brown had told her. The revving of an engine startled her as she thought she was alone. She stepped aside, headlights flashed on, and the car came hurtling towards her as if out of control, swerving inches from her.

'Idiot,' she screamed after it, shaken by the near miss. She heard the car screech to a halt, reverse and come directly towards her again, its tail lights speeding unerringly in her direction. Fear gripped her. Just in time she staggered backwards as the car careered past her and screeched to a stop.

She started to run as she heard the car door slam, sure now that someone was trying to harm her. Heavy steps beat an uneven rhythm behind her as she began to sprint towards the lift, fear catching at her throat. Jabbing the lift button, she knew she was too late. Big hands grabbed her jacket; she tore free. Stairs, where were the stairs? She started to panic as the figure in the dim light grabbed her by the arm and swung her round, roughly pinning her to the wall, a hand around her neck. She kicked and punched the burley figure, determined not to be overcome. He laughed as she struggled against him, appearing to take delight in her dilemma, a hand ready to smack her.

'Who are you?' he demanded.

A rasping sound she didn't recognise as her own voice surfaced with fear and anger, but mostly fear. 'You must know who I am unless you are in the habit of trying to kill strangers.' Anger welled up, and she punched him in the chest with both fists. 'How dare you? Who the hell do you think you are?' she balled at him, stamping on his foot, hoping her heel would penetrate his shoe.

'OK, OK—listen. Just keep away from this stuff in Middleston and stop prowling around my club,' he said, backing away from her as if afraid to touch her again. He walked calmly away as if they had just exchanged pleasantries.

Shaken, she watched the retreating figure. Max Baines. Doing his own dirty work, contrary to what Steve had told her when he had shown her pictures of the loathsome creature. She pressed the lift button and stood proudly, her head held high in disdain as he drove past her.

Helen paced the brown carpet, wondering what to do. She wanted to call the police but held back because she wanted to speak to Steve Brown first. She called his mobile again but received no answer. Where was he when he was needed?

The phone rang and she snatched up the receiver.

'Helen, I have the best news for you,' David Kerr began with no preamble. 'Nicholas Baines had his paintings appraised last week, and he's having his first exhibition at Milford House very soon. He wants you to cover the story. Nobody else. Quite a scoop, eh?'

She absorbed the information: Nicholas's paintings, scoop, Milford House.

'Helen, are you there?'

'Yes, David, that's fantastic news for Nicholas, but I won't be able to cover the story,' she said firmly, knowing that she would have leapt in the air with joy if the venue had not been Milford House.

'We're all going to Milford House tomorrow, Nancy too, and I have my orders that your expected refusal is not an option, so we'll see you there at ten sharp.'

The line went dead, and she looked at the phone in shock. She didn't have to follow orders. She wouldn't follow orders. She couldn't possibly go.

It was nine in the evening, and she poured herself another generous glass of red wine and walked to the window. The city was spread out before her in a carpet of lights, some moving, some static. A plane, seemingly parallel to her window, flew slowly past like a condor lifted and carried by a thermal current. It would be an amazing story; she remembered the paintings and how she had been drawn into them as if they were each telling a story that needed time to be read. 'Fancy Nicholas wanting me to have an exclusive,' she muttered.

If she looked to her right, she could see the road leading to the Zanzibar club. She had deliberately walked past it a few times as if by doing so she might learn something about the notorious Max Baines, and now she had met him. Everyone had been right about him; he was dangerous. He needed to be behind bars. Nicholas Baines was a relative of his—such a contrast in character to the evil, loathsome creature she had encountered.

It would be truly wonderful if Nicholas could bring life back into the Albermarle area and thwart Max Baines's plans, but his story would not only have to be about his paintings, it would have to be about the area that had inspired him. Will another reporter just take his paintings at face value? Is this the weight on the scale that might stop the wharf development? 'Damn, I'll have to do it,' she told her reflection in the window. *I shall be businesslike with Roderick. I'll keep my distance. And I will defy Max Baines.*

22

S HE DROVE SLOWLY up the long driveway, trying to delay her arrival, reluctance invading her body like a heavy hand pushing her into her seat, telling her not to do this, it was madness. She still hadn't spoken to anyone about Max Baines and his murderous ways, and this meeting was delaying that further. Parking, she turned the engine off and waited. She noticed the Kerrs had not arrived yet, even though it was fifteen minutes past ten.

The entrance alone looked intimidating. She took in the beautiful building with its mellow stone. Perfectly proportioned windows looked out onto the grounds. A sports car was parked to the left under a retaining wall. An arched entrance to another set of buildings—stables maybe. The smell of recently mown grass and the sounds of summer wafted across her senses. To think that she had imagined she could be part of this, that Roderick had thought that she could fit in. His insult to her played again like a familiar tape.

'Good morning.'

She turned towards the voice, thankful that it wasn't Roderick.

'Good heavens. Is it Helen? What a surprise.' Her car door was opened. She swung her long legs out and allowed herself to be helped by Jeremy. 'Roddy will be pleased to see you, but we have a meeting scheduled at ten thirty.'

She saw him look flustered as he leant forward to kiss her cheek. 'I know, Jeremy, I have come for the meeting. I'm reporting the story for the *Post*.'

'So you are the one Mr Baines insisted upon,' he laughed. 'Well, well. Come in, Helen, let me show you round before the others arrive.' He took her arm and led her up the steps. 'I didn't know you had moved to these parts. How do you know Mr Baines?'

She was happy to have her arm firmly clasped by Jeremy as they chatted away as if they were old friends, her reason for being there validated. He seemed to be genuinely pleased to see her, and she began to feel less apprehensive as he led her into the great hall with a magnificent staircase sweeping up to the balustraded upper floor.

Shafts of light broke through the double doorway to her right, revealing clean walls painted in the palest of grey. 'Roderick has worked his socks off getting this together,' he said proudly, guiding her into the first room. Framed and hung were Nicholas's paintings; beside each one, a small plaque contained a description and the year. 'He had an army of people in for a week to get it to this stage. We are having a preview with the critics on Friday and will be open to the public after that.'

'He must strongly believe in Nicholas's work to invest so much time and effort.'

'Yes, absolutely. His boss came up and told us to throw caution to the wind when he saw them.'

Still holding her arm, Jeremy led Helen through the room and on through another set of double doors to another room, and another. Three rooms had been transformed into a gallery housing a one-man show. That Nicholas was prolific did not detract from the vibrancy and depth of every piece. His early works were sometimes unframed, letting their vibrancy spill over uncontained, not restricting the idea but letting it seemingly flow into the room, the viewer able to fill the void with imagination. Jeremy and Helen fell into an easy companionship as they looked at each picture in turn. There were no prices displayed as in the better London galleries. She looked at the pictures with renewed interest, realising just how special the brothers believed the paintings to be.

'Have you invited any London buyers?' she asked.

'Yes, everyone of any importance and influence.'

'Everyone?'

'Everyone is here, Helen.' The sound of voices drew them towards the hall. The Kerrs had arrived with Nicholas and George Thomas. Roderick was greeting them. Helen slowed her step. Jeremy momentarily squeezed her arm and smiled encouragingly as if he understood the awkwardness of the situation before leading her to the group.

'Helen, you made it.' Nancy Kerr held her close as she kissed her cheek. 'Don't worry, I'm here to look after you,' she whispered into her ear.

She was aware that Roderick had stepped back into the shadows as she greeted David, Nicholas, and George. She didn't know that she had commanded her legs to walk in his direction until she was holding both hands out in greeting to Roderick as if nothing had ever happened between them.

'Roddy, how good to see you.'

'Helen, my dear. This is most unexpected. I see you are a party to our meeting. Most unexpected, most unexpected,' he repeated as if struggling to find words suitable for the occasion. 'You didn't tell me you were in these parts,' he said, as if accusing her of social negligence.

'I didn't think my news would be of any interest to you, Roderick,' she rejoined, finding humour in his stumbling over niceties. 'Otherwise, I would have informed you.'

'Shall we go through?' Jeremy ushered the group into the library where the smell of freshly made coffee met them. A long table had been prepared with pads of paper, pens, pencils, jugs of water, and glasses. 'We thought it would be easier to have our discussion here.'

Helen entered the library. A young woman was standing by a table waiting to serve coffee.

'Helen,' Jeremy took her arm again, 'can I introduce you to my sister, Miranda, who has offered to serve coffee and to take notes. She has been an enormous help in the last few days.'

Helen took Miranda's hand and on impulse, kissed her cheek, having an overwhelming feeling of compassion for her. She saw the hurt in her eyes and the need for love. Sister Agnes had taught her to see the lost sheep of society, often hidden behind bravado and abuse of substances. 'Miranda, I'm very pleased to meet you. I hope that we can be friends.'

Miranda looked both surprised and pleased at the invitation. 'Thank you, Helen.' She lowered her voice. 'Are you in cahoots with Nancy Kerr? She's also being extraordinarily pleasant to me. I'm not a very nice person, you know,' she added as she started to pour coffee. 'This is the kindest thing I've done for years.' She laughed. 'Do you want to hand these round? I'll probably spill them.'

Jeremy had saved a seat for Helen next to him. Sitting opposite, Nicholas grinned at her mischievously, clearly thrilled to see her. Delighted to see him again, she smiled back as she took out her tape recorder and set it out on the table in front of her. Miranda joined the meeting at the head of the table, pen in hand.

The door burst open. 'Sorry I'm late; just picked up your message this morning. Hello, everyone. Steve Brown from the *Post*,' he announced, taking the spare seat at the end of the table. Rummaging around in a battered briefcase, he drew out a collection of papers and slapped them on the table.

'Thank you for joining us, Steve,' Jeremy greeted him warmly. 'Let me introduce you to everyone: Nicholas Baines, the artist; George Thomas, the leading campaigner for the preservation and conservation of old Middleston; Nancy and Dr David Kerr, good friends and supporters of our project; my brother, Roderick; and my sister, Miranda. Helen, of course, you know.'

'Can I offer you coffee, Mr Brown?' Miranda asked.

'No thanks, sunshine, I tanked up at the office. I'll be pissing for Britain if I have any more.'

Miranda laughed delightedly whilst Roderick adjusted his tie. Jeremy appeared to be totally unfazed by Steve Brown's language. 'Let's get down to business then. We have three main items on the agenda, the first being Nicholas's exhibition and how we want to present the news of a major new artist to the world. Roderick will be leading that item, having consulted extensively with Nicholas over the last week.'

'Second is the wharf development and how Nicholas's talent might be used to stop the desecration of the Albermarle neighbourhood. George will be giving us his ideas on that, and Nicholas is keen that his sister Marjorie be involved when she moves back into the area. Finally,' he said, pausing and looking at each person in turn, 'we will see how we can get Max Baines behind bars. Steve has compiled quite a dossier and is willing to share it with us.'

'I don't think Helen needs to be here for that part, Jeremy,' Nancy said, leaning forward earnestly.

'He tried to kill me last night.'

'Bloody hell, Helen, why didn't you call me?' Steve shouted down the table amidst gasps and cries of horror. 'I told you he was a bloody monster.'

'You didn't answer your phone, Steve. I still haven't told the police because I needed to speak to you. He tried to run me down in the underground car park below my flat. I would like him behind bars as soon as possible,' she stated firmly, looking at Nancy.

'That's settled then. Helen has every right to stay,' David spoke softly to his wife, patting her arm reassuringly.

'Are you sure you want to hear more about Max Baines, Helen?' It was Nicholas speaking to her from across the table, such concern filling his voice that it made her laugh.

'Of course, Nicholas. I wouldn't miss this for the world.'

'Each and every one of us then has a reason for seeing him brought to justice.' Jeremy looked at Miranda as if to show that she was not alone. 'I have a friend at the Yard who is going to make sure there is an outside investigation; Max Baines has too much influence in the local force. But first, let's start with Nicholas. I'd like to hand over to Roderick, who will explain the significance of his work.'

Helen watched and listened as Roderick's animation grew, warming to his subject, piling compliments on Nicholas. She made sure her recorder was on and listened to his voice, so well loved for a long time, but what did she feel now? Had she fallen out of love with him at last? Seeing him again had perhaps been the best medicine. The wound in her heart no longer felt open and raw. Instead, a feeling of peace rested lightly there, and she found herself smiling up at him in between doodling flowers as he talked, not listening closely to what he said but watching him like an old friend who had once made a stupid remark and knew it. Hadn't she been part of the drama and put him in an awkward situation? He had reverted to stereotypical behaviour from a bygone age. It was just as well to know his instincts before marriage; it would have been a disaster had she found out later. She couldn't have lived with it, she knew that.

'And it is Helen who will be writing the piece.' He paused and then addressed her as she looked up into his face. 'I didn't know that when Nicholas mentioned a special person called Helen that it was the Helen I know so well.' His voice wavered as he regarded her tenderly.

She felt herself flush with the attention. 'It's a pleasure to be here, Roddy. I hope that I do justice to all your effort,' she added, bringing him back to the task in hand. She didn't want him to think that she was there for anything else.

Then it was George's turn. He talked of the ideal outcome of any development plans, sounding both excited and sceptical at the same time, as if it was fun to plan and speculate but it was unlikely to come true. He ended his presentation by saying how much he was looking forward to having Marjorie in their midst again.

Steve Brown followed by detailing a brutal account of the activities of Max Baines, including the blackmail and extortion that had brought Milford House to its knees. Everything was out in the open, Miranda portrayed as one more casualty on Max's road to power. She began to weep as she listened to the part she had played in her family's misfortunes, her misery-torn face turned to Jeremy. 'I didn't know. I'm so sorry, I didn't know,' she sobbed.

'Miranda, darling, you were so young, of course you didn't know.' Jeremy looked beseechingly towards Nancy, who had already left her seat.

She put her arms around Miranda's shoulders, and Miranda leant her head on Nancy's arm. 'I feel so ashamed,' she whispered. 'I was so beastly to Daddy when he asked me to stay at home to keep him company. Now I know it was to keep me away from Max. I couldn't keep away. Why couldn't I keep away?' she wailed, turning her tear-streaked face up to Nancy.

'Come, let's go into the drawing room, and we can talk,' Nancy urged her.

'Not yet,' she said firmly. 'I need to tell you all about the girls Max is bringing into the country to be prostitutes.' The room quieted, listening closely. 'I met two of them, and they asked for my help. I feel rotten because I haven't done anything yet, and it was weeks ago. They asked me to go to the police, but how could I? They would have asked what I was doing there, so...I've done nothing.' She shrugged her shoulders, helpless.

'Where is this place?' Jeremy asked.

'Dorrington Road.'

'Ta, Miranda, don't worry, babe, we'll fix it.' Steve flipped his shorthand book open and scribbled incomprehensible hieroglyphics before snapping it shut again.

Roderick leapt to his feet and gave Miranda a brief hug. 'Listen to Nancy,' he said, his voice catching with emotion. 'She will help us all to get back together as a family. Jeremy and I want that more than anything else in the world.'

'I don't know if I deserve it, do I?'

'Of course you do, darling Miranda. Everyone deserves a second chance,' he said forcefully, turning towards the table and looking directly at Helen.

Helen met his gaze and felt acutely embarrassed as his meaning became clear. She shouldn't have come. This was going to be so awkward.

'And now we have attempted murder to add to Max Baines's list of crimes.' Steve continued his summary as if there had been no interruption. 'Are there CCT cameras down there, Helen?'

Everyone turned to her, waiting expectantly.

'Helen, will you stop daydreaming and answer the bloody question? CCT cameras in your bloody car park?'

'Yes, I think there are,' she replied distractedly.

'Bull's eye. Jeremy, your man in Scotland Yard can get him arrested for that, and the rest can follow. Bloody hell, what time is it?' He looked at his watch. 'Jeremy, catch your man at the Yard and get him to preserve that tape.' He shuffled his papers together and pushed them into his briefcase. 'God, I feel fantastic. Any chance of a slug of something, mate?'

'Drinks are in the drawing room, mate,' Jeremy replied cheerfully. 'And lunch at one in the kitchen,' he called to everyone as he left the room to make the call.

'I must excuse myself, everyone, I have a deadline to meet, so I'll see you all on Friday,' Helen announced with what she hoped was conviction. She caught sight of Roderick's dismayed face as she slung her bag over her shoulder, but she studiously ignored him, leaving the assembled group before any well-meaning objections could be voiced.

She needed to be alone but didn't want to go to the office or home. The only place she could think of that would offer safety and privacy was Auntie Daff's cafe in the hills, and that was where she headed, driving more recklessly than was wise.

Cold air rushed in as she wound down the window, blowing her hair in every direction. She didn't care. Her head was spinning. What was to stop Max Baines from trying to harm her again? A trickle of fear travelled through her body as she thought of the previous night's drama.

And Roderick? His apparent change of heart was not only unexpected, but also to her surprise, very unwelcome. She felt angry with him, angry that he should think they might get back together; angry that he should think his behaviour could be excused and forgotten.

She accelerated up the winding hill, negotiating every twist with a tinge of danger that kept her senses alive. She was approaching the cafe from the opposite direction from which Steve and she had done only the day before. It seemed a long time ago; an attempt on her life and now a different kind of attack, this time on her emotions, separated that time when she felt in control of her life.

Auntie Daff's cafe was a single-storey, whitewashed building perched on the brow of the highest point of an otherwise uninhabited landscape. Lichen-covered rocky outcrops were strewn in disorganised clumps surrounded by short grass mown by sheep. Scraps of heather clung to the hill, braced against the ever-blowing wind. It was a hostile environment for someone used to living with life's luxuries, but Helen liked its otherworldliness. Steve was right; it was the perfect place to be private.

She sat at a laminate-topped table, listening to Auntie Daff working in the kitchen, the clattering of china gratefully drowning out her thoughts. She was in no hurry to order and closed her eyes. Unwanted images played in front of her eyelids: Roderick's face, Nicholas's paintings, car lights, Max Baines, Jeremy, and Max Baines again, this time strangling her.

'Cup of tea, is it love?' Auntie Daff stood in front of her, a water-splashed apron circling her girth.

She snapped out of her reverie to enter the comforting presence of this solid Lancashire woman. 'Yes please, Auntie Daff, and a teacake if you have one.'

'You're lucky, you've just missed rush hour. Two lorries and a tour bus in one morning.'

'That's a relief. I came here to be on my own and to think.'

'I can see that. You think away, and I'll get you something nice to eat. A teacake isn't enough, is it?'

Helen laughed. 'Thank you, perhaps I do need to eat some lunch.'

'You don't look well, duck.'

'I do feel a bit shaky, but I'll be all right soon.'

After eating the shepherd's pie Auntie Daff put before her, Helen took out her pad. If she worked on her piece for Nicholas, maybe it would chase the demons away. She played the recording she had made listening to Roderick's voice over and over until she had a sense of detachment as she wove his words in with her own. She jotted down ideas of how to stress the importance of the Albermarle area as Nicholas's inspiration and to explain the council's plans for redevelopment.

The bustling figure of Auntie Daff came and went; a group of hikers ate mountains of food and departed while Helen scribbled away until the sun crept behind the hills to the west.

'Finished, love?' Auntie Daff asked as Helen finally put her notes into her bag.

'Almost. I'll let Steve read it through tomorrow. I think I might come here more often, it's a great place to work.'

'You do that, duck, and bring that nephew of mine up to get fed. He looks emaciated.'

23

ALISON BAINES FELT the dog licking her face. He wanted to go out for a walk, but she felt too drunk to move. It hadn't been her idea to have a dog. She had wanted a child, not a dog. Max had insisted on it saying it was for security. She never went out anywhere except to the shops. She was sick of the shops. She had bought everything there was to buy. Drink was all that was left to do.

'Just wait awhile, I'll take you out, just wait,' she told the dog before passing out again. Lying on the settee, eyes closed with her hands crossed over her chest, she shut out her living room filled with painstakingly chosen coffee tables, lamps, vases, ornaments, and soft furnishings, the result of years of shopping and dreaming. The drinking began when reality had threatened to invade her dreams of children and a happy marriage.

She smelled his presence. The dog had greeted him half an hour before, wildly jumping up and down with unconsumed energy. Max had swiped it across its head and it now lay down, its head on its paws, following his master's movements with nervous eyes.

'Get up, you stupid cow.'

Alison heard her husband but decided to keep her eyes closed. It was better. He would go out soon and leave her alone. She would walk the dog, and when she next saw Max, she would say that she had just been sleeping.

'I said get up.' She sensed him looking down at her. 'All right, Alison, you've only got yourself to blame if I'm not home much. I had thought we might go out, have a nice meal, take in a show, but you spend your life unconscious, so I'll go to the club as usual.' Alison heard him make one of his customary speeches before he picked up his keys and left the house. He always found an excuse to leave, whether she was drunk or not. It made no difference.

Uncurling her legs from the settee, she sat up, feeling muzzy-headed. Her mouth was dry. She staggered towards the kitchen, supporting herself on the furniture. As she passed the hall mirror, it reflected her bruised eyes surrounded by her once-beautiful hair, now a tangled mess. Once she would have paused to admire herself; now she avoided its unexpressed accusation.

The dog followed her, his tail wagging. 'OK, OK, we'll go in a minute.' She rubbed his head affectionately. 'Silly old thing, but I love you, and you love me too, don't you?' She let tap water splash and spill into a glass before gulping it down. 'Where's your lead?'

It was eight o'clock, and she was alone in the street, even though it was a beautiful evening. She felt better now that she was outside, the comfortable dog at her side. She wondered why she resented it sometimes since it was her sole companion.

The matured housing estate on the outskirts of the town offered a short walk before the open countryside with its web of narrow lanes, enticing to the dog, but menacing to Alison.

'I don't want to live here,' she had told Max twenty-five years ago as they walked round the nearly completed site.

'You'll live where I tell you to live. This house is a good investment. Whether you want to live here is immaterial.' He climbed into the car, slammed the door and waited for her to join him. She had learned early on that arguing with him was a pointless exercise.

As a young married girl, she had played at house. Within a couple of years, her neighbours had dutifully produced babies, a common bond established between the young mothers. Alison had gladly babysat, thinking that it was only a matter of time before she would join in the long discussions about her own baby's development. It was not to be. With visits to the doctor, the specialists, and the different treatments tried, the knowledge that she would never have a family or hold her own baby was devastating. She began to drink to soothe the pain. Just a little at first, and then a little more as the effect wore off.

Her parents had been delighted when Max Baines had begun to court their only daughter when she was sixteen. They had known his distant cousin Marjorie for years and knew that she was a nice girl. Their only reservation was Alison's youth, but they felt after three years, Max had shown that he was serious. They were relieved that the passage from teenager to woman was over with the minimum of fuss. Their daughter had made a respectable marriage to someone who had good prospects. Their responsibility was over.

Max had been proud of her then. She knew she turned heads with her thick blond hair. He was the perfect gentleman when they were courting, never making her go further than she wanted. She wanted to be a virgin when she married. It held Max.

It was several years before she knew he had found solace elsewhere during their courtship. A chance remark here, a conversation overheard, the flushed face of his secretary as Alison walked in to his office unexpectedly; all of it put the pieces of jigsaw together, which told her that her husband was unfaithful at any and every opportunity.

She had challenged him one morning over breakfast. She didn't know what his reaction would be, or what she would do if he acknowledged her suspicions. Perhaps she wanted him to ask her forgiveness, that they would start anew, tell her she was the only woman in his life, that he loved her. She was still clinging to the dream portrayed in all the magazines she read avidly. 'Max?' She waited for him to look up from his plate of bacon and eggs.

'What d'you want now?' He hadn't bothered to swallow his food before he spoke.

'Max, have you been unfaithful to me?' Her heart pounded in her chest at her own boldness and she felt a hot flush creep up her neck.

'What difference does it make to you?' he demanded. 'You've got everything you want, haven't you?' He indicated the kitchen gadgets, the food mixer, the gleaming set of pans hanging in graded rows on the wall, the new dishwasher, the only one on the street.

Instantly, she experienced the familiar defeat, out-manoeuvred by a cold logic that was devoid of emotion. Everything in Max's life had a price tag. She knew she had been bought, and that had effectively ended her rights as an individual.

He continued to masticate his food, watching her, as if waiting for his moment when he would go in for the kill. 'You're useless in bed. You can't blame me if I want some excitement, can you? You can't even get pregnant.' He pushed back his chair and stood up, addressing her bowed head. 'I'll fuck whoever I like, whenever I like. All you have to do is to keep this house going, cook a few meals, and spread your legs when I want it.'

Her spirit finally crushed, it had been downhill all the way since then. Keeping up the pretence that all was well had gradually became unimportant. Her parents were disappointed in her and felt that she was letting Max down. She had no friends, just the dog, now walking by her side.

Lately, she had begun to wonder about Marjorie and Nicholas Baines. They had disappeared altogether from her life. She hadn't questioned it at first, thinking that Marjorie was jealous of Max taking her out. She had enjoyed going out with the full consent of her parents. The disappointment of not being allowed to go to school dances with Marjorie had turned into scorn at something so childish. But where had Marjorie gone? Alison had wanted her at the wedding to show off. Old Mr Baines had not been forthcoming, saying he had washed his hands of his son and daughter. It was Max that mattered.

Since having the dog, she had often wondered about Marjorie and the walks they had taken with Barney, the Labrador. Strange that she should be left alone with just her memories of that one friendship.

As she turned into her drive, she was surprised to find two uniformed figures standing on her doorstep.

'Mrs Baines?'

'Yes.'

'Can we go inside?'

'Yes, of course.' She unlocked the door and allowed the dog to go in before them. 'How can I help you?' she asked, indicating the settee she had so recently vacated.

'I'm sorry to inform you, Mrs Baines,' the policeman said sombrely as he pushed a cushion aside, 'that your husband has been arrested on some very serious charges.'

'Oh, that's too bad,' she replied airily. Was she still drunk, she wondered as she registered her lack of feeling for her husband's dilemma.

'We would like to ask you some questions.' The solicitous tone came from the neat little policewoman who stood twirling her hat in her hands.

'Yes of course. Does that mean he won't be coming back for a while?' she asked brightly.

'It may be some time, yes. We have a search warrant to look around your home, but we would prefer to do it with your cooperation,' the policewoman stated very seriously.

'In that case, you may be interested in finding out what is so fascinating about our shed when he doesn't show any interest in gardening,' she blurted.

Had she been waiting all these years for this moment when she could tell everyone what a pig her husband was? She wanted to be liberated and was more than happy to cooperate in her release. An unfamiliar bubble of laughter threatened to rise and spill over. Aware of the inappropriateness of it, she fought to hold it in; her eyes watered, and as the two police officers studied her, it struggled against containment and burst forth. Unfettered, her laughter filled her living room and travelled through the house.

24

HELEN DROVE DOWN the ramp to the underground car park, fear clutching at her heart when she noticed one of the lamps that would light her way to the lift was out. She sat for a moment, plucking up courage before she opened her door. Someone was there, rasping out her name. She ran, leaving her car door open, hearing the rough accent calling out her name, finally recognising it as she hit the lift button. Turning round she saw Steve with his hands up as if she were holding a gun. 'Steve, you idiot. What are you doing here?' Her heart was pounding as relief surged through her body.

He dropped his arms and said, 'I think I'd better come up, don't you?'

There were five messages indicated on her answerphone.

'Hi, Helen. It's Nancy. Can you call when you get in? Just need to know you're safely home.'

'Helen. Roderick here. Can we meet before Friday? I need to talk to you—about us. Please call.'

'Where the hell are you? Jeremy's called the police, but it would be helpful to have the victim around. Stop farting about and get in touch.'

'Helen. Nancy again. David and I are very worried. Please call.'

'The bastard's been arrested. Got the CTV from the car park, no thanks to you. If you don't call back by ten, the cops are going to start looking for you.'

'Better call your friends first,' Steve Brown belched as he walked over from the window.

'I really have caused you all a lot of worry. I didn't mean to,' she said as she started to call the Kerrs' number.

'Hello, David. It's Helen.'

'Thank God. Are you safely home?'

'Yes, Steve was waiting for me in the car park. He gave me a bit of a fright, but I was very relieved to see him there. He's in the flat with me now, telling me off.'

'Good. Don't do a disappearing act again, Helen, until we're sure that all of Max Baines's stooges are with him behind bars where they belong. Steve told you, I assume?'

'Yes, I didn't think it would all move so quickly.'

'Jeremy, it seems, has some powerful friends. Nancy is blowing kisses in my direction; I think they're meant for you. We'll see you on Friday, if not before. Keep safe, Helen dear.'

'Where's the beer?' Steve held the fridge door open, revealing salad ingredients and salmon steaks.

'Sorry, only wine. I wasn't expecting visitors.'

'Better get something stronger for when Master Roderick comes courting,' he said, uncorking a bottle and splashing wine into two glasses. 'He's obviously soft on you.'

'Roderick won't be courting me, as you put it. Cheers.'

'Jeremy, then? He's not a bad bloke for a toff.'

'Steve Brown, are you trying to marry me off to get rid of me?'

'No, you're all right. Bit of a liability, but all right—for a girl.'

'I'll take that as a compliment.' She looked at his pitted face with affection. 'Steve?'

'Yeah?'

'Thanks.'

25

HELEN'S ARTICLE WAS timed to come out the same day as the preview. A champagne reception was being held for the critics, art collectors, and investors scouting for the next big name and anyone influential in the art world that Roderick could think of. Accommodation in the house was offered as an added incentive to travel the extra miles.

Nicholas was applauded and sought after, a great novelty to him, making him want to laugh at the absurdity of the situation. Red circles indicated some of his most cherished paintings were sold at what he considered silly prices. He was sorry to let his work go; his paintings were like children to him, nurtured and worked at until they were ready to stand alone in the world. The money meant little to him other than being able to influence the decision not to destroy the Albermarle area. Not every painting was for sale. Roderick wanted to test the market by releasing a limited number at first. He hoped that they would command higher prices as the word spread.

The champagne was going to his head. Miranda kept taking his glass and replacing it. He had no idea how much he had drunk. Roderick steered him around, working the room, as he put it. He occasionally caught sight of Helen, looking very beautiful in a simple black dress. He would have preferred to chat to her and share the moment with her. She would understand how he felt. Marjorie too would understand his feeling of intimidation as these well-dressed people spoke in riddles about his work. He tried to match their language, but he could have been in a foreign country, making him feel like an imposter.

He felt hot in his new jacket and was longing to discard it, but there was something about the casual air with which these people carried their expensive clothes that made it impossible for him to reveal his cheap shirt, so he soldiered on, hoping the end to come soon. George, on the other hand, he noticed, was loving every minute of his friend's success, standing tall and confident, his infectious laughter inviting people into his circle as if an opening night was just another social occasion in a busy round of engagements. He envied George being free of the searing spotlight which glared down at him and his paintings. He returned George's wave as he was steered towards another group. Thankfully the Kerrs were there giving off a quiet, cultured air, Nancy's soft American accent slicing through the British establishment with ease.

'Nicholas, congratulations.' Nancy kissed him on one cheek and then the other, something he was getting used to. Once had been too much for him before today, but he had kissed cheeks up to four times, depending on the nationality of the ladies. Jasmine, the Italian teetering on her high heels, had hugged and kissed him, enveloping him in her expensive perfume, making him feel quite giddy. Even the men were not against giving him a hug and a kiss.

'Can I introduce Jason Ruffle-Smith, the arts editor of the *Independent*; Timothy Parsons, *Observer*; and of course you know Nancy and David Kerr.' Roderick held his arm as if he might escape, as indeed he would given the chance. He felt weary and waited for the usual questions. What were his influences? Where had he trained? Had he shown his work previously? Which school did he align himself to? What was his reaction to a successful opening night? What was his personal story? They liked a good story, Roderick had told him. He replied, giving a variation of the same answer to each question.

Nancy came to his rescue. 'Nicholas, have you talked to Helen yet? Would you excuse us?' Her voice was filled with charm as she effortlessly extracted him from the group. 'You look ready to drop; let's see if we can rustle up a coffee and a seat,' she said conspiratorially.

Nancy took his hand and expertly wove through the crowded room. 'Join us for a coffee?' she whispered into Helen's ear as they brushed passed her.

In the kitchen they found Jeremy supervising a boiling kettle. 'Coffee anyone?' he asked as if anticipating their arrival and divining their thoughts.

'Bless you, Jeremy. Poor Nicholas is in need of a break from all the adulation, and my feet are killing me. Can we sit with you for ten minutes before we return to the fray?'

'There you are.' Helen looked stunning as she entered the kitchen. From where he sat, Nicholas saw Jeremy's expression and wondered if there was something going on between them. He'd noticed both brothers' admiration at the meeting on Monday. *This would tickle Marjorie*, he thought.

'Helen, you look beautiful.' Jeremy forgot his coffee making as he walked towards her, drawn like a magnet.

'Thank you, Jeremy,' she said simply, smiling up at him. 'Have you escaped too? It's all very exhausting, isn't it? Nicholas,' she said, turning to him, 'you must be thrilled with the reaction to your exhibition.'

'Yes, I am, but a bit overwhelmed by it too. I'm not used to all this fuss. I'm glad I have friends with me to keep my feet on the ground; otherwise I might have lifted off into the stratosphere with all this talk, half of which I don't understand.'

He gratefully took the offered coffee from Nancy, who had taken over host duties since Jeremy had forgotten in his paralysis at the sight of Helen. *Funny how things turn out*, Nicholas mused as he looked around him. He'd eaten here on Monday, he was having his first exhibition, and now he was looking on as the lord of the manor mooned over his niece—not that she was aware of it. She was relaxed and friendly, unselfconscious of her own beauty.

The sound of brisk footsteps coming down the hall heralded the arrival of Roderick. 'What on earth is going on here?' he demanded. 'We have a major function going on, and the hosts are in the kitchen.' He raised his voice in bewilderment.

'Right, coffee break over, chaps; let's return to battle.' Jeremy led the way with Nancy Kerr.

Nicholas began to follow Helen, but their way was blocked by Roderick. 'Helen, I must speak to you—about us,' he added.

He sat down again. *I'll just be invisible*, he thought.

'You never answered my call.'

'No, I thought it best. There is no "us," Roddy,' she said gently.

'Helen, I made a terrible mistake. I love you. It doesn't matter a jot about your background. I'd like to marry you in spite of it.'

'There lies the problem, Roderick. I couldn't think of marrying you when you hold a belief that I am inferior to you in some way.' She took a deep breath. 'I no longer love you, Roderick,' she said tenderly, as though talking to a child.

Poor chap, Nicholas thought as he watched Roderick's wounded face regain composure before he turned on his heel and disappeared down the hall.

'Oh God, Nicholas. Sorry you had to witness my tragic love life.' She was trying to sound cheerful, but he knew that she was a bit shaken.

'Come on, you breaker of men's hearts.' He held his arm out for her. 'Let's get back to the party to take your mind off throwing up an opportunity to marry one of the most eligible bachelors in the country.'

'Thank you, Nicholas.' She leant on his arm as they began to saunter towards the sounds of laughter and clinking glasses. 'You must think I'm mad, but it's the principle of it,' she said with indignation in her voice.

'I'm proud of you.' Without a foundation of mutual re-spect, where was love? Even he could understand that. He pat-ted her hand thinking that she was the most special person in the world.

26

MARJORIE LAID HER new dresses on top and closed the lid of her suitcase. She looked in the dressing table mirror again, not quite believing the transformation her new haircut had brought not only to her appearance but also to her feeling of well-being. She had spent money lavishly on herself, surprising her colleagues at work with her tailored suits and daring shoes. Her promotion as team leader of her group of draughtsmen before Jack's death now rested on her shoulders with authority. She moved more assuredly and talked with confidence, as if she were a butterfly finally emerged from its cocoon.

She carried the case along the path to where her silver-grey car was parked and heaved it into the boot alongside her briefcase. She was thrilled with her new purchase, loving all its controls and the smell of new leather. She felt like a pilot about to take off as she pointed its nose in the direction of Middleston.

It had been four months since she had ventured southwards and learned that her first daughter was alive and well. That knowledge had lifted her spirit, giving her energy and purpose. Her daughter Sally had listened to her story with extraordinary understanding and compassion and was excited at the prospect of having a half sister. Marjorie didn't know if Helen was ready to meet her, but just the thought of being in close proximity to her first child again filled her with wonder.

It was early evening when she rang the bell and walked into Auntie Ollie's house.

'I'm home, Nicholas,' she called as he came running down the stairs to greet her with a bear hug.

'Hello, Sis. My, don't you look smart?' he exclaimed as he held her at arm's length. 'You've changed. I don't think Albermarle Street is ready for someone so sophisticated.'

'Has the street become accustomed to someone so famous?' she asked him, affectionately punching his arm.

He laughed. 'Come on. Let's get you some tea, and we can have a long chat—in the front room,' he added proudly as he opened the door with a flourish.

'Have you stopped painting, Nicholas?' she exclaimed incredulously as she saw the room devoid of canvasses. In their place were two settees, a coffee table, and some lamps lighting up the newly decorated walls. Coir matting now covered the paint-splattered floor, giving the room a soft, welcoming feel.

'No. I have a studio now that I'm a rich and famous artist,' he said with self-mockery. 'Come on then, make yourself comfortable.'

'Fancy all those years of work,' she said as she gratefully sank into the settee closest to the fireplace. 'I got the newspaper article—very posh and la-di-da we've become.'

'Helen did a good job.'

'Yes, she did you proud. Do you think she has any idea that she was writing about her uncle Nicholas Baines?'

'No, not yet, but Nancy Kerr thinks that she's working up to wanting to know about her birth family. Intuition, she said, when I asked her why she thought that. Trouble is, Marjorie,' he said, rubbing his chin, smiling mischievously, 'Helen's taken to dropping round here quite often to say hello, so you may meet her soon anyway.'

The following morning Nicholas picked up a key from the mantelpiece and followed Marjorie out of the door. They didn't have far to go to the wharf building, but those moments were filled with eager anticipation. Marjorie carried her briefcase, which contained a portable computer and drawings she had made under the instruction of her firm of architects. Her boss had taken a personal interest in the project after Marjorie explained the fight for the restoration of Nicholas's beloved buildings and the corruption that had nearly destroyed them. The fact that it was more than a hundred miles away in Newcastle hadn't deterred him; his high regard for Marjorie and her unusual request intrigued him, and it wasn't long before he had arranged a week's stay in Middleston to view the site and the surrounding area.

'Come on, Marjorie, let me carry your case.'

'No, I don't trust you,' she said, laughing and swinging it tantalisingly towards him.

'I'm not going to run off with it, I promise.'

'Don't believe you. This represents weeks of work, and knowing you, you'll open it up right now and let it fly all over the town.'

'Race you then.'

'Don't be daft. We'll be there in a minute.'

As they turned the corner onto the towpath, a familiar figure was waiting by the bridge. Shyness crept over Marjorie, slowing her step as she approached his solid presence.

'George, glad you made it. You remember Marjorie?'

'Of course I remember, I've never forgotten,' he spoke softly as he held his arms out to her.

She stepped inside his embrace and kissed his cheek, feeling the roughened skin and breathing in the fresh soap smell of him. 'George, it is so wonderful to see you,' she exclaimed, surprising herself at her sudden lack of inhibition. 'I've never forgotten you, either,' she stated frankly, looking into his sun-crinkled eyes.

'Right then.' Nicholas interrupted the moment. 'Let's have a look at the plans.' He gazed up at the flat-fronted building he had so often painted and took the giant key from his pocket. He turned towards Marjorie and George. 'I think this moment calls for a small speech,' he said, standing on the doorstep. As if addressing a large crowd, he raised his voice. 'Lady and gentleman, we have a long way to go, but I hope one day to open this door to local people and visitors who will come to see Middleston's heritage and its arts and crafts and even have a cup of tea and scone. It is my greatest pleasure to invite my greatest fans in this endeavour to put on their hard hats, courtesy of George, and inspect the plans, courtesy of our Marjorie.' With a flourish he inserted the key into the ancient door.

Scuffling sounds met them as Nicholas eased the door open, careful not to let the last hinge holding it in place come away. Startled mice ran for cover. Along with spiders and rats, they had shared this territory for so long it was as if the visitors were entering a private home.

'This is what remains of our cotton industry,' George said, looking round at the remnants of storage shelves and hoists scattered across the ground floor, most having been removed to melt down for the war. 'The finished materials from the mill were stored in these warehouses, ready to be lowered onto the barges,' Nicholas added. 'Wasn't it the Cotton Crisis in 1955 that ruined the business, George?'

'Yes. It was thriving until the Japanese imports killed it. The mill was torn down along with loads of others in the area to make way for new housing.'

'It's a miracle this has survived,' Marjorie said, looking up at the wooden ceiling, some of the rafters, clearly rotten, hanging on to the beams for dear life. 'If Middleston had been closer to Manchester, it would have been already developed.'

'It's the rise in the leisure boat industry that is making it attractive to Baines and Baines to develop now,' George said. 'That's what's given them some urgency. Before, they were happy to destroy the area house by house, street by street, until all the residents had left.'

'But this used to be a community which pulled together,' Nicholas said, 'and that's what we're fighting for. There are still enough folk who live here who would like to see it restored, but their voices are not heard.'

'Past tense, Nicholas,' George said. 'They now have you and Marjorie.'

Marjorie felt herself blush at the undisguised admiration from George. 'Come on, let's go upstairs; careful though, some of the steps are weak.'

'Can I carry your case for you?'

'Thank you, George. That's very kind.' She saw Nicholas smile before he led the way up the wooden structure that towered above them, the stairs branching off to each vast floor, telling their own story in the straggled bits of machinery left behind like old men too old for active service but still able to speak.

Marjorie looked on as the two men unfolded the plans and laid them out on the trestle table in the centre of the cavernous room. Nicholas's excitement was at fever pitch. He had spent days working with her boss in the attempt to realise his vision, and now she had presented him with the blueprint of his long-held dream.

'Come on, Marjorie, take us through the plan.' George waved her over from the cobwebbed window overlooking the canal. She smiled warmly at him as she went to his side, their hard hats occasionally touching as she walked them through each level, the structures that had to be reinforced, the areas that would be subdivided into artist's studios, the gallery and heritage centre on the first and second floors, a visitors' centre on the ground floor.

'It's hard to imagine what it will look like from these, so I've brought my computer to give you a better idea.' She saw their astonished faces and laughed as she pulled a portable computer from her briefcase and swiftly entered details to bring up the finished project.

'That's why you wouldn't let me carry your case.' Nicholas chuckled as she opened the CAD programme. To their astonishment, she expertly guided them through rooms. The gallery, a tea shop, a newly constructed wooden staircase... Nicholas's dream was alive and nearer to reality than he could have imagined.

'Flipping heck, you've worked wonders, Marjorie,' George exclaimed, clearly impressed by her skill. 'This will bowl them over at the meeting when you give your presentation.'

'I also have plans for the vicinity which should help to persuade the undecided that Albermarle should have protection by becoming a conservation area.'

27

'HELEN, WE HAVE a surprise for you.'

'A nice one?'

'You'll be thrilled. Can you come for lunch?'

As she walked through the Kerrs' door, she knew at once what her surprise was. Her mother's laughter filled the house. She hurried into the kitchen and threw her arms around her, squeezing her tight, drinking in her love.

'Ah, child, it's good to see my beautiful girl again. Let me have a look at you before you smother me. You look well again, so that's fine.'

Helen reluctantly let go of her to give Nancy and David a kiss. 'Thank you for a wonderful surprise,' she said, swiftly turning to her mother again. 'Have they let you out on parole?'

'Cheeky girl. Nancy and David thought it was high time I visited you all in Middleston. Parole indeed! You see what I've had to contend with all these years.' Agnes laughed as she took out a lace handkerchief to dab her eyes. 'Come and sit with me, child, and I'll tell you why I'm here. I can see you're puzzling.'

She indicated the large settee filling the corner of the large kitchen.

David sat two glasses of sherry on the coffee table before them.

'Are you trying to loosen my tongue, David?' she asked before taking a large sip. 'Now then, Helen,' she said, setting her glass down, 'let me talk.'

Helen was filled with a sense of foreboding as she watched her mother uncharacteristically search for words.

'Nancy and David visited me yesterday, long overdue I might add. They were worried about you, and I didn't need much persuasion to journey back with them, arriving in the small hours of this morning.'

'I don't understand, why the concern?' She looked mystified at Nancy, who had sat at the table to prepare vegetables.

'Agnes will explain, dear.'

Her mother took hold of her hands, a signal for her just to listen.

'Helen, my dear heart.' She paused and drew breath. 'Your natural mother came from Middleston, and it's very likely you will meet her in the next few days. We wanted to prepare you.'

A jolt of emotion travelled through her body as she took in the implications. 'I'm not sure I'm ready for this.'

'It's your choice, my heart, but'—she paused, as though wondering how she should continue—'do you remember long ago, you asked me if I was your real mother? A friend at school had told you it was impossible for a nun to have a child. I told you then that although I didn't give birth to you, I was your mother and that would never change. We have an unbreak-able bond that will not be shaken by your meeting your natural mother, Helen.'

Her head was whirling. She felt as though she were being given no choice and didn't like the fact that she was being pres-sured, however gently, into doing something she was not ready for. Of course over the years she had thought about her natural mother and thought one day she would find her, but her being in Middleston was a shock. She took a sip of sherry, then an-other, aware that they were waiting for her to speak. She could run away, but that wouldn't alter the fact that she now knew where her birth mother was and that one day she would want to meet her. She didn't want to leave the area she had come to love; she had been thinking that she might live in Middleston and commute into the city. A lot of her work was done on her home computer nowadays, and she didn't need to go into the office every day.

'OK,' she said simply. 'Tell me.'

Agnes patted her hand. 'I'm sure it's the right decision,' she said in her soft, lilting tones. She took a deep breath. 'Your mother's name is Marjorie Baines.'

'Nicholas's sister?'

'Nicholas Baines is your uncle.' David grinned at her from the dresser where he was collecting plates.

She left her mother's side and started pacing the kitchen, around the table and back again. What trickery was this, she wondered, that everyone knew all about her before she did? And Nicholas, she couldn't wish for a more perfect uncle; she loved his dry humour and unassuming demeanour. 'Does he know we're related?'

'Yes, he's known for some time and pleased as punch you are his niece,' David told her.

'He asked me to choose his new living room furniture for when Marjorie came to stay. He said anything I liked his sister would like. I thought it was a funny thing to say at the time, but now it makes sense.' She shook her head at the memory. 'Does she know I'm here?'

'She's longing to meet you,' Nancy told her.

She felt another wave of pressure as she thought of Marjorie waiting for her to make contact. She wanted to, but in her own time, when she had stopped reeling from all the revelations and had processed the information. She didn't have all the facts, however.

'And who is my father? Oh God, I know those looks by now, Nancy and David,' she exclaimed as she saw them exchange glances.

'Marjorie was in a pitiful state when she came to the convent,' Agnes began, neatly altering the focus. 'She was black and blue with bruises, and it was a miracle you both survived the ordeal. Whoever did that to her was a monster.'

'You think it could have been my father?'

'Or grandfather. Either was capable,' David answered.

'So you know who my father is.' In the stillness that followed, an uneasy germ of knowledge planted itself in Helen's mind. Please no, she begged silently, not him. She felt nausea rising in her throat as she fitted the pieces together. What other reason was there for everyone being so against her story when she first came to Middleston? It made sense now, the last piece of the jigsaw with a face on it to complete the picture. They had all been so protective, which she had put down to an idiosyncrasy of her new friends, but they all had knowledge of her which they wanted to keep secret, and not without reason, she reflected ruefully.

She sat beside her mother again and leant her head on Agnes's shoulder, just as she had done since childhood. She needed strength to get her through all this, but all she wanted to do now was to cling to her rock and cry, for Marjorie and for herself.

'We'll take it one step at a time. I'm here for a week, plenty of time for us to get used to the idea.'

Helen closed her eyes as her mother stroked her hair. She didn't want her world to change, but it would never be the same again. She listened to the bustle of the kitchen; pots and pans; oven door opening, emitting the delicious smell of roast lamb with rosemary; Nancy and David trying to sound cheerful and normal. She nestled closer to her mother, feeling the familiar starched wimple under her cheek.

'Will you help me?'

'Course I will.'

28

NICHOLAS AND MARJORIE followed the white-uniformed young woman along the corridor on the first floor. Some of the doors were open, revealing solitary men and women in various states of undress sitting on plastic armchairs, television channels arguing with each other as they passed each door. She stopped at number twelve and rapped on the door before swinging it wide. 'Visitors, Ernest,' she called. 'Phew, I'll change you when they've gone,' she added as a waft of warm, fetid air met their nostrils. 'Go on,' she urged them as they held back, 'you'll get used to it after a few minutes.'

Their father sat in his chair watching television. He was in his pyjamas, a newspaper covering his knees. At his feet was a bottle of whisky and an overturned glass. He didn't bother to turn round as they entered the room.

'So you've come.'

'Hello, Dad.' Marjorie kept her distance, thinking that other families would warmly greet their parent with a hug. She had no urge to even touch her father.

'Dad.' Nicholas let his presence be known.

'Is that my pansy son? I cut you out, so I don't know what you're doing here.'

'I believe you asked to see both of us,' Nicholas stated with a note of sarcasm.

'I was curious to know what an airy-fairy famous artist looks like, that's all.' He turned and looked Nicholas up and down. 'Just the same, a scrawny excuse for a man. That's a pity.'

'Dad, have you asked us here to insult us, because if so we'll go now.' She was not afraid of this old man and wondered why she had let the memories of him haunt her nights.

'I want to talk to you, our Marjorie, and you can stop your hoity-toity ways right now. Sit down before I change my mind,' he ordered as he fought with the television control to turn the volume down.

She sat on the edge of the bed while Nicholas continued to stand near the door, keeping his distance.

'I want you to take over Baines and Baines. Don't look so bloody surprised. Who else is there? Max won't see a penny of it now he's in the clink, I've seen to that.'

'Dad, I can't…' The thought was ridiculous. Why would she want to associate herself with Baines and Baines, all that she reviled?

'Hear me out, our Marjorie. I haven't got that long before I kick the bucket; I need to know my business is well out of Max's greedy paws before I go. With a bit of prudence'—he grinned, revealing his cigar-stained teeth—'I contacted my solicitors when Max was arrested. This hotshot young solicitor, Lee Osborne, found something really interesting in the original contract. I got him to write it down for me in English. Hang on.' He pulled out a crumpled piece of paper from his pyjama pocket. 'Read it.'

Marjorie leant over and took the grimy piece of paper from her father. She read it out to include Nicholas. 'Clause in Memorandum and Articles of Association stating in the event of criminal activity on the part of one of the shareholders, the shareholder who has acted in good faith has the right to buy the shares at a nominal value.' She handed the bit of paper back to her father. 'Have you acted in good faith, Dad?'

'Compared to that rattlesnake, I've been a bloody angel. It was him that dragged me here, you know. Told me to get out of my own company, that I was a liability. He's been trying to put the squeezers on me to let go of the business and my money, but I've held tight. I told him to go to hell. Well, he's on his way to hell now, and I'm free of his slippery ways. Now, what d'you think? D'you fancy it? Mind you'—he went on without waiting for an answer—'I'd make you promise not to support the restoration of Albermarle that your stupid brother's so keen on, according to the papers.'

'I wouldn't make that promise, because I do support Nicholas and his project, and I'm not going to sit here listening to you insulting him.' She got up. 'Good luck with finding someone else.' She turned to go. 'Come on, Nicholas, let's get out of here.'

'Wait, wait,' he rasped. 'You can't go yet. Thirty years and that's it? Where's the gratitude? All I've done for you. All I've bloody done for you,' he spluttered.

'Can you remind us, Dad?' Nicholas asked reasonably.

'You little shit. You'll never see a penny of mine.' Marjorie watched him turn his attention back to her as though he had just commented on the weather. 'Marjorie, you're getting the business whether you like it or not. It's all signed and ready to go as soon as Max is sentenced, but you've got to make that promise.'

'No, Dad.' How could he think that she would betray her brother?

She watched her father slump back into his chair. He reached down to the bottle by the side of the chair and felt for the overturned glass. 'What does it matter now,' he muttered, as he poured a generous measure. As if trounced by age and infirmity, he looked at her steadily, defeated. 'Do what you like, it's yours anyway. I've told the office you're taking over, so go in as soon as you like. If you want to support that fairy in his arty-farty project, that's your choice, but you won't make a penny out of it. The money's in new housing, not the rat-in-fested holes that your brother likes to live in. How I produced two lefty brats, I'll never know. Must have been your mother's fault. You look like your mother,' he stated, as if seeing her for the first time. 'Bloody woman died on me,' he added, spoiling a moment that could have signalled to Marjorie a softening, even regret at his past behaviour.

So she had no choice. It was going to be hers whether she liked it or not. Her heart began to pound, with nerves or excitement, Marjorie couldn't tell, but she was aware of a great rush of adrenaline surging through her body at the prospect of not only managing but also owning a construction company. She had seen the large building again outside of town on her way to Middleston. It looked prestigious, with its own drive and parking areas. Vans and trucks with Baines and Baines blazoned on their sides were going to and fro; it appeared the business was in full flow. She didn't know what projects were ongoing or projected, or for that matter what financial state the company was in.

'If you have no alternative, I'll accept your offer,' she found herself saying, 'but with one proviso. I need to look at the books to make sure I'm not taking on a white elephant.'

'A white elephant!' Ernest Baines nearly choked as he heaved himself round in his chair, clouds of putrid air billowing up into Marjorie's face as he wrenched his body towards her. 'I'll have you know there's millions locked up in that company and a few million sitting in my bank account gaining enough interest to keep you going without your ever having to lift a finger again. White bloody elephant,' he said incredulously, staring at her, his mouth hanging open as if the insult had loosened his facial muscles.

What she thought was that his money had been made on the backs of people's misery, but she kept that thought to herself and instead said, 'Sorry, Dad. I know you must have worked hard, and I hope that you will be proud of both of us one day.'

'Highly unlikely,' he said, taking in both of them with a sweep of his glass. 'You've both been nothing but trouble since the day you were born. Your only use to me is to get Max out of my company. I should never have let the little shit in with his smarmy talk.' He scrutinised his son's face, a curl of contempt forming. 'It's all your doing.' He jabbed his finger. 'If you'd been a proper son, but no, your head was in the clouds, and any talk of the family business sailed right over your weasel head without even registering that it put food in your mouth. Always clever, clever, and too good to get your hands mucky. Well, you're getting nothing now as payment.'

'That's fine with me, Dad. I'm glad Marjorie is getting it.'

Ernest Baines turned away from them to face the television again. He watched the picture without the sound, swirling the last drop of whisky mechanically, years of drinking having perfected the motion.

Marjorie didn't know if that was a signal for them to go or not. Nicholas tugged at her sleeve and indicated with his eyes that they should leave.

'I want to be cremated,' their father announced as he drained his glass.

Nicholas looked at his watch. 'We haven't time now, Dad, and I don't think I have any matches, but maybe next time we see you?'

'Bugger off, the pair of you, and tell that stupid girl to come and change my nappy.' He turned the volume of the television up, which drowned out Marjorie's attempt to say goodbye to her father. Nicholas was already walking down the corridor.

'You weren't tempted to tell him?'

'No, what's the point? He didn't even ask about Jack, never mind whether he had grandchildren.'

'Will you take over the business, like you said?'

'I can't wait, our Nicholas. Just think, I can have some influence over the type of housing that's being put up. I'll start as soon as I can.'

'Hecky thump, this is a turnup for the books.'

She laughed joyfully as she started the car to begin their journey home. 'I don't know if I'm more pleased about Max being in prison and forfeiting his share in the company or because it's giving me a chance of a lifetime to fulfil my dreams.'

'Both reasons are worth celebrating. Let's eat out tonight.'

'We could go to the George, Dad's old haunt. We could give him a toast.' She looked at Nicholas from the corner of her eye as she negotiated the unfamiliar streets. A sense of fun bubbled up as she waited for his reaction.

Time passed while Nicholas looked out of the window as if she hadn't spoken. 'Some stuff he said struck home,' he said at last. 'It's true I didn't care about what he did or where the money came from, and I wasn't the son he wanted.'

'Nicholas, I can't believe what I'm hearing! Dad was and still is a foul-mouthed bully. He's spent his life trying to get the better of other people, including us. Albermarle has been a thorn in his side because he knew Mum was happy there and that buying a big house and moving away to a posh area didn't impress her. All she wanted was her friends and books around her, both of which he sneered at because he couldn't control them. It was him who kicked and punched me before I had Helen. You didn't know that, did you?' she cried, anger exploding in her head, shattering any sense of where she was.

'Jesus, slow down,' Nicholas yelled as they ran a red light and careered into a dual carriageway, horns blaring and fists raised towards them. 'Bloody hell, Marjorie, I've just started to enjoy myself, I want to live.'

The road came into focus again, and she indicated her intention to go into the slow lane, settling behind a lorry struggling to keep moving. 'Sorry,' she said as her anger subsided. 'Just don't ever think that you've done anything wrong. Your only crime is being a good, normal, decent human being.'

'Thanks. Maybe you're right. I'm just a paragon after all.' He grinned wryly at her before continuing. 'I thought it was Max that beat you up, but Auntie Ollie always said it was probably Dad because she'd seen Mum often enough after being kicked around.'

'So stop feeling guilty, our Nicholas; that old man was a brute. We might have been visiting Mum now if it wasn't for him. For her sake, let's start the rest of our lives now, from this moment on. Agreed?'

'Agreed.'

They drove on in companionable silence for a few minutes. 'I don't want to go to the George.'

'Neither do I.'

29

HELEN DREW INTO Albermarle Street, her mother at her side. She had grown used to its wretched appearance in her frequent visits, but as Agnes tut-tutted beside her, she registered anew the enormous project the restoration programme would be.

'So this is what all the fuss is about. I can see how the developers were having their own way.'

'But it was the developers who helped to create this barren landscape. It's only Nicholas and a handful of neighbours who've held out against them.' She manoeuvred the car through the beer bottles and litter. 'I'm so nervous. I hope they're not in,' she said as she stopped the car outside number forty-one.

'Fine thing to say when they're expecting us. I'll stay put until you want me,' Agnes said, patting Helen's knee.

Nicholas's door opened as Helen climbed out. She knew her birth mother immediately. Marjorie was tall, like herself, slim and elegant. No wonder Nicholas had acted strangely when he first met her. It was like looking in a mirror.

'Helen?' Marjorie stepped towards her.

'Hello,' Helen said, taking the outstretched hands. There was a moment's awkwardness. 'Can I call you Marjorie?' She searched the face that she had so often thought of and saw the beautiful tear-filled eyes, the lines and creases around them only serving to enhance the beauty of her natural mother. She put her arms around Marjorie and held her, feeling the pain coursing from her birth mother, informing her of suffering and loss.

'Helen, dear Helen, I have longed for this moment.' Marjorie continued to hold her as if she would never let go. 'I want to know every detail of your life, but what I need to know most of all is if you have been happy.'

'I think you might recognise the person who has been a wonderful mother to me.' She gently released herself from Marjorie's arms and went to open the passenger door to help Agnes out.

Nicholas appeared beside Marjorie, a lopsided grin on his face. 'The kettle's on if everyone would like to come inside,' he announced before disappearing again.

Agnes reached up to kiss Marjorie's cheek. 'Look at you. I wouldn't have known you from the memory I have of you. You see what a wonderful girl you gave birth to? Now, did someone mention a cup of tea? Where's the kitchen?'

Helen and Marjorie smiled as they followed Agnes's bustling form into the house.

—◈—

Marjorie's heart was filled with emotion. Here was her first child sitting poised and relaxed in the chair before her. She had last seen her as a tiny infant clinging to life, and it was hard for her to think that this beautiful, healthy-looking girl was one and the same being. She had given up her baby, and it was the loss of a baby that had splintered her heart into shards of pain. It was the image of Helen as a baby that was seared into her memory. Now, as she looked at Helen in wonder, she found it difficult to bring the baby and the adult into one. She thought it would be easy; after all, Sally was just three years younger, so she knew about daughters. She thought of Sally and their easy relationship and how Sally would love Helen as a sister; but again, they hadn't grown up together with shared experiences that sisters would normally have.

Agnes is Helen's real mother, she thought with clarity as a new sense of loss layered on top of the old. Agnes was the one who had nurtured her child, who had mothered her, shared all the delights and dilemmas of her childhood. She was the one who Helen had relied on to be there at all times, to soothe the tears, plaster the cuts, to answer all her questions, to tell and to share stories. They had a shared history that she would never have access to.

What could she offer Helen except her own pain? Was that fair to her? Helen had grown up in a loving community, adored and cherished by all who came into contact with her. She would never understand the sordid surroundings of her conception, nor should she have to. This beautiful young woman shouldn't be contaminated by her own experiences, she resolved. She smoothed her skirt over her knees. *I don't know where to begin*, she thought. *I don't know you.*

'It'll take time for us to get to know one another,' Helen said as if reading her mind. 'I've thought about meeting you for so long, but it's difficult to know where to begin, isn't it?

'Yes, it is,' she acknowledged. *Is it because I can see Max in Helen, in the turn of the head, the thick, straight hair, the self-assuredness?* she wondered.

'Do I remind you of my father?' Helen asked.

It caught her off guard. 'A little bit,' she admitted. 'The good bits,' she added quickly.

'My father is Max Baines.' It was a statement, not a question.

Marjorie nodded, looking into her daughter's eyes, hating to admit that Max had any connection to her. Helen suddenly leapt up and came to sit beside her.

'I know he's a bastard,' she said, resting her hand lightly on Marjorie's arm, 'and I don't suppose he was any different when he was younger.'

'Yes, he was a bastard then.' She put her hand over Helen's and at last felt a strong connection to her, her vision blurring as she fell in love with her adult daughter.

Agnes came into the living room carrying a tray, Nicholas following with a teapot. 'Now this is nice and cosy,' she declared.

Marjorie didn't know if Agnes was referring to the room or to Helen and herself sitting side by side in tears, sharing a packet of tissues.

'Nicholas has been telling me that you're taking over your father's business, Marjorie.'

'What?' Helen didn't disguise her astonishment. 'Are you really?' she asked Marjorie delightedly, her eyes shining.

'Yes, I am.' Marjorie laughed, wiping her tears away. 'Dad's handing the lot over to me, and I intend to keep it going. I'll need lots of help, but I think I can do it.'

'That means you can put in a tender for Albermarle…if that's what you want,' Helen added deferentially.

'I want that more than anything else, apart from being with the people I love and care for.'

'Nicholas, this is a dream come true.' Helen got up to pour the tea. 'I'm dying to see the plans, Marjorie, and now you can see the whole project through. I'd love to help.'

She's completely at home here, Marjorie thought as she watched her daughter move around. No wonder Nicholas has been so enchanted with her, her enthusiasm and radiance lighting up Auntie Ollie's house, giving strength to everyone around her. She's pulling us all in the right direction; everything is going to be all right. She felt herself relax and began to enjoy her daughter.

She became aware of Agnes watching her. 'Thank you,' she said to this angel who had stepped in to guard her child as if she were her own. Her family had grown in numbers: Helen of course, but Agnes also. A bond had been created when she had first met her all those years ago; she had acted as a mother to her then and even now. That is how she considered Agnes—a mother to them all.

'Perhaps one day you might want to visit me at the convent?'

'I'd love to. I'd also like you to meet Sally; she's coming tomorrow.'

'Sally? My sister, Sally, is coming tomorrow?' Helen's face lit up. 'I can't wait! Are you taking Sally to see your exhibition, Nicholas? Or should I call you Uncle Nicholas from now on?'

'You can call me what you like, Helen, but I prefer plain old Nicholas.' He put his arm round her shoulder. 'We were thinking of going up to the house on Wednesday. Marjorie hasn't been there either. Do you want to come with us?'

'I for one would love to see your work, Nicholas. What time shall we meet there?' Agnes asked innocently.

Marjorie noticed alarm register on Helen's face.

'Come on, Helen, let's make a day of it. His Lordship's brother is probably in London during the week. We'll just go as tourists like everyone else,' Nicholas said.

30

THE EXHIBITION HAD been a great success, firmly placed on the map of places to visit in the area. Nicholas had said that busloads of people were paying to look at his paintings. Helen had thought he was exaggerating, but as she and Agnes passed through the gated entrance to drive up to Milford House, she saw that Nicholas had indeed been right. On both sides of the drive, several coaches were parked parallel to one another in amongst cars in what seemed to be a packed car park. They followed the arrows into a newly gravelled area and found a space in the shadow of a gaudily coloured coach advertising Supa Valu Day Trips.

'Very classy,' Agnes said, making Helen laugh for the first time that morning.

'That's more like it. Let's just concentrate on meeting your new sister and getting to know Marjorie better. Forget about that young upstart Roderick; he doesn't deserve you if he can't think of you as his equal. Little pipsqueak,' she added, indignation in her voice.

'I wonder what he will think when he learns who my father is.'

'I think it might be too much information for him, Helen,' Agnes said as she linked arms with her daughter. 'Don't go too fast, all this gravel is leaping into my shoes.'

'They've worked really hard to get this up and running in such a short time,' Helen said as they unhurriedly passed a sign for a tea shop with a finger pointing in the direction of the old stables.

A banner reading 'Nicholas Baines' had been hung above the entrance of the house, and underneath it stood a group of people waving towards them. Helen waved back, making out Nicholas, Marjorie, and three other people, one a young woman about her own age hand in hand with a tall, slim man. Slightly behind them, she could make out another man. She saw him break away and make his way down the steps before running towards them. A collection of tourists passed them, blocking her view.

'Is it Roderick?'

'I don't know. It could be Jeremy.'

'Whoever it is, he's pleased to see you.'

'Helen,' Jeremy shouted, beaming, as he emerged from the group, 'how good to see you.' Relief and happiness flooded through her as he put his cheek next to hers, lingering a moment. 'And you must be Sister Agnes,' he said warmly, kissing her on both cheeks. 'I'm Jeremy. Welcome to Milford House,' he said, taking her mother's other arm as if it were the most natural thing in the world. 'Helen, why don't you go ahead and meet your sister?'

Helen hesitated, torn between wanting to look after Agnes and longing to meet Sally and to see Marjorie again.

'I'm in very good hands, Helen. Go on. Jeremy and I will just take our time.'

'After the gallery, maybe you would like to see the gardens,' she heard Jeremy say as she started to walk, then jog towards the house, running up the steps into the arms of her new family.

She liked Sally immediately, a quieter, more restful person than herself, more contained, with neat features and neat clothes. Her only nod to flamboyance was her thick chestnut hair, cut to chin length but having a life of its own as if it were rebelling against the orderliness of its owner. Her soft but clear voice had a quiet authority. *Probably developed from her years of teaching in a junior school*, Helen thought. They were very different, but as she hugged her new sister, she knew that they could be friends; she could imagine being able to share confidences and being able to trust her.

'This is my husband, Tom,' Sally said with an unmistakeable note of pride.

'I'm really pleased to meet you,' he said as he shook hands and pecked her cheek. 'Sally's been jumping up and down, waiting for this day.'

'Me too.' Helen laughed as she turned to Marjorie to give her a tight hug while Nicholas looked on with satisfaction written across his face, as if he had designed this family tableau and was pleased with the result.

Agnes and Jeremy joined them, and there were introductions made again, Agnes in her black and white, an incongruous figure being welcomed into the circle. Helen caught Jeremy's eye, and she found herself smiling foolishly at him, her happiness extended to include him.

A crowd gathered around Nicholas as they entered the gallery. Amidst squeals and cries of delight, he began to sign outstretched catalogues as though he had been doing so for years, not just a few weeks. Jeremy took Helen's arm while they waited for him. She couldn't resist looking round to see if Roderick was there too.

'We'll do the tour while you wait for Nicholas,' Agnes called to them as Sally, Tom, and Marjorie sauntered past them into the gallery, already captivated by the exhibition. She began gesturing excitedly as if giving the others a lesson in art appreciation, which she probably was, Helen thought, as the small group dutifully listened to her mother.

'Roderick's in London during the week, now that the exhibition is established,' Jeremy said.

'Thank you for telling me.' Had he sensed her anxiety? She was grateful that he had seemed to understand her dilemma without her having to explain. She looked up into the kind face, so like Roderick in appearance, but a different character altogether. She couldn't imagine Roderick embracing her family in such a welcoming way. Indeed, he had let her know that he would never do so. Compassion came naturally to Jeremy, and she had been impressed with his patience with Miranda.

'How is Miranda?'

'It's difficult to tell. It's been tough for her withdrawing from the drugs she was taking, but Nancy and David Kerr have been very supportive and encouraging. She's now talking of training for something and getting a job. It would have been anathema to her only a few weeks ago, but...' He paused as though hesitant about sharing his thoughts. He drew her away from any listening ears. 'I'm still very worried about her. Sometimes I catch her with tears pouring down her cheeks as though she has been saving them up for years.'

'She probably has,' Helen said gently.

'David Kerr suggested a residential rehabilitation centre where she could receive counselling while she withdraws from the drugs. It seems it would be the most effective treatment for her, but she has refused, saying that she needs to be at home. I have to be in London tomorrow. The staff have promised to keep a watchful eye over her until Roderick gets here later in the day. We try to be here as often as we can, but still...' He looked around the room as though seeking answers.

'Has she friends she can turn to?'

'She has old school friends who all seem to be in London. I've suggested she stays with Roderick and me in the London house, but again she has refused, saying she needs to be here.'

'I wonder why she feels that way?'

'I don't know. I really don't know.'

'If I can do anything, please ask.'

'Thank you, I will.'

She felt that their friendship had been cemented. Sharing his concern for Miranda had crossed the line of acquaintance to a deeper level of understanding, bringing with it a not-unwelcome fondness for this thoughtful man by her side.

They stood in comfortable silence, watching the scrum of visitors still wanting Nicholas's signature.

'I hope the meeting goes well tomorrow. You must feel very proud of Marjorie.'

'Yes I do. I'm looking forward to getting to know her better and of course Sally. It is a very odd mixture of belonging to them but not knowing them. We can't re-create the past, but we can make a good future together. I'm sure it will have its problems, but there's such a lot of goodwill that we will all make it work. My natural father is another matter. You know who he is, don't you?'

'Yes, Nicholas told me. I think he wanted me to absorb the information before I saw you again. I hope you don't mind my knowing.'

'No, it makes it easier. I'm glad you heard it from Nicholas. I feel so ashamed; being part of him makes me want to compensate for his appalling behaviour.'

'Helen, you are not connected to him other than sharing some genes, and can I suggest that you have inherited a fine set of genes, even if some of them are from Max Baines.'

His kindness was almost overwhelming, and she fought off the tears of relief. She felt Jeremy squeeze her arm, but she didn't trust herself to speak for a few moments.

She saw Nicholas about to be inundated by more fans. 'Shall we rescue Nicholas before another group comes in?' she suggested.

'Good idea. I shall leave you to enjoy your family, but perhaps I can persuade you to have some tea in our newly designated drawing room next to the kitchen when you've finished in the gallery? I also promised your mother a walk round the rose garden if she has time.'

'That's very kind of you, but you don't have to go to all this trouble.'

'It's no trouble, my dear Helen,' he said softly.

She and Nicholas joined the others, who were absorbed in the exhibition. She was right about her mother; she was making a fine job of being a tour guide; her knowledge of painting technique, perspective, and form was impressive. Where and when she had learned this, Helen didn't know, but she felt an enormous pride in her mother's knowledge. Nicholas too became an observer of his own paintings. *It is like a play or a book*, Helen thought. There can be so many interpretations that it takes on a life of its own; it doesn't belong to the writer anymore but becomes public property, open to new ideas as to its meaning and significance. So it was with Nicholas's paintings; separated from their owner, they were now in the public domain, open to new insights. Nicholas seemed to be totally absorbed.

She turned her attention to Marjorie and Sally as they listened attentively; they both had a quiet demeanour, leaning towards each other occasionally, checking the catalogue listing, and making the occasional comment. She felt a pang of jealousy, thinking that it should have been her with her natural mother. She tuned into Agnes's lilting Irish voice, which sent a warm glow through her, seeing her bringing her family—new and old—together. Marjorie and her mother were so different, and yet they both had qualities she admired: admired in Marjorie but adored in her mother.

Tom too was listening but seemed to be less absorbed, looking around at his surroundings. She caught his eye and smiled, understanding that perhaps art exhibitions were not his favourite pastime. He joined her.

'Our families have grown,' he observed. 'It is such a pleasure for Sally and I to have you all in our lives.' He turned to Nicholas, who had peeled away from the family group as Agnes led the way into the next room as if she knew exactly where she was going. 'I was thinking that you may want some help with accounting.'

'I've been told I need an accountant, Tom, but I haven't given it a thought. It would be great if you could help. I haven't a clue about that stuff.'

'Perhaps we can get together in the coming weeks and see what your needs will be.'

'Smashing, any time.'

'Marjorie might also need some help now that she's taking over Baines and Baines,' Helen said.

'My firm is already looking at the books, which are proving to be an interesting case of creative accounting.'

'That's a nice way of putting it; wholesale plunder of a town would be more honest,' Nicholas said.

'Mrs Willis is determined to change the image of the company, and of course it will start with tomorrow's meeting when she gives her presentation. She holds all the cards in her hands, so her ideas should prevail. Her plans are based on a sound financial basis, will benefit the community immediately in and around the Albermarle area, and will bring in revenue to the town through tourism.' Tom had turned into an accountant again. His business manner was impressive.

'I can't wait to see Ron Thompson's reaction when he finds out,' Helen said with a note of glee in her voice. 'He's the town planner,' she explained to Tom. 'He thinks he has it all stitched up.'

'There's going to be a lot of disgruntled folk who will see their bribe money coming to a sudden stop,' Nicholas commented.

'Nicholas, you have real talent,' Agnes said without preamble as she, Sally, and Marjorie joined them. 'I often wondered where Helen got her artistic talent from, and now I know it runs in the family.'

'Jeremy has offered tea in the drawing room. Are we ready to join him?' Helen asked the group before a discussion about her minor forays into painting were enlarged upon. 'May I?' she asked Marjorie as she offered her arm.

The rest of the afternoon was spent in pleasant conversation, with Jeremy asking lots of questions about everyone, making them all feel comfortable as they got to know one another. *He's like an angel, helping us to negotiate this difficult road*, Helen thought as the afternoon sun dipped behind the great trees in the park. They were walking in the gardens, and she was feeling tired and knew that the others must be too.

'Jeremy, thank you so much for a wonderful day,' she said as they reached the steps leading up to the house.

'It's been a great pleasure to have spent time with your family. Marjorie's ideas are an inspiration, almost a throwback in time when benevolence was a trademark of being civilised.'

'It appears that I've been lucky with both my mothers.'

'You have a precious family, Helen.' He took both of her hands into his own. 'Come again soon, won't you?' He kissed her on the cheek.

She felt very happy as he shook hands with everyone and they said their farewells.

'What an angel,' Agnes declared, echoing her thoughts as they sauntered down the drive behind her new family. 'I think he's soft on you.'

'No, I think we have found a friend in each other, that's all.'

'Really, is that what you call it nowadays?'

31

THE SCHOOL HALL was packed with those who hadn't managed to get seats standing in ever-increasing numbers around the periphery. The Baines family was out in force. Helen sat between Sally and Nicholas and Tom next to Agnes, who had delayed her departure, saying she wouldn't miss it for the world. The Kerrs were next to George Thomas with Marjorie taking the aisle seat beside him.

Ron Thompson was to give a presentation to the audience first and was already on the stage with a projector and a pile of plans and transparencies next to it on a table. The hall hushed as he tested the microphone: one two, one two three. He looked confident and had said in the press that the public meeting was just a formality.

He cleared his throat, and the hall fell completely silent. 'Ladies and gentlemen,' he began. 'We are here today to look at the plans for the redevelopment of the Albermarle district. As you know, the streets are a disgrace to our town, and for several months now, we have been working on a plan to raze

the existing houses and replace them with a modern development fit for the needs of the town.

'We have had several tenders for the building of these new
homes, but of course it is our very own Baines and Baines that
has come through with a sensible cost for the scheme, and despite the unfortunate temporary indisposition of the owner,
Max Baines, we believe that Baines and Baines will fulfil its
promise to the town and deliver a first-rate product.

'The plans of course include the demolition of the unsight-
ly wharf buildings we have lived with for so long. Having been
empty for years, they are a magnet for rats, and the health of
our local population is at risk if we continue to let them stand.

'Now, if I can draw your attention to my first drawing…'

Helen had to admit that he was doing a good job and
wondered if their counterargument would hold sway. He was
smooth and slick in his delivery as he displayed pretty pictures
of houses with children playing outside on the grassed areas.
Fully grown trees dotted the ground, giving shade to seats
where a couple sat reading the papers while their baby slept
in its pram. Cars were parked in neat driveways; neighbours
hailed each other across the picket fence as they tended to their
gardens. It was an idyll that would be hard to beat, and she felt
nervous for Marjorie. Could she pull this off?

'Finally, as you know, there has been some opposition to
the scheme, and that is why we are here today—to let reason prevail. I am your friend. I am on your side. Most of you
know me as Ron, and I believe you know that I have the town's

interest at heart. I must emphasise that the council is listening and doing its best to make the right decision for the future of the town and the district, taking into account a wide range of evidence as well as the views of the public.'

'That's right, Ron, you tell 'em,' a voice called out.

Helen looked round and saw a group of leather-jacketed individuals holding up a banner with RON THOMPSON FOR MAYOR blazoned across it.

'Do we have a mayor?' Nicholas leaned across Helen to ask David Kerr.

'Not now, but clearly he wants to create the position for himself.'

'Of course we will hear the opposition group's argument with interest.' He paused for his followers to laugh at the thought of any opposition. 'We live in a democracy, and it is our duty to listen to them, but you will find their reasons for opposing the council's plan weak, without an alternative viable solution.'

He looked pleased with himself as he said, 'I think there is a Mrs Marjorie Willis who wishes to speak. I'm sure this won't take too long,' he sneered.

There was hearty applause from one side of the hall, which continued for far too long, Helen thought. She felt concern for Marjorie, who was gathering her things together and approaching the stage. With a nod to Ron Thompson as though telling him that 'it is my turn now, so get off the stage,' she opened her computer and connected it to the projector screen.

She appeared calm and fully in control as she faced the audience. 'Ladies and gentlemen.' She waited for silence before continuing. 'Many of you may not know me, but some may remember that Ernest Baines had two children, Nicholas and Marjorie. I am Marjorie.'

Murmurs of recognition ran through the hall.

'I have returned to Middleston after an absence of over twenty-five years. As you know, my brother Nicholas has been recognised as a painter of some stature, painting local scenes and in particular, scenes around the Albermarle area. Over the years he has captured on canvas the decline of the area; a decline he knew was not brought about voluntarily but by the manipulation and greed of our father and Max Baines.'

A burst of chatter ran through the hall as if everyone were asking whether they had heard correctly.

'This area used to have a strong community, a community which was vibrant and caring. A community that pulled together and had grown in strength because it was a good place to live. You may remember the street parties, the may-pole dancing on the green, neighbours sitting out on summer evenings telling stories of the old days. You may remember The Albermarle Arms, our local pub on the corner, inviting whole families in because at one time they had the only television in the street.' She paused to allow the picture of the old days to be rekindled in the public's memory before continuing. 'You also may remember the fires and the council kindly buying up the burned-out shells from landlords for peanuts. You may remember the playground now used as an overnight parking lot for buses and the green now used as a council dumping ground.' She looked across at where Ron Thompson was sitting and held his gaze.

Helen saw Ron Thompson shift in his chair and look down at his papers. She was not the only one; most of the audience was looking his way.

'I am here to right the wrong done to this community in the name of progress.'

Helen listened to her birth mother in awe as point by point, she built up her argument for the preservation of the area and the reasons why they should not accept the so-called affordable housing scheme. She brought up a map of the area showing the canal basin and the probable reasons behind the scheme. 'These are not going to be affordable houses,' she said. 'These homes are for those who can buy in to the larger scheme, which includes the clearing of the basin and the development of the area as a high-cost residential area where those who can afford it will keep their boats.

'I suppose you are wondering how we can counter Ron Thompson's proposal and make it a scheme to benefit all the people of Middleston, not just the chosen few? Here are my plans.'

One by one, she brought up on the screen the alternative plans, which included the wharf buildings as an arts centre, a tourist centre, a restaurant, and shops. She had illustrated the canal basin so that it was bobbing with colourful boats with pedestrian walkways and cafes on its banks. She walked everyone through the 3-D images, making the scheme alive and tangible.

'So how can the town afford to do this?' Marjorie surveyed her audience as if savouring the moment. 'As a result of criminal charges being brought against Max Baines for drug dealing, extortion, money laundering, and running a prostitution ring, my father has asked me to take over Baines and Baines.'

'That can't be right!' Ron Thompson stood up and shouted out. 'Max would never allow that to happen. He promised me—'

'What did he promise you, Mr Thompson?' Marjorie coolly asked. 'A slice of the profits maybe? Support in your becoming mayor?' She laughed at the group holding up the banner. 'Really, Mr Thompson, you are rather too transparent.'

Laughter rippled through the hall. Everyone seemed to be enjoying the scene, especially the press photographers snapping away. Helen felt a tap on her shoulder. It was Steve Brown. 'Now I know where you get your belligerence from,' he said before turning his attention back to Marjorie, who was holding her audience in the palm of her hand.

'Again, how can the town afford this? Where will the money come from?' She left her questions hanging in the air. Helen thought of the proverbial pin being dropped as the audience waited for her to reply to her rhetorical question.

'From Baines and Baines,' she declared. 'It is Baines and Baines that has destroyed the area, and under my ownership, it will be Baines and Baines that restores it. I will right the wrongs done in this town and bring back decency and account-ability to the people of Middleston.

'The schemes submitted by Baines and Baines under my leadership will be scored against strict, preset criteria, including quality and sympathy with the surrounding envi-ronment, and they will satisfy the council's non-negotiable terms. At all stages the views of the public will be taken into consideration. This will involve exhibitions of models and ar-chitects' drawings to enable detailed scrutiny and comment on the design.

'My brother, Nicholas, and my family fully support me in this venture, and I sincerely hope that you will support our proposal. Thank you.'

Marjorie stepped down from the stage amidst a stand-ing ovation. Only those near Ron Thompson started to leave, pushing cameras out of their way as they exited the hall. Helen watched as her mother was surrounded by well-wish-ers, feeling extraordinary admiration for this woman who had given birth to her. She saw George Thomas make his way to Marjorie's side as if to protect her from the crowds gather-ing around.

Sally took her hand and squeezed it. 'I never knew our mother had this in her.' She laughed.

Our mother, Sally had said. She turned and hugged her sister. 'I feel very proud of her too.' As she sat companion-ably with Sally, she saw a black leather–clad figure tap Ron Thompson's shoulder and whisper into his ear. Thompson leapt to his feet as if glad of an excuse to get out of the hall. Steve

Brown, notebook in hand, seizing his chance for an interview, blocked his path. Thompson raised his fist as if to strike but instead thrust his hand into Steve's chest, knocking him aside, before pushing the swing doors open and disappearing into the night.

32

MIRANDA WAS THINKING with clarity for the first time since her mother's death. She remembered her sweet mother succumbing to breast cancer and her father's grief, but she hadn't registered, let alone recognised, the full depth of her own feelings about the loss of her mother until now. Her father's death and the part she had played in it had unlocked the door to the area of her heart that had been inaccessible for all these years.

Put on a brave face and get on with the job was her father's mantra to her, reinforced by Roddy's clipped remarks about how boarding school would help her to get over their mother's death. She remembered Jeremy giving her an unexpected hug but otherwise being completely silent on the subject of life without their mother. No wonder she didn't know her feelings. A picture formed in her mind of a small rudderless boat trying to survive in heavy seas. Confusion in a world without her mother had crowded out sensible thought, but now she had a plan.

Being packed off to boarding school at thirteen, she had successfully buried the ache in her heart beneath new friendships and the buzz of high jinks and pranks that constantly put her in the principal's office to account for her behaviour. She couldn't explain why she was not like the girls who got their kicks out of studying hard and getting good grades. Over and over, Mrs Howard would ask her kindly how an intelligent girl like her could waste her time with such nonsense. She couldn't give a plausible answer because she didn't have one. In the last few weeks, she had come to realise that the constant activity and mischief were worth being hauled up before Mrs Howard and ticked off because of the kindness shown to her. In that room she felt close to her mother again.

She had acted in the same way to get her father's attention when she had left school, but this time the stakes had been higher, the games more dangerous, and the consequence worse. It was not a fifteen-minute chat in the principal's office but the death of her beloved father. She had seen the way Roddy looked at her with a mixture of incomprehension and loathing. Yes, he tried to cover his true feelings with platitudes that failed to convince her that she was, in his opinion, the creature that had brought the family into disrepute, killed their father, and been instrumental in bringing the family fortune crashing down. Nicholas Baines's exhibition had been a lifesaver, but was it enough to reverse their fortunes? Enough to keep the house but not enough for Roddy.

Jeremy was different. His compassion and pity for her were genuine, but his sympathy for her only highlighted how far she had brought the family down. All his kind words could not take away the disgust she felt for herself. It would never get better; what was done was done; she couldn't change the past, but she could change the future. Without her as a constant reminder of her evil nature, both her brothers would be better off. They could draw a line over the past and work on their future without the encumbrance of their little sister.

She had needed to be at home close to where all her good memories were—to savour them, to treasure them, and to lock them in her heart forever before she left for good.

The rat poison had been easy to obtain and the dosage dangerous to human health easily exceeded. Posted this morning, the carefully labelled parcel addressed to Her Majesty's Prison enclosing a lovesick letter to Max had given her huge satisfaction. The letter of apology, explaining her actions to Jeremy and Roddy, was on her dressing table. Jeremy had caught the early train to London, and Roddy wasn't expected back until late evening. Perfect timing.

Telling the hovering figure of Roberts, who was pretending to adjust the ornaments in the hall, that she was having an early night, she made her way up the stairs. Out of sight, she continued past her bedroom and opened the narrow door with stairs leading up to the servants' quarters. Their doors were closed as expected; the staff gathered in their television room, watching the final episode of a serial. She tiptoed along the corridor until she reached the wooden stairs leading to the kitchen. Below her the sturdy table and chairs were lit by an outside lamp, the corners of the room unexplored by the diffused glow. She opened the kitchen door and let herself out into the night.

She drew up outside the school hall, and with relief, she saw Benny leaning up against the wall, smoking as usual, the rolled-up cigarette pinched between finger and thumb as though he were sipping tea from a porcelain cup. She knew Ron would be there. Benny was his sidekick.

'Benny.'

He didn't move. She produced a five-pound note and waved it at him. He stubbed his cigarette underfoot, taking his time to grind it into the pavement before dawdling over to her. She watched this slime ball with disgust; she had been a willing participant in this world of sleaze, but now she saw only the sordidness of this wretched creature.

She waved the note in his face as he leant into her car. 'This is yours if you fetch Ron. Tell him I'm feeling hot.'

He leered at her. 'I could help you with your hot pants, Mandy.'

He was no James Dean. 'Don't be silly; just get Ron, or you won't get your money.'

She kept the engine running as he slouched off into the building, defeat written across his shoulders. If she switched the engine off, she might change her mind. She knew her drug-free resolution was precarious, and she didn't want anything to interfere with it.

She didn't have long to wait. Ron burst out of the building and jumped in beside her.

'Jesus, Miranda. Am I glad to see you.'

Benny appeared, and she thrust the crumpled money into his hand before revving up the engine, Ron's hand already creeping up her leg. Why she had never felt repulsed by him before was bewildering. *That's right, Ron, run your hand up my thigh.* With care, she drove the car through the streets of Middleston before accelerating when she hit the road leading to open countryside. She had studied the map, driven her route, and was confident, even though the night was closing in, that she could find her spot.

'Where are we going, Mandy?'

'I've found a great place. You'll love it.'

'God, I need a good fuck after that bloody awful meeting. I'm finished, Mandy. Fucking finished.'

Not quite, she thought.

'Unless Max can weave his magic and buy his way out of jail, I'm done for. This bloody woman turns up, turns out she's old man Baines's long-lost daughter. Since when did he have a daughter? He'd never spoken about her. Anyway, she turns up and says she's the boss now. Going to put right the wrongs of yours truly. I'm finished. Bloody Max is safe in prison. I'm going to be skinned alive.'

She half-listened to his ramblings, most of his words whipped away by the wind. Thankfully, he had forgotten about her thigh. She couldn't make sure of Max but smiled at the thought of him gorging on the chocolate-slathered cake and the poison eating him away, thinning his blood. She imagined him refusing to share, taking it to his cell and dying a painful death, unable to call for help.

She had the neatly folded newspaper report of his arrest in her bag. She had memorised it, distaste for herself, wanting to have it on her person as a reminder of how bad she was.

RACKETEER ARRESTED, screamed the headline.

Max Baines is arrested on charges of drug dealing, extortion, people smuggling, and running a string of houses used for prostitution. The Zanzibar Club, owned by Max Baines, was raided by police on Tuesday evening. Evidence was gathered which puts him squarely behind a substantial operation involving corrupt local police and officials. Further incriminating evidence in the form of illegal drugs was discovered in a heavily padlocked garden shed at his home in a prestigious residential area on the outskirts of the city.

A well-known figure in the city, Max Baines built up his business empire on the proceeds of Baines and Baines, the well-known construction company where he is a major shareholder, the other major shareholder being Ernest Baines, who has been living in an old people's home for the last two years and who is believed no longer to be active in the company.

Further arrests are expected.

An article on the effects on individuals, property, and community, of racketeers like Max Baines, had followed, written by Steve Brown, who was the only person who had made her laugh in years. If it hadn't been for the pimples, she might well have fancied him.

Ron was still ranting on about the injustice of it all—the petulance in his voice rising above the wind and engine noise—about Marjorie Baines resurfacing, not only taking over Baines and Baines but also quashing all his carefully laid-out plans to make a mint.

'Max will be out soon,' he declared, as if trying to reassure himself that this nightmare was an aberration of the normal state of affairs he had grown used to.

Greed. She had been greedy too, but for attention. At what point would she have taken responsibility for her own life if her father had lived? Well, she was taking responsibility now, she thought, as she accelerated into the hills, leaving the last houses behind.

'Bloody hell. What are you doing?' It seemed Ron only now had noticed his surroundings as her car rounded tight bends, her headlights searching the hills, her tyres complaining as they gripped the road at high speed, the darkness descending on them like a heavy blanket. His hands gripped the dashboard. She saw his feet pressing imaginary brake pedals. She laughed at his fear as the wind tore through her hair.

'Slow down. You're going to kill us,' he yelled, the fear in his voice spurring her on.

She was close now. The lone tree was her landmark. She passed it with relief, knowing that the end was near. A sharp bend was indicated which gave her the signal to press her foot down to the floor. Ron screamed, a piercing, shrill cry that echoed her adult life. *It's just like flying*, she thought, as relief and peace swept through her.

—m—

The funeral took place at the picturesque Norman church in the village two miles from Milford House. It was a quiet affair. A tragic road accident was the official cause of death, but most mourners knew otherwise. They kept up the pretence, however, for the sake of appearances. No one wanted to remind Jeremy and Roderick at this awful time why their sister had taken her own life; the fact that she was dead was enough pain to deal with.

Along with Nicholas and the Kerrs, Helen sat behind the chief mourners. She felt stunned and helpless at the tragic turn of events. She knew that Jeremy was blaming himself for leaving the morning of Miranda's death; that Roberts was grief-stricken at not being more vigilant; that Roderick was feeling guilty at not returning sooner and not realising she wasn't in the house until the following morning, when the police knocked on the door to deliver the news.

Steve Brown was hunched over in the opposite pew, an ill-fitting grey suit swallowing his thin frame, a dirty handkerchief pressed into his hand which he used alternately to dab his eyes and blow his nose. At this moment she felt very fond of him, knowing that he too took part in the blame. She had tried to console him in the last few days, but he insisted on being instrumental in Max's downfall and the subsequent collapse of the house of cards; it was he who had started the process.

They knew how Miranda felt from the letter she had left in her bedroom. Jeremy had shared it with David Kerr, Steve, and herself, wanting to make some sense of his sister's suicide when her future seemed so promising. David had expressed his wretchedness at not being more persuasive about Miranda attending a residential clinic. Helen too could have been more insistent about staying with Miranda when she knew she would be in the house without her family. It seemed that they all carried some guilt at the awful turn of events.

The coffin was draped in a cloth bearing the family crest. What remained of Miranda after the fire that engulfed the car as it crashed down the hillside was an image that Helen fought to dispel. Ron Thompson had miraculously escaped certain death by being thrown out of the open-topped car, landing in a clump of heather with only a few broken bones to nurse. That Miranda had intended to kill him was clear to those closest to the family, but a tactful silence was maintained as they said their farewell to the mangled body. Steve Brown had nearly choked with laughter when he heard that a doctored cake had been sent to Max Baines. He would have liked to have done it himself, he said, only he would have made sure it got to him.

The house staff was there in the two pews in front of Steve. Miranda had been a handful in life, but that fact did not stop the flow of tears. Even the dignified figure of Roberts seemed to be crushed by the tragedy, Helen noticed, his bowed head held in his hands, as if by looking ahead at the coffin, it would confirm all that he feared.

Ahead of the Milford House staff were relatives of the family. Helen studied their aristocratic backs. Their expensive, understated clothes hung elegantly, worn with confidence and practice. She thought of her own wardrobe made up of middle-of-the-range, high-street attire and bits and bobs from second-hand–clothes stores she loved to frequent. She couldn't have lived up to this family's image; Roderick had done her a favour by rejecting her. She thought fondly of the dreams she had cherished. Such a lot had happened in her life since then that it was as though she were another person looking at a foolish child's fantasies.

She glanced round at Marjorie, who was in the pew behind her with George Thomas. These were her people—down to earth like her mother Agnes with realistic expectations of life, their dreams to suit the cut of cloth. Marjorie gave her an encouraging smile as if she had read all her thoughts. Perhaps she had; she was her natural mother, after all.

They sang the final hymn and received the blessing. Following Marjorie and George, Helen made her way out of the church.

33

MARJORIE'S TENDER FOR the Albermarle Scheme was accepted by a unanimous vote once the planning committee members realised their jobs were on the line. They followed all of her suggestions without a murmur of objection, knowing that she had all the information she wanted to bring the majority of them down if necessary. She had no intention of doing so personally, but they didn't know that. No doubt they thought she was cut from the same cloth as her father, and it was in their interests to be obedient. She wasn't about to disabuse them of their assumptions because their subservience played into her hands.

Those hands were now spreading the revised plans in front of the committee members after a period of public consultation. She was following all the planning rules and regulations to the letter, fastidious in her dealings with all concerned. Every meeting had been minuted, every proposal given serious consideration. She was delighted when the council voted to clear the basin of debris that had been dumped there over the years, saving her a considerable sum in time and money. Her plans were ambitious, and they were going to take the lion's share of the Baines and Baines reserves and borrowing power to fulfil them. She needed all the help she could get to deliver what she had promised.

'As you can see from these revised plans, we have preserved the pocket of streets closest to the canal. These will be restored, keeping the facades but updating the interiors to meet today's criteria. This one, the one closest to the old pub, will be left, acting as an extension to the museum. It is particularly interesting because the interior hasn't been updated since the mill was in use. It acts as a snapshot of life in those times. The outside privy and coal-hole are still there, as is the kitchen range, complete with the iron tub in front of it.'

She watched their faces, some feigning interest; two or three looked intrigued. She was mischievous these days, and a great sense of fun bubbled up, spilling over in the most inappropriate places. 'I know it's hard to believe that pieces of historical interest have been discovered. I have to thank you for not following my father's instructions to the letter.'

After delivering her salvo, some scribbled, some scratched, some just bowed their heads. She didn't care how they felt. Most had taken bribes in brown envelopes. She knew exactly who had accepted what and why. The information had been meticulously recorded by her father and continued by Max, kept in a log book in the company's safe. She had nothing but contempt for their duplicity in their dealings with her father. As representatives of their community, they should be shamed and held accountable. It was not her job to help them, but nevertheless she was using their compliance for her own ends. If in the process they received brownie points, then so be it. She had given the offending log book to Steve Brown, who would hand it over to the police when he had completed his trawl through the books of Baines and Baines. Tom had helped him to decipher the history of deals and point out the discrepancies. She wanted to clean up Baines and Baines before she took the company forward.

'I'm aiming for transparency in this project, and I hope that we can work together in giving the people of Middleston what they want. I appreciate your cooperation in this venture. It is a U-turn on the previous plans, but I think you will agree that the benefits outweigh all the extra work involved. It is more profitable to tear down and rebuild; restoration is always more work than starting from scratch.'

'We will need to meet several times to monitor the progress,' a young man called Guy said. 'Ron Thompson has always done that, but he will be out of action for some time with his injuries.' He was the youngest member of the committee, one of two who had not accepted a bribe in the past.

'When will Ron be back, does anyone know?' Another member had come alive.

'No one else has done this overseeing work for years,' another complained.

They are rudderless, Marjorie thought. Ron Thompson had led them into the abyss, and now he wasn't amongst them to lead them out.

'I would like to do it if no one objects,' Guy piped up. 'I have all the necessary qualifications, and I would like to have the opportunity to use them. I believe in this project,' he said, turning to Marjorie. 'I would be very happy to help you see it through.'

'We'll have to clear it with Ron.'

'Bugger Ron,' the sole lady member, Mary Baker said, the only other person in the room not to have taken a bribe. 'He's not here, and we should make the decision ourselves in his absence. Anyway, it seems he will be arrested soon because of his involvement in Max Baines's empire. I don't think we will be seeing Ron again round this table.'

'Is there anyone else who wishes to put themselves forward?' a self-elected chairperson asked. 'No? Any objections to Guy having this?' He looked around the table. 'Good, that's settled then.'

Guy turned to Marjorie. 'I took Town and Country Planning at Manchester, and we had several examples of urban regeneration projects in the area to study. As far as I was concerned, it was the most interesting part of my degree.'

Marjorie liked what she saw of him. He was young and idealistic and would have the energy to get involved in the spirit of the enterprise.

'I would appreciate your input. Thank you.'

She continued her tour of the revised plans, Guy at her elbow making notes. She then fielded questions.

'Will anyone be able to keep a boat in the yacht basin, or will it be restricted to residents in the area?' 'Will the corner shop stay?' 'Will there be sufficient parking for the residents and visitors in the high season?' 'You're asking for cobbles around the wharf buildings. Won't that be a hazard?' What about a safety barrier around the water?'

The questions kept coming for the next hour, and soon she knew that they were all, without exception, taking an interest. This was no rubber-stamping exercise; she was getting them involved, and they were taking responsibility. Perhaps they would realise that life without Ron Thompson was better.

The last question was about the new housing. 'The design of the town houses has been drawn up by my old firm of architects in Newcastle. As you can see, they have understated elegance to marry in with the existing streets. They will be built using superior materials to stand the test of time but still be affordable in the local property market.'

She saw scepticism in some faces. 'It is similar to a design that has worked well in comparable areas of regeneration further north. I'd be happy to arrange for the committee to visit to see the quality of construction and the way these houses complement the older ones.'

'Splendid idea,' Mary Baker said. 'I'll book the minibus. Shall we agree on a date now?'

She had allies on the committee. In the next few weeks, she would bring them all a 100 per cent on board with her plans. They were good, but she needed their support in dealing with all the unforeseen problems that this type of project always threw up.

A glow of pride spread through her as she thought about the last few months. It had been a roller-coaster ride from feeling utterly distraught at her not being able to feel the happiness she expected when she gained her independence, to managing her own project as owner of a building company. Her boss in Newcastle had supported her all the way, giving her confidence in her abilities and instincts. She felt heady with the freedom she had gained to make her own decisions, but she also felt a sense of responsibility to the community who had placed their trust in her. She was determined not to disappoint.

34

HAD SHE EVER spoken about her marriage like this before? It was a new experience knowing that she could trust George. She was safe, at home with him. This older George was a haven for her true self. He knew who she really was. Unaccountably, tears welled up and spilled over. George put his arm around her and drew her close, kissing her forehead. She felt engulfed by grief and happiness rolled into one. He didn't try to stop the tears. He didn't offer words but just held her close as they sat on the bank of the canal.

'What happened to your wife?' she asked to take the attention away from herself.

'There hangs a tale,' he said, standing abruptly. 'According to her, I didn't love her enough, and she may have been right. Yes, we had the lads, and that's why we stayed together for twelve years. Then she met Derek, who was crazy about her. She's really happy now, and I'm happy for her. Our lads seem to have survived it all. When they were younger, they'd spend weekends and holidays helping me out on the boat, so I saw a lot of them. Talk of the devil.'

'Dad.' A younger version of George waved from a narrow boat passing by. 'Who's your lady friend?'

'Marjorie.' He called back.

'Not *the* Marjorie,' he shouted back.

'Yes, *the* Marjorie.' George laughed.

The young man saluted Marjorie as though she were the admiral of the fleet.

She allowed herself to be pulled up, and for a moment they stood facing each other. Marjorie longed for him to kiss her. Instead he held her at arm's length and looked into her eyes with such an amused expression that she began to smile back at him. She took in his weathered face, his once rich brown hair now turning grey but still flopping into his eyes. She loved his face. 'Come on then, show me this boat of yours.'

She'd never let him kiss her on the lips, but now she was longing for his embrace. She wanted to be crushed with love. Why had she denied herself? She knew the answer, but now it all seemed very simple being with this man. That he hadn't thought any less of her she understood and believed now.

Now she stood side by side with George while he manoeuvred his thirty-foot motor boat into the main stream, taking them away from the town. A cool breeze was picking up, but the sun was strong. She felt exhilarated, full of life.

'Where are you taking me?'

'I want you to see all the improvements since you left,' he said, grinning, 'and I want to show you my other boats.'

'How many do you have?'

'I have my own fleet, my dear, an armada, all booked up this season. Look!'

On cue, they drew into a turning bay filled with canal boats all identical in colour to the one George's son had steered by. A deep green base colour was brightly decorated, some with flowers, Marjorie could see, some with birds, fish, butterflies. Each had a name; she spotted his boys' names, Nicholas's even, but three boats moored together as if sharing a bed were named *Marjorie One*, *Marjorie Two*, and *Marjorie Three*.

'What were you thinking of, George Thomas?'

'You, Marjorie, all the bloody time.' He turned to her and drew her to him, kissing her with gentleness and passion. She relaxed and returned his love, wondering at what she had been missing. What a fool she had been, but now, as she allowed herself to be wrapped yet more tightly in George Thomas's embrace, she knew she was where she belonged.

—∞—

She listened to the water lapping the side of the boat as it rocked to and fro on its mooring, the reflection dancing on the ceiling as the morning sun streamed into the window. It matched her mood as she lay in George's arms, which were holding her tight. She closed her eyes again to savour the moment, to let the love she felt for him course through her mind and body. It had all seemed so natural when she had given herself freely for the first time in her life. So this was making love. The fierce desire that had gripped them both, sending them on a tangled route of exploration and wonder, had given way to a gentle coming together in the early hours of the morning as if to cement their union for the future. She wanted to sear these last hours into her memory.

'Are you awake?'

'Yes. I'm just treasuring the moment. I don't want to let it go in case I can't get it back.'

'We've missed out on a few years, my dearest, but I hope we can have many moments like this. Will you marry me?'

'Yes.'

Epilogue

Two Years Later

MARJORIE SLIPPED THE line and pressed hard on the dock with her foot to ease the narrow boat off its dock. She coiled the rope on the deck of *Marjorie Two* before joining George at the helm. It would take twenty minutes to reach the yacht basin, twenty minutes to savour the moment.

'We're on our way, my darling,' George called to her.

A great rush of happiness swept over her as she turned to him. How she loved this man who adored her in a way she had never thought possible, who had supported her throughout the project, who had helped steer her through the minefield of local politics, and all with good humour. *This is my husband*, she thought with wonder for the millionth time since their wedding.

Her life had returned to its original course, taking up the baton as if the last twenty-eight years had been a diversion. If only she hadn't been so enamoured with Max all those years ago…And yet she wouldn't have Sally, and she wouldn't have Helen. How could she wish for her life to be different? Life had thrown her off course, but looking back now, what would she change? She would change the crushing shame that had prevented her from telling those people who loved her about Helen, but times were different then. Girls were supposed to disappear until they had got rid of the problem of having a child outside marriage. Admitting to George that she was not the nice girl he thought she was had been impossible. She couldn't do it even though over the two years after she had given birth to Helen, she knew she loved him. She had let Jack take her away rather than admit that she was dirty and soiled.

Having Helen back in her life had been the most precious gift she had ever received. Far from keeping her existence quiet, she wanted to shout it from the rooftops for everyone to hear. This is Helen, my other beautiful daughter, she told everyone now without a hint of shame or regret. Her cowering in the dark and nursing her secrets had evaporated since her marriage. If only she had been able to talk about it all those years ago. But life is full of *if only*s, she had decided, and it was pointless to let past mistakes or errors of judgement cloud the present when you were using the only tools you had at the time. She felt compassion for her younger self, as if she were another person who needed her love. Loving who she was had been her greatest achievement, along with realising her potential at last. She had thrown every ounce of energy and creativity into the restoration of the wharf and the development of the new housing where the old mill had stood. Now as they neared the pristine yacht basin, she felt light-headed with pride.

She could see the crowd gathered on the newly extended dock. She waved to all the people who had come for the opening of her project, and they in turn shouted and cheered as George guided the first pleasure boat into the new marina. A light breeze brushed her face as she took in the sight ahead of her. The restored wharf buildings were just beautiful, gracing the scene enfolding before them. The stone had been pointed and cleaned, new bespoke wooden windows installed, an exact replica of the old door made, and beside it a plaque which at this moment was covered in ceremonial curtains ready for the official opening.

Nicholas was waiting to help secure the boat. He had become quite adept at helping George, their old friendship renewed. His face was tanned, and he looked strong and healthy, having taken to messing around in boats with surprising enthusiasm. He had abandoned his post office round when his paintings were commanding ever higher prices. He had become quite a celebrity in Middleston, people coming out of their houses when he was delivering their post to pat him on his back and congratulate him. His paintings were in demand, but he had never lost the uncertainty of the value of his efforts, making him continue to strive for perfection.

She glanced up at the windows to his new studio overlooking the yacht basin, his dream since boyhood. The day their mother died flashed across her mind.

'Mum would have loved this,' she called to George as she gathered up the line, ready to throw to Nicholas.

'She would have been proud of you and of Nicholas. Look at you both, the toast of the town.' He laughed as the press cameras began to snap and more cheers went up.

Helen stepped forward to help Nicholas as the boat drew alongside. Next to Sally, Tom was holding Sam on his shoulders so that he could see; her first grandchild was now sixteen months old, and she doted on him. Beside them, wrapped up in a blanket, sat an old man in a wheelchair.

The Kerrs were there too; they had asked Sister Agnes to come, but she was nursing Sister Marcia, who was now very ill. Marjorie had visited Appleford with George earlier in the year, taking the same road she had travelled all those years ago when she was expecting Helen. It was comforting to see where Helen had grown up, the small living room that was set aside as a private family room for Helen and her mother, her school, and even the site of the old coal store that she had heard about in vivid detail. Sister Agnes was Helen's mother in the true sense—the bond between them was strong and unbreakable, just as it was with Sally and herself. She felt gratitude for being allowed into Helen's life, not to take over the role of mother but to be something in between a sister and an aunt. It was a strange situation, but somehow everyone was eager for it to work.

George was very protective of her during that visit, knowing that her joy at being reunited with Helen was mixed with memories of having left her baby behind. The loss of the baby and the finding of an adult were hard to reconcile, but time was working its magic, and the two stories were being knit together to become one. The similarities in their personalities were not obvious at first, but in the process of Marjorie rediscovering herself, the likenesses were becoming apparent.

It had been the wharf project that had highlighted their shared attributes, a readiness to fight for what they believed in, to take risks, to bulldoze through problems as though they were molehills to be kicked out of the way, to challenge those who didn't want to do a first-class job for a good wage, to keep going back to the drawing board to improve on their plans. Marjorie was thrilled when Helen took a real interest in the project, their relationship strengthened in getting to know one another through a shared enthusiasm for a worthy goal.

Nicholas teased Helen about her friendship with Jeremy, but she refused to say that there was any romance, even though it was clear that Jeremy doted on her. Roderick had married. Helen was happy for him, and Marjorie knew that she was relieved that it let her off the hook after his embarrassing efforts to rekindle their relationship.

Helen continued to work at the *Post* and had gained respect in the area for her ability to uncover nests of injustice. Steve Brown was steadfast in his regard for her, and they had often shared stories when their lines of enquiry collided. They accused each other of stealing and spying until they called a truce and began working together as a team, often making the trek up to Auntie Daff's to get away from the office to hone their stories. The downfall of Max Baines and Ron Thompson, who was also now languishing in prison for his involvement in the drug and prostitution trade, was a testament to their reporting abilities, and the newspaper had given them free rein to follow where their noses led them.

Helen had decided to buy one of the new homes which now graced the canal side. The first phase of mixed housing had been completed, giving access to first-time buyers as well as those further up the property ladder. The fact that the reservations were coming in faster than they were able to build was a tribute to her trust in her old boss as architect and to her building company that had taken up the challenge when she had breathed fresh air through the corridors. The new regime was met with distrust at first, but when she had demonstrated her professionalism and her determination to restore the reputation of Baines and Baines while maintaining the existing staff, the majority had been won over. A few chose to leave when it became clear that honesty was to be the foundation of the company and that their 'perks' of the job were curtailed. She had no problem with their exit from her company.

For the second time, she made the journey to see her father in the nursing home. She had wanted to show him her plans, and to her surprise, he was pleased to see them. He made no mention of his opposition to saving the wharf buildings; instead, he peered closely at the plans and the photos she had taken of the first phase of the new housing. She also showed him photos of Albermarle Street, now spruced up to become a desirable place to live. She told him about the changes she had made at Baines and Baines and her plans for the future of the company.

'I'm really happy that you gave me the opportunity to do this, Dad. That's why I wanted to come. To thank you.'

'You were always drawing houses, expecting me to build them.'

'I wanted to be an architect.'

'You should've stayed on at school then.'

She almost laughed at him but managed not to. There was no point in telling him what had happened to her. Instead she dug into her handbag to find more photographs. 'You have two granddaughters. This is Helen'—*Max's daughter and the baby you nearly killed*, she thought as she held the picture in front of him—'and here's Sally.'

He took his time peering into one face and then the other.

'Aren't they beautiful? All grown up.'

'I can see your mother in them. I've been thinking a lot about her, while sitting here,' he said as he handed the photos back.

'You didn't treat Mum very well, Dad.'

'I know, lass. She was too good for me. She didn't have to do anything, but she was better than me.'

This was such a revelation to Marjorie. Had Jack felt the same? Was it OK to be foul to someone just to make yourself feel better? 'Mum only wanted you to be nice to her,' she said.

'I didn't like it when she didn't join in,' her father grunted.

'What do you mean, join in?'

'No matter what I said to her, she never said anything back. That's what was wrong with her. She kept tight-lipped all the bloody time, playing the martyr.'

'Playing the martyr? Playing the martyr?' Her voice rose in anger. 'You thought she was on the moral high ground, so you thought you'd bully her into being like you. Very nice,' she spat out. 'You were awful, Dad. You bullied all of us just because we weren't like you, wanting to bring people down all the time.'

She was standing over him now, shouting, but she couldn't stop. 'Mum was a lovely, intelligent person, but you didn't see that. You only saw what you made her, which was ill with unhappiness. She might have been here today if you'd been different.' She snatched up the photograph of Helen. 'Does she remind you of anyone, Dad, other than Mum? I wonder where the straight hair comes from? Look more closely, Dad, and who do you see? Anyone familiar?' She was shaking with rage now. 'Max is Helen's father.' She flung the information at him. 'At the very time you were thinking he was better than your own children, throwing out your insults like manure, your protégé was plotting to rape me. You may as well have given him permission, such was your adoration. I couldn't come to you because you would have believed his story, that it was my fault, that I'd encouraged him. Your own children were worthless in your eyes. It's because he made me pregnant, Dad, that I left school and home. And would you have cared? All you wanted was the house to be cleaned and the cooking done.' All the years of suppressed anger rained down on her father. 'Did you know he paid Nicholas to stay away? Did you know that you nearly killed Helen when you beat me up just because your tea wasn't up to standard?'

Oh, God, she couldn't believe that she had said all that. She stepped away from him and slumped down on the bed.

She watched him reach for the bottle of whisky under his chair and pour a measure into his glass. He was taking his time, swilling it round, examining the contents as if it were a drink that was new to him. Gone was the moment of normal family life. Her own bitterness had surfaced to ruin the visit. She felt ashamed of her outburst as her simmering hatred quieted. Silence invaded the room. She watched him down his drink in one gulp and then stare into the bottom of the glass as if reading his fortune—or was it his past? But where was the charging bull? The vitriol? The venomous essence of his younger self seemed to have flown away, the fight in him evaporated. How odd, she thought, to see this man who had been such a brute when she was young turn into a benign human being. How odd that it was she who had lost control and was being hurtful.

'I'm sorry, Dad, I didn't mean to bring all that up.'

He continued to study the bottom of his glass as if trying to read what he was supposed to say.

'Anyway, it's all over now,' he said finally. 'You better be going.'

So that was it. He glanced up at her as she gathered up her papers and stuffed them into her briefcase.

'Bye, lass.'

'Bye, Dad.'

She looked back to see him watching her, his eyes looking soft. Were those tears? She felt too embarrassed to find out as she walked away, closing the door firmly behind her. One day she might forgive him, but she wasn't ready yet. She hoped that he would forgive her too for her explosion. She felt ragged with discomfort. That was no way to treat an old man. It hadn't been necessary to drag up the past, especially using Helen as a weapon to wound him. She was disgusted with herself.

It was George who suggested that their father be present at the opening. She had told him about her disastrous visit and how wretched she felt. Nicholas had protested, saying that their dad would not be welcome by anyone, but George thought it was time to bury the hatchet for everyone's sake, and his cool logic prevailed.

As she stepped off the boat, she saw her father in his wheelchair, bundled up to keep warm amongst his family as if the intervening years of estrangement hadn't existed. Sally had offered to look after him and was now fussing over him, adjusting the woolly hat she had bought him. Marjorie caught Nicholas's eye, and he began laughing.

'The irony of it,' she said.

10671294R00200

Printed in Great Britain
by Amazon.co.uk, Ltd.,
Marston Gate.